The Everest Enigma

An Abbie Bradford Mystery

Jeannette de Beauvoir

Beckett Books

The Everest Enigma
Copyright © 2025 by Jeannette de Beauvoir

Published by Beckett Books
PO Box 326
Provincetown, MA 02657

ISBN 979-8-9925942-0-1
eISBN 979-8-9925942-1-8

Cover design by Miladinka Milic

The Everest Enigma is a work of fiction. Names, characters, places, situations, and incidents are the products of the author's imagination and used fictitiously. Any resemblance to actual events, locales, or persons, living or dead, is purely coincidental.

Other books by Jeannette de Beauvoir

Mysteries:
The Sydney Riley mystery series:
Death of a Bear
Murder at Fantasia Fair
The Deadliest Blessing
A Killer Carnival
A Fatal Folly
The Matinée Murders
The Lethal Legacy
Dead in the Water
The Fine Art of Deception
The Honeymoon Homicides

The Martine LeDuc mystery series:
Deadly Jewels
Asylum
Trapped

Murder Most Academic (as Alicia Stone)
Assignment: Nepal (as J.A. Squires)

Historical Fiction:
Lethal Alliances
Our Lady of the Dunes

Chapter One

I saw my first dead body when I was nine years old.

That sounds scary, but oddly enough, it didn't feel that way at the time—something about the resilience of childhood, I expect.

We'd gone to Algeria for my father to take celestial measurements in the Sahara, and one day the local expat group asked him to accompany a doctor going to see a woman in a village outside of town—she was an American, they said, and would be reassured by the presence of other Americans.

We went along with him because my mother wanted to, and that was back in the good days, the days before she started having serious conversations with the bust of Shakespeare in the front hall of our mansion in Boston's Back Bay.

My family members each embrace obsession in their own way. My younger brother Martin went so mad for God he had to become a priest—albeit an Episcopal one, so he can still enjoy some of the finer things in life. My father, following a patriarchal tradition of obsessive eccentricities, devotes his life to stargazing—and traveling to stargaze—while my older brother Phillip turned those same stars into scientific objects and spends his days teaching astrophysics. And my mother... well, the less said about my mother, some days, the better.

I expect we each have something terribly wrong with us.

So my parents and I went along the bumpy track in the Land Rover, with the doctor explaining that she'd been screaming, the American woman, something about great birds blotting out the sun. Ergot poisoning, he added. It happens.

By the time we arrived, the woman had died, and there was fear still etched in her face, fear of those dark wings she'd seen in the sky. Memorable. And so I saw my first body when I was nine.

I wonder, now, if that meant anything, pointed me in a direction I didn't even know I was taking, that would be revealed only once I went to Nepal.

***

The visitor came soon after I was contemplating the dispiriting contents of my refrigerator.

I periodically go on diets, and the first step in any diet is clearing out anything remotely delicious from your kitchen. And then, of course, that first night finds you staring at a hard-boiled egg, a can of tomato juice, some healthy-looking grain, and an apple that's seen better days.

I pulled up the online delivery menu from The Q, my favorite local Chinese restaurant. I could go back to the diet tomorrow.

So when the buzzer rang downstairs, I flung the door open with enthusiasm achieved only by a person who's been dieting for a full eight hours. Instead of the delivery guy with a bag full of goodies, however, I was looking at a slightly older-than-middle-aged woman in an anorak with the hood up.

"Yes?"

She sniffed, wiping an errant snowflake from her cheek. "Are you Abigail Bradford?"

"Yes," I said automatically. "Can I help you?"

The gray eyes looked me over, shrewd, intelligent, and extremely thorough. I wondered what she made of what she saw, because I can be a little startling at first: a tall youngish woman, chin-length hair currently an experimental vivid blue, brown eyes behind glasses. "You answered my post," she said calmly.

I stared at her. "Excuse me?"

"My post," she repeated, exasperation creeping into her voice. "I put a post up on the intranet. At *Harvard*."

At that moment the dinner delivery arrived, the driver impatiently shouldering past her. "Here you go."

I had the tip ready. "Thanks," I said, grabbing the food and hoping this woman would take the hint and leave.

"Well," she said, eyeing the bag, "you'll want to get to your dinner."

"Yes," I agreed.

She stepped forward. "So let's get inside. There's supposed to be heavy snow after midnight." She caught my eye. "Well, of course I won't be staying past midnight," she said. "But with the timing of things—well, I wanted to do the interview as soon as possible. Of course."

Interview?

The wind was screaming down Acorn Street—the most-photographed street in Boston is also one of the narrowest, a perfect wind tunnel—and my dinner was getting cold. I gave up and let her in.

Five minutes later we were sitting rather cozily in my living room, her coat and hat hung up in the hall, fire blazing merrily along, boxes of fragrant Chinese food between us. "You're sure you don't want anything?" I asked for about the third time. I am nothing if not polite, even to people who are clearly off their rockers.

"No, no, you go ahead, dear," she said, fluffing the pillow beside her, settling in. Seen in the light, she had no-nonsense, short salt-and-pepper hair, with lots of laugh wrinkles around her gray eyes.

Nothing distracted, however, from the sharpness in those eyes.

"Since your memory is clearly failing you," she said, "I'll remind you. I'm Emma Caulfield. I put up an ad for a research assistant to go with me to Nepal."

I'd just opened the chopsticks packet. "Nepal?"

"Well, yes, of course, Nepal," she said, frowning. "Really, dear, do you usually repeat what people say to you? Do you want the job, or not?"

I put everything down. There was a glimmer of an idea at the back of my mind. Harvard perforce means Phillip, and this was *exactly* something Phillip would think was funny. "I have a feeling my brother answered your post on my behalf," I said carefully.

She was unfazed. "Then he must have known you'd want the job."

"Going to Nepal."

She nodded. "Going to Nepal."

I thought about it. It wasn't actually *totally* insane. My brothers and I are that most hated of species, trust-fund babies, and Phillip and I have spent a substantial part of our inheritances collecting academic letters after our names, probably to prove something to someone... well, I've never quite worked that part out. I was into the second year of holding my doctorate in history, and hadn't yet found any work in academia. Boston and Cambridge might together be the hub of higher education, but even lectureships are harder and harder to come by, and guarded jealously.

And—here's the thing—truth be told, I was slowly coming to the conclusion that I didn't actually *want* a career in higher education. I liked the research part: I liked being a detective, figuring out what really happened, the story behind the story preserved for posterity. Learning about people who weren't just stick-figures, real people who lived and loved and breathed and should be remembered. Bringing them back to life, somehow, if only on paper.

Teaching... yeah, maybe not so much. Faculty interactions, definitely not. And while it's true I'd never *need* to work for a living, that didn't mean I didn't actually *want* to. To contribute to the world in some way. I just wasn't yet seeing how.

All that meant, of course, was there wasn't anything tying me to Boston at the moment.

"What," I asked, "are you going to Nepal for?"

"Well, research, of course, dear." She looked puzzled. "I thought that would be obvious." I didn't say anything, and she sighed gustily. "I'm *Emma Caulfield,*" she said again.

"Yes, I got that part."

"I'm a *writer.*"

I continued to stare blankly at her, and she started looking annoyed. "I write historical romances," she said. "I'm on the New York Times *bestseller list.*"

And there it was. I hadn't heard of her for good reason: I subscribe to the academic historian's dim view of historical fiction in general, and historical romances in particular. It's an automatic judgment we make: slipshod research, damsels in distress,

4

Regency dresses. I met her eyes. "Bodice-rippers," I suggested, nodding.

To my surprise, she laughed. "Well, good for you, Abigail Bradford," she said. "I was starting to think you didn't have any gumption at all."

There it was again, that sharp mind behind those eyes. "You fraud," I said slowly. "You knew I'd react like that."

Emma nodded. She looked thoroughly satisfied. "I am researching my next novel," she said crisply. "I am going to Kathmandu, and then on to some trekking. I'm planning on getting up to Everest Base Camp, and I certainly don't want to do that alone." Her expression dared me to say anything. "I'm good at asking questions, and taking in the scenery, and all that. But I'm not always able to organize what I'm doing, and this time around I need some specialist help. I want you to help research what it was like for people on the mountain, people in the country, people in the *world*, in the early nineteen-twenties."

She paused, and a trace of something vulnerable slipped into her voice. "I also need someone to—well, to go with me. I used to like traveling on my own, have done it for years, but not so much anymore. There's too much to keep track of, and I need to be thinking and writing. So I need someone to go with me."

"As a researcher," I said.

She didn't meet my eyes. "I've never done this before," she confessed. "I've always done everything on my own. But this time feels different—and I'm not about to get a reputation for slipshod work, so I need some help. Some research, some organizing, some travel… and someone to tell me when I'm going off in the wrong direction. That's why I need a historian—you."

Not just any historian: me. I'd remember that, later. "You're looking for facts?" I asked sweetly. "That must be a first for a romance novelist."

"Historical romance novelist," she corrected. Her eyes were steely. "So are you in, or what?"

I had a feeling I was going to regret this. "I'm in," I said. "And now, can we eat?"

***

I Googled her, of course. The moment she was out the door.

Emma Caulfield, it transpired, was indeed a Big Name in the genre. She'd been writing novels for the past thirty-odd years. She'd been part of the big Regency romance movement, had switched things around for a while with an American Colonial period, even set a small series in prehistoric Britain.

And she was right: her novels were consistently on the bestseller list. She must be making a fortune.

"The *romance* bestseller list," I reminded my friend Justine when I told her about the late-night visit. We were still deep in February, and we'd come off the ice-skating at Boston Common to the warmth of my fireplace, a pot of tea, and a bag of popcorn.

"You know," Justine said, stretching out a leg toward the heat, "you could manage to be just a *little* more judgmental if you tried."

"Do you think?" I smiled and refilled her tea. I was only half-serious.

"What *I* think," she said carefully, "is that you might be surprised. Romance novels have come a long way since the *oh, John, oh, Mary* days."

"And you would know this, how?"

She laughed. "Come on, Abbie. *Sex and the City* changed everything. There are feminist romances now. And your Emma Caulfield—she has a good reputation. I think she might surprise you, I really do. God, I think my toes are finally thawing." She slanted a look at me. "So you're going with her? To Kathmandu?"

I nodded. "I think so."

"You know, you don't have to, just because Phillip had one of his harebrained ideas."

"Trouble is," I said slowly, "he's usually right, and it actually sounds like it could be fun. And... interesting. The work, the travel, the research—there's a goal, you know? Something that might mean something."

She nodded, her eyes on the flames. Justine knows about my past. Phillip and Martin and I are the thirteenth generation of an old, old Massachusetts family: check it out, the first governor of what would eventually become the Commonwealth was named Bradford, he was on the *Mayflower* that first miserable winter in Provincetown and Plymouth. Later, during the Gilded Age, the Bradfords became rich beyond understanding, though they had one saving grace—philanthropy. Hospitals, learning institutions, the arts … my ancestors helped build the knowledge-based economy that still characterizes Boston.

I have an ambivalent relationship with my family wealth— well, to be fair, with much of my family itself, too—and am always looking for ways to put it to good use; I'm not interested in a trust fund that does nothing but increase itself. I give away a lot of money, in a whole lot of ways, and that's good, that's important… but I'd like to be *doing* something important, too. I just hadn't yet figured out what.

"So what's the plan?" Justine asked. "What exactly is she researching?"

I shut my eyes; I can nearly always visualize conversations when I do. "She's doing something about an Everest expedition back in the 1920s," I said. "There was an Englishman called George Mallory who went up and didn't come down, and there's controversy about whether he reached the summit or not, which is an important question among mountaineers." I paused. "And apparently he was incredible eye-candy, as was his wife, so maybe it's a love story between them." I found I was smiling. Okay, so maybe there *was* something more to romance novels than I'd assumed. "She wants me to go to Kathmandu ahead of her, and she'll join me after she's done some sort of conference in New York."

"Well, it sounds exotic anyway," said Justine. "Why not? It might be just what you need while you decide what you're going to do with your life."

That was, of course, the question. "I'm intrigued," I admitted. "Phillip was right. It sounds exotic, it sounds interesting, and it's the other side of the world."

"Top of the world," said Justine. "Everest's the highest mountain on Earth."

"I'm not actually *climbing* Everest," I reminded her.

"No," she conceded. "You'd need to be a little more of an Outdoors Girl for that. Still, it might lead to other things."

"Like what?" I asked suspiciously.

Justine grinned. "Romance?" she suggested.

I threw the popcorn at her.

Excerpt from the journal of George Mallory

Mont Vélan, Swiss-Italian Alps, 1904: Just when I thought I was going to be all right, the heaves started again.

Harry was looking miserable, though it was unclear to me whether that was because of sitting so long in the cold or because of my constant sickness. I've been near others who are throwing up and I know what that sound triggers in the listener's gut. "Sorry," I managed to gasp.

"S'alright," he said, though I don't for a moment think his heart was in it.

I didn't know what was the worst thing about my predicament, that the rest of the climbing party had trusted Harry and me to crack on to the summit and we were within grasp of it, or that I so very sincerely wished I could die. "When you're well enough," Harry said, almost conversationally, "we'll start down again."

It was ignoble. I'd been a member of the Ice Club for almost six years, having ascended several substantive peaks and even practised snowcraft in the Scottish Highlands, so I absolutely shouldn't have been bothered by altitude.

Once a year, Graham Irving—my own old schoolmaster from Winchester—chose a few "recruits," as he called us, for an annual trip to the Alps. This year, this brilliant year, he'd chosen me, George Mallory, taking me away from the schoolroom, offering me a window on the world from far above it. It was a thundering great honour, and I'd botched it completely.

"Never mind," said Graham when at length we made it down to the camp. "Louis and Harry can go up tomorrow. And you," he added, turning to me, "need to do more climbing."

That night I lay awake long after the fire had been extinguished, listening to the wind catching at the tent flaps and planning my physical regimen. I was realising one cannot treat mountaineering as a hobby, to be taken up or put down at will.

Well, that would all change, I vowed to myself. Never again would the name George Mallory be associated with altitude sickness. Never again would I fail so miserably at something I wanted so badly to attain.

Toward dawn, Harry poked his head into the tent. "Well, then," he drawled, looking at me. "Time for the odd egg and toast before we leave."

That time, my stomach stayed where it was supposed to. And in the end, we made it up the Grand Combin and of course the view from the top was simply ripping.

We were all sure it was the very best day of our lives.

Chapter Two

Emma had been clear with me about one thing. "You have to be as fit as possible," she said. "We're trekking up into the mountains, there are steep paths, and some days we'll be on the trail for five hours or more. Go do some cardio work at your favorite gym, dear."

Oh, right. Like I had a favorite gym.

But a cursory Internet search had me convinced she was spot-on: I could either spend the next month pushing my strength and endurance, or I was going to experience a very unhappy couple of weeks on the trail.

And who likes being unhappy?

I joined my new favorite gym and hired a personal trainer who proceeded to torture my body almost every day; but the truth is I live in a part of the city that's called Beacon Hill for good reason, and I was noticing that I was getting less and less winded every time I walked home. Definitely a bonus.

Going to the gym every day really puts a dent in one's schedule, though, and I had a lot of work still to do before leaving for Nepal.

I started with the Internet. And an hour later felt like I, too, might be experiencing altitude sickness. Some of the videos were... scary. To say the least.

It turns out Mount Everest in the past decade or so has become, from one perspective, something of a Disney ride for some rich would-be adventurers. Buy the gear, run around the block a few thousand times to tone your muscles, hire an expedition company, and Bob was apparently very much your uncle.

Or could be; YouTube was filled with operators and mountaineering outfits earnestly demonstrating how they were different from the seat-of-your-pants organizations that proliferated after the last king of Nepal was deposed and the new secular government very much wanted tourist dollars, thank you very much. When it came to climbing Everest, the "cheap" option meant merely that there was someone doing the extensive necessary paperwork, including securing the permits, handing you some oxygen bottles, and then sending you up to Base Camp. Good luck, and good night.

The more positive spin was that it seemed most of the outfits were experienced, cautious, and professional, and the people who engage them true mountaineers. I tore my eyes away from the blinding white of the snow and turned to the past, my own favorite foreign country.

It is apparently accepted wisdom that the first two people to get to the top of Mount Everest did it in 1953, but that was hardly the beginning of interest in summiting, at least from Europeans, and especially the English. In the late 1800s there was some interest in "conquering" this mountain, and several expeditions were put together without any noticeable success. It was a sideline, of course: to the south lay India, the jewel in the crown of the British Empire; already a generation of soldiers had found the terrain to be challenging and had to think up ways of coping: better tents, bottled oxygen, something oddly called hobnails on the soldiers' boots.

Nepal, my own destination, was closed to these early would-be mountaineers: ruled by a maharaja who wanted nothing to do with the West, the country's borders were sealed until the 1950s; so the northern—and more difficult—route through Tibet was the only one available. I was amused to see that even these early expeditions had their share of wealthy amateur incompetent tourists: when the Alpine Club tried to organize an expedition in 1906, there was a financial shortfall and a publisher called A.L. Munn offered to make up the difference—as long as he could come, too.

Plus ça change...

And then world events took over. The First World War shook Great Britain to its core. Like the knights of the medieval era, my own area of specialization, the young officers who went into the war believed in civilized conduct, a gentleman's code; war was conducted with dignity and fairness. They were proven wildly and tragically wrong, and despite their final victory on the battlefield, the people who returned from it were forever changed.

They also returned to a life into which they no longer fit. So, many of them—those who had, or could amass, the where-withal—turned to travel and exploration, to "conquering" other worlds and other challenges. The war for them had never really ended; staying home felt impossible.

And for some of them, the triumph of summiting Everest would be way to erase the horrors of the war. A path, perhaps, to redemption.

A number of authors leaned on something called the "Third Pole" theory—that Everest was all that remained for rugged ad-venturers to put their names on something hitherto unattainable, once Peary had "discovered" the North Pole and Amundsen the South; but that seemed a little too reductive to me.

I leaned back and chewed on my purple felt-tip pen. The Eu-ropean conquest of Everest, it seemed, was very much a product of the war, in that the mountain was an enemy that wouldn't fight back (well, okay, as it turns out, it pretty much *does*, but no one was thinking about that), and it engaged the minds and hearts of those who had returned from France and Flanders different peo-ple than when they'd set out.

There was a deep gulf between those who had fought and those who hadn't. People who'd stayed home still clung to the illusion of imaginary glories, still dreaming the dream that had been so completely shattered in the trenches, while the others knew the truth, that the world had changed irrevocably in the sod-den fields of Ypres and Verdun. Hating the old men who had talked the nations into a conflict that in Britain alone left a million dead, two and a half million wounded, and the same number on disability ten years on, including 65,000 men who would never re-cover from post-traumatic stress disorder.

Worse, they returned to a country that passionately wanted to forget the war had even happened. It wasn't a unique story: the same thing had played out in my own country after the hapless American war in Vietnam.

I could imagine them, those survivors, doing everything they could to stay normal during the day, to pick up where they'd left off, going to their jobs, reading Scripture lessons or singing at church on Sundays, trying to be the same father and husband they'd been when they'd left... and then to awaken, screaming, in the night, the smell of mustard gas in their nostrils, the sounds of shells exploding all around them, bayonets and blood and how do you survive something like that?

You go to Everest.

So those early expeditions through China and Tibet were about more than just empire-building and machismo. They were also, somehow, about some kind of salvation. About repairing lives ripped apart at the seams. About finding a new challenge, a new motivation to get up in the morning, a new reason, perhaps, to not think about the world that was lost and focus instead on a new world they could create.

And into this scenario stepped the clearly irresistible George Mallory.

He'd already made quite a splash on the scene in one way or another. George was everything we want a legend to be: handsome (okay, *gorgeous*), brilliant, creative, brave. He'd done some rock-climbing early on while in school, but then went up to Cambridge, where sports took a poor third to his social life and his studies. It was 1905, and if Europe wasn't trembling in expectation of the war, it was certainly moving toward it at ever-increasing speed, and the obsessive way that people seemed to embrace frivolity showed there was a doomed kind of anticipation lurking in the shadows of their gaiety.

George became part of the Bloomsbury set, where recreation and education were pursued with the same intense eagerness: they grabbed for a lightness, an insouciance that the world would never know again; they grabbed it with both hands and sucked every bit of joy they could from it.

I had vaguely heard of the Bloomsbury group, but still checked them out on Wikipedia: Rupert Brooke, John Maynard Keynes, Lytton Strachey, Virginia Woolf, Duncan Grant, familiar names. It was a pleasant way to spend one's time, pursuing intellectual endeavors, writing—it hadn't escaped me that the Bloomsburies, if I might call them that, were predominantly writers—punting on the Cam, throwing outrageous parties in each other's rooms at college, drinking and arguing and generally having the time of their lives.

Until they couldn't. The war came, and everything changed.

Mallory went, of course, but not before he'd met and quite fallen for a non-Bloomsbury girl, Ruth Turner, every bit as beautiful in her own way as he was in his. They'd met at a dinner party in 1914 and apparently both came away from the experience equally smitten; they got married within months of the meeting. Their daughter Frances Clare was born in 1915, and another daughter was born the following year; eventually there would be a son as well.

The most famous photograph of the couple is a twin headshot taken in 1916, presumably on the eve of his departure for France. In it, Ruth is wide-eyed and elegant, while he looks every bit the dashing young officer. I was beginning to see why Emma was so interested in writing about them. There was enough in that photograph alone, I thought, to fill up at least one novel, romance or not.

George had a good war, in the sense that he returned from it; but that was about all you could say. He'd been deeply shocked by the war's outbreak; like many other intellectuals, he believed international disputes could—and should—be solved by diplomacy. However, some of his friends, including Robert Graves and Rupert Brooke, had gone into the British Army, and George himself joined the Royal Artillery after Brooke was killed in 1915. His bad luck was that his first posting was at the Battle of the Somme, one of the deadliest battles in human history.

British forces suffered more than 57,000 casualties—including more than 19,000 soldiers killed—on the first *day* alone; by the time the "battle" ended nearly five months later, more than three million soldiers on both sides had fought, and more than one million were killed or wounded.

How did the delicate sporty boy from the literary haunts of Cambridge manage to keep his sanity in the trenches? It was hard to imagine.

Viewed through this lens, it seemed clear that the spate of expeditions that birthed the conquest of Mount Everest were meant, more than anything else, to help exorcise the myriad ghosts of the war dead.

I emerged from my reading with a headache and a lot of questions about where I was heading and what was going to happen there. I finished my cocktail—just for fun, I'd looked up what people were drinking in the 1920s and discovered that I could make a mean Boulevardier—and headed upstairs to bed. George's further adventures could wait; this mountain-climbing thing was tiring me out already.

***

Emma's voice on the telephone sounded like there was heavy machinery working nearby. "Are you sure you'll be fine going on ahead of me, dear?"

"Yes," I said, my own voice just below shouting level. "Where are you?"

"Getting a coffee."

At a building site? "It's fine," I said. "I'll be fine. Enjoy your conference."

The noise abruptly subsided, as though a switch had been thrown. "Oh, the *conference*," she said and laughed. "It's just a bunch of old ladies wanting to find out what each other is working on, really."

"Then don't go."

"Bite your tongue, child," she said, her voice shocked. "It's *also* filled with fans, and the first rule of romance writing is *honor thy readers*."

I found myself smiling. When I think romance, I think Barbara Cartland in her bathtub. Emma was shooting all my preconceptions to hell. I was liking it. "So, your George Mallory," I began.

"Yes?"

"Pretty hot stuff, in his time," I said.

"Huh," she said. "Wait till you read his letters to Ruth. Amazingly beautiful." She took a loud slurp of her coffee. "Jack Bailey will pick you up at the airport—*if* he remembers. He's Australian." As though the two, forgetfulness and being Australian, were connected. "I'll be in Kathmandu on Sunday. See you then."

Kathmandu! Even as I ended the phone conversation, I carried the word with me, conjuring up nineteenth-century paintings of "Oriental" life, a Western gaze for sure, but the only frame of reference I had.

Well, I still had three days before I left. And a lot of stuff to learn in that time.

Jeannette de Beauvoir

Excerpt from the journal of George Mallory

Magdalene College, Cambridge University, 1905-07: I tried to explain to my father why I'm reading history at Cambridge instead of mathematics. Life is too short, I told him, to be limited; and while I am still held in marvelment at the sheer beauty of mathematics, the exquisiteness of that perfect language, I think history will give me a better grip on what the world is about. I don't know that he'll understand. Perhaps I don't, either.

But I'm not terribly worried. The material is interesting, which is a good thing, because there's so much more here to entice one to leave one's studies behind. It seems there will be many opportunities to excel at sports, especially—I hope—climbing.

My tutor is a fellow called Benson, and his rooms are in a converted granary. He's somewhat nervous—keeps twisting a cigarette between his fingers as he conducts his tutorials—and he's already inspired me. "The best rule," he told me on that first day, "is to read what interests one."

That thought is part of a new sort of thinking that's sweeping across Cambridge, sweeping aside the old, dusty notions of life, sweeping in exploration and questioning like never before. A new century, and a new mindset.

It's all terribly thrilling, really.

Had a sumptuous dinner some weeks ago at Christ's College—old Benson, my tutor, brought me along with him—and met some interesting chaps, among them Charles Sayles, who is, I am told, one of the patrons of Cambridge's intellectual social life, holding salons and effecting introductions to the university's overlapping and interlocking social cliques.

Sayles, it turns out, is a founding member of the Climbers' Club, which focuses its assaults on mountains in Great Britain (though he did say my experience in the Alps is what led him to recommend me). So I've been round and invited Geoffrey Keynes, Rupert Brooke, and Hugh Wilson, to head out to North Wales with me and do some climbing there. Rupert's dropped out— he sent me a damned postcard, of all things, of Rodin's Penseur, *and he wrote on the back, "My soul yearns for mountains, which I adore from the bottom. But the pale gods have forbidden it." I haven't a clue what he's trying to say, other than that perhaps he's had a spot of fright in thinking about climbing. If he only knew how easy it is.*

18

Snowdonia. Even the name beckons one! I can scarcely wait. We leave a week Monday and will be going to locales with such exotic names as Craig yr Ysfa, Lliwedd, and Ffynnon Llugwy, the latter being a lake in which we will no doubt be resting our limbs after a day of climbing.

Cambridge is a marvellous place… but the peaks are there, waiting for me. I can feel it… I can hear it. And soon I'll answer their call.

Chapter Three

My first impression—and, in fact, what would be my lasting impression—of Nepal was one of color. Bright, swirling, riotous colors everywhere, worn as clothing, painted on buildings, on signs, draped across animals.

When I went to collect my bags, a smiling woman stopped me to place a string of bright orange and white carnations around my neck. I lost her almost immediately in the crush of people; but for days I smiled when I remembered that brief lovely welcome.

It was hot, and the air was bright, glittering almost, with little prisms of suspended dust dancing all around me. Like diamonds. It was magical, dazzling, different from anything I'd ever seen—or breathed—before.

A voice behind me drawled, "If you were here in November, you'd see the mountains."

I turned and found myself looking into the eyes of a middle-aged white westerner, a large, rugged-looking man wearing a decidedly non-Nepalese uniform of jeans and a t-shirt and with twinkling blue eyes above a slightly out-of-control beard. "Dr. Bradford? I'm Jack Bailey." He dragged out the name. "Emma Caulfield's friend. She told me to look for someone with—unusual hair."

I shook his hand. "Call me Abbie, please. And—well, it's not *always* blue." I suddenly wondered if I was going to regret my impulsive visit to the hairdresser's. Of course, last time around, it had been purple.

"Of course not. Amy, then. Are these your bags? Did you have a good trip?"

I didn't correct the name. I wasn't sure how to answer him. I'd been in transit for forty-eight hours; it had been cold and raining in Amsterdam for the layover, and ninety-two degrees Fahrenheit—in the shade—in New Delhi, with four hours to wait for the flight to Kathmandu. "Long," I said at last. "And they misplaced my bags in India."

He chuckled. "But miraculously found them again when you came up with the fee," he said. "Welcome to the subcontinent. Come on, I have transport."

Wedged into the front passenger seat of a ridiculously small car, my two bags taking up all the space there was in the back, I found I had to shout over the noise. There were, apparently, no windows in this vehicle. "What did you mean, about the mountains?"

"What's that?"

I leaned farther over. "Back there, you said in November I'd see the mountains."

"Right." He downshifted as we turned into a narrow street where life seemed to be crowding in on us: open storefronts with wares spilling out onto the pavement, an assortment of vehicles, bicycles, and motorcycles that seemed a combination of the two. Jack drove deftly and very fast. "Used to be, even in the spring, you'd get off the airplane," he shouted, "and you'd see the Himalayas. Still can, occasionally, actually, but it's more and more unusual. Now you see a lot of pollution."

I didn't know what the right rejoinder to that might be. "What a loss," I said.

He glanced at me. "Your loss," he said. "Nepal's changed. Still changing."

I looked around me; the air still shimmered, the colors were still riotous. It was pretty exotic to me, anyway, invisible mountains notwithstanding. And besides, his complaint was familiar—every place I've ever lived or visited has the same lament: *it's not like it used to be.*

There was a traffic snarl-up a few blocks from our destination, which Jack negotiated with a lot of muttering I couldn't quite make out. We were, it transpired, all maneuvering around a pair of small cows lying on the pavement, apparently oblivious to the traffic flow.

I was fascinated. "Why doesn't someone move them?"

Jack shrugged. "Where to?" he asked, the question clearly rhetorical. "Nowhere for them to go."

I stared at him. I've always associated cows with green pastures. Vermont, maybe, or Wisconsin. "How do they live? Does someone feed them?"

He shook his head, apparently amused by my naïveté. "There's not enough food in this city for the *people* to eat. Who's going to feed the cows? Nepal's an incredibly poor country. The minimum wage here works out to one hundred fourteen American dollars a month. That's right well below the poverty line."

I wasn't ready to give up on the cows. "But where do they come from?"

"Farmers drop them off," he said, unconcerned, as we gathered speed again. "They only keep the female cows, the ones that'll give milk, the ones that'll reproduce. No one wants to pay for extra mouths. It's always been a thing, but since the earthquake it's gotten worse. Cows, dogs... you'll see the most pitiful things here. I don't spend much time in the city if I can help it."

And with that dismal introduction, we pulled into a walled courtyard in front of a low cement building. "Home sweet home," said Jack. He didn't turn off the ignition.

A young woman wearing a tunic—I later learned it was a South Asian garment called a *kurta*—of riotous oranges and reds, over more prosaic jeans and flip-flops, came out of the house. "Mr. Jack," she greeted him, putting her palms together and executing a brief bow.

He returned it. "Laxsmi," he said. "This is Anna—um, Amy?—Bradford. Annie, Laxsmi runs things here. I'll leave you to get settled." Even as he was talking, he was taking my bags out of the backseat.

I hadn't thought my name was that difficult to master.

Laxsmi gave me the briefest of glances, taking in the glasses, the blue hair, the rumpled clothing, and dismissed me. "Dinner," she said to him. "You don't forget."

"Yeah, yeah."

"I mean it! You don't forget?"

The car backed out of the courtyard, with Jack waving dismissively out the open window, and the young woman and I looked at each other. She was shorter than me, with honey-colored skin and thick dark hair worn in a plait down her back. Her eyes were speculative, and I found myself wondering who else Jack may have brought here, and for what purpose. She repeated the palms-together bow and I had the sense to make an attempt at one as well. In Japan, where I'd spent some time a few years back, westerners never get the bowing correctly. I wondered if it were the same here.

"He will be late," she predicted, and then moved past me to pick up my bags. I managed to wrestle one of them from her and followed her into the house. "Only a few people here now," she was saying in a slightly singsong voice. "So you have a room all to you. Later you will share it. They will start coming soon. Tomorrow, perhaps. Or tonight, I do not know."

"Who?" I managed to ask. The only person I was expecting was Emma, and not for a couple of days still. I'd somehow in the back of my mind expected to find myself in a hotel, not in what felt like someone's house, without even learning who Emma's mysterious friend Jack actually was.

Ah, well. When in Rome... I looked around me with some curiosity. We were standing in a low-ceilinged room that looked a lot like the Tibetan tea rooms I'd seen on the Internet: every wall covered with a bright textile, clashing colors on the rug under our feet, wooden furniture also painted in bright and brilliant intricate designs.

Laxsmi turned to look at me. "The other members. The rest of your team," she said, her voice registering surprise.

"I have a team?"

There was something else in her eyes now, and I'm sure it wasn't my imagination that she edged slightly away from me before turning and heading out of the room, wheeling my suitcase behind her. "This way," she said.

Okay, let's take the crazy white lady where she's going.

24

Down a hallway, passing a couple of rooms off to either side, and we'd arrived at my temporary home away from home. Four single beds, each one covered with a sober beige bed-spread, a small stack of towels on the foot, fluffed-up pillows at the head. One long wall was covered with a built-in wardrobe, and at the end of the room large glass doors stood open to trees and a garden.

Laxsmi stood to the side for me to enter. "The bed at the end is best," she said. "You choose it now."

"Okay." What was this, a dormitory? Back in boarding school? Who were the other three occupants to be? "Do you know when my friend is arriving?" I asked hesitantly. Maybe I'd gotten this wrong. Maybe *Emma* had gotten this wrong.

"Mr. Jack is here for dinner," she said.

"Not Mr.—Jack," I stammered. "Emma Caulfield. The writer."

She looked at me impassively. "The others are here soon enough," she said, her voice firm, brooking no discussion. "Dinner is at seven o'clock."

"Yes, but—"

"Seven o'clock," she said again, and executed her bow. I was dismissed. She closed the door behind her.

And that, it seemed, was that.

***

The garden, when explored, proved enchanting. I was glad I'd followed Laxsmi's instructions to secure the bed beside it.

The colors didn't disappoint out here, either. Marigolds, lush with brilliant yellows and oranges pushing up against each other, and sitting back from them as though suspicious of their riotous jostling, tall red rhododendrons. Something purple and delicate that I didn't recognize, something else that was probably in the orchid family, another tall plant with red spikes. And an intoxicating scent, filling the nostrils with promise of even more lushness to come.

Statues were scattered around seemingly at random, including one I recognized—from my recent dives into Wikipedia—as Vasudhārā, the Buddhist goddess of wealth and prosperity, wearing her so-over-the-top headdresses and jewelry. I sat near her for a long time on a bench, watching a cat clean itself, thoroughly and fastidiously; and then I went back inside.

A card placed on my bed announced access to Wi-Fi, hours of meals, and transportation options to Hanuman Dhoka. Since I had no idea what Hanuman Dhoka might be, I contented myself with clicking online and checking email. Nothing from Emma, who was presumably still shaking hands with her fans and signing autographs and determining what the competition was writing about. Nothing else that required a response; I closed my MacBook and looked around me again.

The bathroom was equipped with a shower head but no discrete stall, so I locked the door and kept it quick. The tiredness seeped from my skin and escaped down the drain along with the grunge and soap, and I emerged feeling much more positive about my situation. If nothing else, this mysterious place was going to provide some excellent anecdotes once I got back to Boston; I could hear Justine laughing already.

Dinner was served in a large room accommodating a tremendous slab of wood for a table with about twenty chairs around it. I waited to go in until I heard some voices, and arrived to find two youngish men already seated, looking relaxed; one of them was laughing.

They stopped talking—I only had time to briefly clock their English accents—when I came into the room. Westerners of Jack's ilk: tanned skin, fit bodies, loose cotton sweaters. One of them stood up, a little awkwardly. "Hey, welcome to Kathmandu," he said, sticking out his hand.

I had to travel down the length of the table to shake it. "Thanks," I said. "Abbie Bradford. Nice to meet you."

"You as well." He grinned; he was my age, somewhere in his thirties, I thought, but with an air of mischief that would probably keep him young forever. "I'm Richard; this is Mark."

"Abbie," I said, leaning across to shake Mark's hand.

"Ah, yes, we heard you were coming," he said, nodding; he hadn't tried to stand up, but his handshake was firm-leaning-toward-hard. "Jack went off like a bat out of hell to pick you up."

"To be fair, he'd forgotten you were coming," explained Richard, sitting down again and lounging back lazily in his chair. "If it doesn't have to do directly with work, he can be a little disorganized. Have a seat. It's just us tonight, I'm afraid, but we'll try to be entertaining. Jack will be back at some point."

"He'll be late," drawled Mark. "He'll come in at the end of dinner and ask us why we started without him. It's what he does. Do sit down, Abbie, and tell us what brings you to Nepal."

I pulled out one of the many chairs and sat. "I'm wondering if there's some mix-up, actually," I said. "I'm supposed to be meeting a friend, but the woman who let me in—Laxsmi, right?—seems to think I'm part of some group?" I let my voice trail upward into a question mark.

Instead of answering, Richard said, "Who's your friend?"

Alice in Wonderland, I thought. "Emma Caulfield," I said. "We're not actually friends—I don't know her very well, I'm her—um, researcher and—um—traveling companion." Put that way, we sounded decidedly Victorian.

"Except you're not traveling together," Mark pointed out.

"There's that," I conceded with a smile. "We will be. She's at a conference; she'll be here Sunday. She's an old friend of Jack's, I gather, and I'm guessing he offered her hospitality and a place to write." That garden, I thought, would be perfect for it. "In the meantime, though, it would actually be really, really helpful if you'd tell me what's going on here."

"We're Supreme Summits," Mark said.

I stared at him. They did in fact look fit, but *supreme* seemed a little boastful. "Um, okay, but—"

Richard started laughing. "Give the girl a break," he said and turned to me. "Jack's company is called Supreme Summits Expeditions," he said. "Jack owns it; we're guides." He noted my look of incomprehension. "Mountaineering," he clarified.

"We're taking a climbing team up Everest," said Mark, probably by this time biting his tongue to refrain from asking if I'd heard of Everest.

Anything I had to add to that was on hold, as Laxsmi had appeared. There were a few moments of quiet as she put steaming dishes in front of us, added a whole array of small bowls containing sauces and chutneys to the table, and poured water. I thanked her; the men weren't wasting time with courtesies, attacking the food. She didn't seem to expect them to say anything, and in fact neither had she.

"What *is* this?" I asked at length, sensing a pause, gesturing toward my plate. It was a mélange of vegetables and meat and eggs all heaped on a large piece of flatbread. It was amazing.

"It's called *chatamari*," said Richard, his mouth full. He swallowed, and laughed. "Sorry, Abbie. Don't mean to be rude. We've been at the gym all day, working out, we're starving. That water's okay to drink, by the way; it's bottled."

"Thank you," I said faintly.

I gave them a few moments to replenish their electrolytes before I reverted to being a pain in the neck. "I still think there's a mistake," I said. "Emma and I are supposed to be trekking. I'm not here to climb Everest."

"Of course you're not," said Richard.

"We know that," said Mark, nodding, before taking a quick drink of water. "Don't worry, don't look like that, we don't know anything about *you*. It's just, it's our job to know who's coming. They sign on with our outfit. We know everything about them. Their names, their occupations, what peaks they've climbed, what their fitness level is, who their families are. We've talked to them, assessed them. We screen our teams, unlike some other outfits I could name, but won't." He was scowling.

"Don't start that again," Richard said to him. "It's not useful."

"It's speaking from my heart," said Mark. He caught my look. "Sorry, Abbie," he said. "It's an old gripe."

"About what?" I asked. As long as they weren't expecting me to climb any mountains, I was happy to listen to them talk about it.

"Everest as theme park," said Mark. "Not for us, and not for everybody, but some of the expeditions? They'll take anybody up. No fitness tests. No high-altitude experience. You pays your money and you takes your chances."

"It's a lot of money," Richard told me. "Starts at around sixty thousand American dollars and can go up from there. And you need to be able to be free for two or three months—take that much time out of your life. So it's an exclusive club."

Mark snorted. "Exclusive my ass!" he said. "Last season there was a guy at Camp Two, didn't know which way his crampons attached. He was on the *mountain*. And he'd never used his *gear*." He shook his head. "Thought it was hilarious. Big joke."

"Not one of ours, he wasn't," Richard said, and looked at me, still being helpful. "For us, it's about two things, the safety of everyone, and the camaraderie we experience together. We don't take inexperienced climbers, and we reserve the right to send anyone back once we've seen what they can do."

"Or can't do," said Mark.

"So why do other companies take beginners?" I asked. I was almost finished with the chatamari, and could easily have eaten another whole plate of it. My diet was a distant memory.

"Money," they said, more or less in unison.

Richard sighed. "It's not really that simple, of course," he said. He was striking me as the more thoughtful of the two, or at least the more diplomatic. "There are political considerations. It would help if the government set more standards. There could be more uniformity in safety requirements. They tried new rules last year." He'd sketched quotation marks in the air when he said *rules*. "No non-emergency helicopters. Tracking chips on climbers—"

"Which didn't work at altitude," said Mark.

Richard finished smoothly, "And limiting the number of permits they issue."

"But they want the tourist dollars," said Mark. He wasn't talking to me. I had a feeling they'd had this conversation already, and more than once. "It really *is* that simple, Rich." He turned to me. "You have to understand, Nepal's issuing close to four hundred permits a season," he said.

"That's a lot?"

Richard nodded. "It's a lot when you consider for every one of those permits, it's one or two sherpas, and sometimes Western guides too. So it's a lot more people on the mountain. And the season lasts for just one month, *if* we're lucky." He wasn't looking at either of us now. "Usually less, to tell the truth. Once you get on the mountain, if you're using fixed ropes, and you'd be crazy not to, then there's one path up—and it's the same path down."

"You might have seen the pictures," Mark added. "Freaking traffic jams. On *Mount Everest.*"

I didn't remember seeing them, but I nodded anyway. "Why is the number of people climbing a problem?"

Richard said, "It only takes one person, one inexperienced climber, one individual who starts feeling ill or tired or has altitude sickness. Or someone who doesn't know how to climb a ladder. They stop, and everyone behind them stops. And waits. And probably there's more than one person in that condition, so there's more than one bottleneck. And so you've got people standing still for bloody *hours* in freezing temperatures, which is one hundred percent inviting frostbite, because there's nowhere to move, nowhere to go. All you can do is flex your fingers and toes, and that's not enough. *And* they use up all their oxygen and don't have enough for the descent, which is where most people get in trouble anyway."

"What oxygen?"

A quick crossfire of looks; they hadn't anticipated someone not knowing the basics. "You have to have a lot of supplemental oxygen," explained Mark. "We call 'em O's. The top of Everest is at the cruising altitude of jet airplanes; breathing up there is close to impossible on your own. But you only have a finite amount, there's only so much you and your sherpa guide can carry, and when you run out, you're in trouble."

"The companies we're talking about, they all keep banging on about making people's dreams come true," said Richard. "But you have to understand—this shit isn't about dreams. What *we* want is to keep people *alive*. Dreams come way down the list."

"That means—" I didn't get to finish the sentence.

There was a booming sound in the hallway, a couple of muttered expletives, and Jack Bailey crashed into the doorway.

I hardly knew the man, and even *I* could see he was in bad shape. His face looked gray.

Mark was already on his feet. "What is it? What's going on?"

"It's Ang Pemba Sherpa," Jack said. He looked dazed. He was shaking his head. "He's dead."

There was a moment of shocked silence. "What happened?" asked Mark finally.

Jack looked at him. "They're saying he fell," he said.

"I don't understand," said Richard. "It's too early to be—"

"—at Lukla," said Jack.

Another silence. "That's not possible," said Richard slowly. Jack was nodding, his expression grim, his eyes rimmed with white; he looked in that moment like a wild man.

"Which makes it murder," concluded Mark.

Jeannette de Beauvoir

Excerpt from the journal of George Mallory

Magdalene College, Cambridge University, 1908: It is to Cambridge that I return, after all. I've officially finished my studies, but Benson thinks I need another year here. I can re-sit my exams and perhaps do a bit better than the first time around, and it's not as if I have any idea what to do with my future.

And there's a literary prize in the offing: the best essay on James Boswell, the biographer of Dr. Johnson, and as I've read excessively about Boswell, Benson thinks I have a shot at it.

Of course, before I came up, I had to go back to Snowdonia. The experience was magical, and, as my brother Trafford is becoming an age where he is interesting and interested, I took him along. We had a ripping time of it, and I followed it up with a climbing adventure in the Lake District before arriving in Cambridge.

Whatever else you can say about us, we don't lack for drama.

Chapter Four

He came to find me in the garden.

"Not much of a welcome to Nepal, was it?" Jack said sympathetically, sitting down next to me on the bench. I was looking at the goddess of prosperity, who hadn't done much, apparently, for the dead man.

"I'm sorry for your loss," I said awkwardly. It was uncomfortable, being a stranger in a house of mourning. I had heard Laxsmi's voice, shrill and in pain, wailing. "This person—he was a friend of yours?"

He nodded. "Ang Pemba, one of our climbing sherpas," he said. "And, yeah, a friend. Almost twenty years of friendship, of working together."

I had about a thousand questions, and didn't know how to ask any of them. The only thing I *did* have a glimmer of understanding of was who he was talking about. Along with reading about the delectable George Mallory, my pre-Nepal research had taught me that the Sherpa (with a capital S) were an ethnic group, some of whom were sherpas (with a lowercase s), mountain workers providing guidance and support for Everest expeditions.

Now I nodded, acknowledging Jack's comment. I removed my glasses and polished them on the edge of my shirt to give myself a moment. There was still an elephant in the room—or garden, as the case may be. "So... why did Mark say he was *murdered?*"

"Mark is impulsive," he said. "I don't know much about what happened, no one does, I'm still waiting to hear. But there's no need to jump to conclusions. Not yet, anyway."

"But why would he even *say* so?"

The sun had disappeared, and now a thin mist was moving in around us, almost imperceptibly, weaving through the flowers and the statuary, lending an unreal feeling to the garden. Jack seemed to be looking through it, at something far away. He sighed. "It's *where* it happened that's the problem," he said at last. "Lukla—that's the name of the village—you have to understand, it isn't on the mountain. Well, it's in the mountains, but not on *the* mountain. If someone dies at Lukla, if it isn't natural causes, and it usually is, but if it isn't, it's probably related to a plane crash." He glanced at me. "There are two ways to trek to Base Camp from here," he explained. "You can take the bus to Jiri, or go by air to Lukla. Lukla's closer to Everest."

"But planes crash at Lukla?" I didn't like the casual way he'd said it, especially if a landing there was going to figure anywhere in my future.

He shrugged. "What do you expect? The runway's short. It's in the mountains. It's an airport where there shouldn't be an airport." His voice grew impatient. "Look, there's an element of risk in everything here. No one goes to Everest without knowing at some level they might not come back."

I decided to let the question of the airplanes go. *For now.* "So tell me why no one falls at Lukla."

He didn't look at me. "The thing is, the climbing sherpas, a lot of them die up there on the mountain," he said pensively and—seemingly—irrelevantly. "They account for between a third and a half of the deaths on Everest. Hell, I run one of the best expeditions, one of the safest ones, and *I've* lost climbing sherpas from my team. Mostly it's due to avalanches." He shrugged. "Well, it is for us, anyway; some climbing sherpas get killed because of the stupidity of the climbers they're there to protect, because their companies haven't trained their clients." He was staring off into the distance, seeing something I wasn't, something far away.

Something that haunted him.

"It's part of the devil's deal," he said at length. "It's the most dangerous job in the world, and believe me when I tell you that if any of them had a choice? They'd never do it. But like I said before—Nepal's poor, and the Sherpa people are poorer than most. And you have to understand, expeditions like ours can pay thousands of American dollars, with a bonus if they have a track record of summiting—and that's enough to support an extended family for a year or more, enough to send a kid to school here in Kathmandu. They all know the stakes, and they have to accept them. They don't really have a choice."

I didn't say anything, and he stretched out his legs and sighed again. "Okay. That's the background. Two things wrong here," he said. "First of all, you have to understand, Lukla's *nothing*. It's an airport and a bunch of teahouses and hotels with a village built up around them. It's a week's trek down from Base Camp. It's just a way station for trekkers and climbing teams. No one spends any time there, and there was especially no reason for Ang Pemba to be in Lukla, not when he's supposed to be making preparations up above Base Camp to start the season."

"And the other thing?"

His eyes came to rest on me. "Well, that's it, isn't it." It wasn't a question. "Ang Pemba is—he *was*—what we call an icefall doctor. Before the expeditions even arrive, before anyone sets up Base Camp, there's a team goes out over the Khumbu Icefall. That's the most dangerous part of the Everest climb. It's unstable, you know? The ice there's constantly shifting, and there are crevasses, really big ones, opening up with no notice, there are avalanches coming down, the whole area's in bloody motion all the time. Climate change is making it a lot worse, a lot more dangerous."

He looked at me, and shook his head, tried again. "These are the guys who go out there at the beginning of the season when the weather's bad, and I mean really bad, high winds that don't let up, avalanches, the whole thing, and they secure ropes and ladders for the expeditions to use. They figure out a safe passage—well, the safest path, anyway—across the glacier and up to Camp One, and beyond."

He sighed, settled in. "Base Camp gets set up in March, and the first camp to be established is generally the Sagarmāthā Pollution Control Committee's. Then the dedicated icefall doctor team has a puja and embarks on their fixing duties. Things change all season, so they work the entire season as a separate entity. Ang Pemba did that before he came to work for me. Sometimes they

35

have to rope three ladders together to go over a crevasse. It's crazy dangerous, and they're careful as hell." He paused. "Paying clients only have to go through the icefall a few times, but the sherpas? They can cross it twice a *night* to carry luggage. People who can do that, they just don't trip and fall in a village built around an airstrip."

I nodded. "So what do you think happened?"

"Damned if I know." He paused, and I thought he was about to say something else, but then he made a show of dusting off his knees and stood up. "But you can bet I'm going to find out. Anyway, it won't affect you and Emma. Just wanted to make sure you're okay. And—well, I have things to do, I'm sorry."

"Of course—"

"She'll be here day after tomorrow," he said, with an air of passing on responsibility. "We're clearing out of here then, when the members arrive."

It sounded like a club. "Members?"

"That's what we call our clients. The expedition members." He flashed a tired smile. "Sorry; niche jargon, right? Anyway, I went ahead and made some arrangements for you. Emma is chuffed about the trek up and I've asked Anish—he works here in our city office, I count on him for just about everything—to make the arrangements along the trekking route up to Base Camp. There'll be tents there for you, and you can stay on the mountain as long as you like. I know she's particularly keen to experience the altitude, so she can write about it. Maybe you can go talk to him in the morning."

I was still stuck a few thoughts back. "The mountain? Wait—we're going up Everest?"

He stared at me. "You're going to *Base Camp*," he said, as though addressing a child or a madwoman. "You're not *climbing*. Didn't you know? She's writing about Mallory, isn't she? Where else would you go for inspiration?" He cleared his throat. "Sorry, Alice—um, Amy—"

"Abbie," I said automatically.

He nodded. "Yes, well, Abbie. I really have to go."

The mist in the garden was dissipating, probably because it was gathering in my mind instead. I stared after him.

As I got ready for bed, I reviewed what I knew about this trip. Emma hadn't shared anything about her specific literary plot, so I'd just focused on learning about George Mallory and what had led him—and Britain—to decide to climb the highest mountain on Earth. But perhaps I should have spent more of that time on less historical research—as in, what was waiting for us up in the mountains. Dodgy plane landings and dead Sherpas. Maybe, I thought fancifully, Emma should change her genre to mystery writing instead.

I was almost asleep when Jack's voice intruded on my thoughts. Hadn't he said that Mark was impulsive?

Was that really a good quality in someone whose job is to ensure others' safety on the highest mountain in the world?

***

Anish was in his thirties, a small slightly tubby man with an apparently perpetually delighted expression. "Namaste! Namaste! Of course I know who you are! You are Miss Abigail Bradford, Miss Emma's friend! Come in, come in. You'll take some tea?"

"Thanks, but I—"

"Of course you'll take some tea," he said, nodding vigorously and grasping both my hands at the same time. "All peoples take tea at the office of Supreme Summits Expeditions in Kathmandu!"

Bemused, I allowed him to guide me safely to a chair. "You're too kind," I said. "Actually, Jack—"

"Jack is the Boss-Man," Anish said, nodding quickly, beaming. He seemed to do everything quickly. "Very good man to work for." He busied himself at a counter running the length of the narrow shop, and I looked around me. His desk was a utilitarian affair of metal, but the posters on the wall behind it were vivid, filled with bright tents and colorful snowsuits and Buddhist prayer flags. "Ah, I see you are looking at the flags. Yes! I will tell you about them, Miss Abigail! The flags are in five colors. Why five colors, you ask?"

I hadn't, but that didn't deter him. "They correspond to our five Buddhist elements: earth, wind, fire, water, and consciousness."

There didn't seem to be anything to say to that, though truth was I hadn't really paid attention to the colors other than noting they were bright. Consciousness as an *element*? I'd have to give that some thought. Later. I cleared my throat. "What exactly do you do here, Anish?"

He turned, a delighted smile already on his face, as though he'd been waiting for exactly that question. "I do everything, Miss Abigail! Everything! I schedule the journeys, I watch the weather, I pay the bills, I hire the helicopters. Everything!" He turned back to the counter and carefully poured liquid from a Thermos into two mugs. "Here you are," he said, handing me one, and taking the other around the desk with him.

I took a cautious sip. The tea was strong and very milky, with a slightly sour aftertaste that wasn't unpleasant. "Thank you."

He nodded energetically. "The Sherpas make tea like this on the mountain," he said. "Me, I am not Sherpa, but I make their tea to perfection. This will give you a taste before you go, so you become accustomed to it."

"Anish," I said carefully, "you know I'm not on the actual expedition, right?"

The smile became, if anything, broader. "But of course I know! Miss Emma and Miss Abigail, not good climbers. Boss-Man told me so."

"Not any kind of climbers at all," I said firmly.

"Only to Base Camp," he agreed. "And that, you find I think, is high enough." He gave a dramatic shudder. "Me, I never go above Base Camp! It is very high, and I have delicate hands, me!"

"Hands?" They looked pretty normal to me.

He nodded. "They are the first to go," he said seriously. "Frostbite. Often the fingers, they must be removed—

amputated? Yes? But you do not wish to think of such unpleasant things."

"On the contrary," I said, "I'd rather know what's going on."

"It will not affect you at Base Camp," he said, projecting reassurance into his voice. "But higher up, in the Death Zone—"

"Death Zone?" I think I may have actually squeaked.

He nodded again. "The Death Zone, it is very dangerous, yes? It is the part of the mountain that is highest—above eight thousand meters. Er—just over twenty-six thousand feet for you, dear lady. That far above sea level, Miss Abigail, it is impossible for your body to get the oxygen it needs. And your brain gets larger, you see, it swells up, and then… but never mind what happens to the brain! We are not here to speak of unpleasantness! You will find it difficult to breathe at Base Camp, too, Miss Abigail, but no need to worry! Because we will take good care of you! We will do acclimatization on your trek up!"

"As long as I'm not losing limbs," I said. "I want to be absolutely clear about that. No one said anything about limb loss." I wasn't going to pursue the brain thing.

He rubbed his hands together, perhaps unconsciously reacting to his own words, to the conjured image of blackened fingers. "I will tell you what you need to know. You must of course take care. Up there, it is very cold, terribly cold," he said. "And your body, when it is threatened, it directs the blood to flow away from the tips of your body so it can protect your vital organs. So your toes and your fingers, sometimes your nose—they die."

I must have been giving something away with my expression, because he held up his hands in mock horror. "But this will never happen to you, Miss Abigail! Not at all! No one at Supreme Summits Expeditions gets frostbite!"

I was glad to hear it.

"Now," Anish said, with an air of getting down to business, "We talk about your schedule."

"Emma will be here tomorrow," I said. I couldn't wait; I had a *whole* lot of questions for Emma.

"Yes," he agreed. "It is good. You will have time to set off on your trek before the members arrive. That is good; they can be a rowdy bunch, I think that is the expression Mr. Jack uses? Rowdy? It will be just you and Miss Emma, and of course your guide. I myself have chosen our very best trekking guide for you, Dawa Sherpa. He is so named because he was born on a Tuesday."

"Okay," I said cautiously. I had no idea what he was talking about.

Anish was nodding again, his sunny smile back in place. "You will like him very much," he promised, beaming in delight. "All peoples like Dawa. He is good guide for the ladies to take the trek into the mountains. And a porter; you will need a porter. I have arranged that also. I have your permits already. Everything is in order, that is how Supreme Summits Expeditions works. There is never, ever a problem with paperwork."

"Um—good," I managed to say. "Anish, can you explain exactly where you've got us going?"

His very white teeth flashed in appreciation. "The schedule! Yes, Miss Abigail, you are right to remind me, the schedule is so important! Of course we have a schedule. And maps. At Supreme Summits, there is never a problem!"

I doubted that, somehow, but decided to go along for the ride. "Okay," I said. "So show me."

"We begin," he said sunnily, "at Lukla. This is a village—"

"Wait," I said. *Bad beginning*, I thought. I'd looked it up online after my conversation with Jack, and none of what I'd read had made me very happy. Nepal's Lukla and Bhutan's Paro—both in the Himalayas—were in competition for the World's Most Dangerous Airport Award. The most dangerous *anywhere*. Literally *in the world*. "Lukla? Do we *have* to go there? It's a really scary airport, isn't it?"

He looked pained. "It *is* difficult," he conceded. "But not for the great pilots Supreme Summits uses. They are skilled, all of them, very safe. The best pilots! They know Lukla well. Never have they had a crash! Never! You are in good hands, Supreme

Summits hands! You do not have to worry. In fact, I will tell you this straight out: do not worry!"

Why is it when someone tells you not to do something, it becomes the *only* thing you can subsequently think of doing? I remembered a meme I'd seen once on Facebook: "Never in the history of calming down has saying 'calm down' calmed anyone down." *Never mind, Abbie. Get with the program.* "And we're flying in," I said, still a little faintly.

"You must be brave, Miss Abigail! Lukla is the beginning of your great Supreme Summits adventure!"

"Uh-huh," I said. I wondered if he was being paid per mention of the company name. "And one of your climbing sherpas just died there, at Lukla, didn't he?"

He closed his eyes, briefly. "Ang Pemba Sherpa," he agreed, nodding. "May he have a fortunate rebirth. But he was not in an airplane crash, Miss Abigail."

"He was an icefall doctor who fell in a village he wasn't even supposed to be in," I countered, and felt instantly guilty. There was no need for me to say that, contribute to Anish's anguish. I didn't know why I had. "Jack said he was going to look into it."

Anish nodded. "Very good friends, they were, Ang Pemba and Mr. Jack Boss-Man," he said sadly. "But you must not to worry. Supreme Summits Expeditions will keep you safe."

Even at Lukla? I wondered. The company hadn't exactly been able to keep Ang Pemba Sherpa safe, had it? But I was starting to spook myself, and that wasn't helpful. Emma, my employer, would be here tomorrow, and she was looking for a research assistant who was fit, cool, calm, and collected.

Right now I could just about offer the "fit" part. I wasn't too sure about the rest.

"Okay," I said. "Let's move on. What happens at Lukla?"

"You have dinner, you go to sleep," Anish said, visibly relieved that we were back on the right conversational track. "And then very early indeed on Monday morning, you will set off. It is an easy day, it is your first, we are considerate of travelers' needs at Supreme Summits Expeditions. You will hike—here, we say trek, but just between us, Miss Abigail, it is the same thing—you will hike to Phakding, this is another village in the mountains. There is much beautiful scenery along the way, and no extra elevation after Lukla. There you sleep in the teahouse—"

"Teahouse?" I thought those were places where one drank tea.

Another fast nod. "Yes, you do not know this yet, they are small hotels," he explained. "With a big dining room, so you can meet other travelers. Many friendships have begun in Nepal, even some romances. You will see!"

"We have enough romance on board as it is," I said. "Okay, go on. Proceed," I clarified, as he seemed to be waiting for me to say something else.

"Yes," he said a little uncertainly before gathering steam again. "Now is the first day to test your muscles. It is a little more steep, the terrain is somewhat more of a challenge, but you will overcome it, I am sure! Your destination is Namche Bazaar, where you will see many other trekkers. But also here you will start seeing members of other expeditions. You will enjoy Namche Bazaar," he added, smiling, nodding, and I found myself automatically nodding with him.

"What's there?" I asked.

"You will have time to explore it all," he promised. "It is a larger village, with much commerce—many members of other expeditions buy excellent high-altitude gear at Namche Bazaar."

"But not Supreme Summits?" It was half a tease: I was getting to know Anish.

"Never Supreme Summits!" He'd become indignant. "Every member we take is fully outfitted before leaving the city."

"So what else is there?"

"There are many shops you will enjoy," he promised. "So many Nepali handicrafts from the mountains, made by the people of the mountains. It has long been a point of commerce. It is part of the old Silk Road, have you heard of this? You are sitting on it right now! Kathmandu is part of the Silk Road. It is the route that connects the mysterious exotic East to the West." There was more than a flicker of irony there. "You stay an extra night in Namche

Bazaar, because your body must get used to the altitude. At Everest Base Camp, you will have only fifty percent of the air you are breathing now. You must acclimatize. The best way is to take your extra day and hike farther up. And this will be the day of a most auspicious occurrence, too: it is your first look at Sagarmāthā, or as the Sherpa say, Chomolungma, the mountain itself, the goddess herself, it is a special moment for all peoples." He nodded knowingly and leaned forward, lowering his voice, secretive. "Here is what you need to know, Miss Abigail." I leaned in with him, as he seemed to expect it. "The key to success, I have it, and I will tell it to you now." He took a deep breath before intoning, "Climb high, sleep low."

"Climb high, sleep low," I repeated, as though receiving an ancient and treasured mantra.

He leaned back and nodded, beaming. "You do that, you will be fine," he said, his voice now brisk. "And then you will go farther up, to Dingboche—here you will stay an extra day, also, for your body to come into harmony with the mountains. After that, it is Lobuche, this is an interesting day, you will start out in flat fields but then come to the toe of the Khumbu Glacier. There will not be ice, oh no, but the path is very rocky, some large boulders, many places to turn your ankle. You will be especially careful."

"I promise."

He nodded. "Dawa will be sure of it," he said, as though Dawa were to be trusted more with my welfare than I was. For all I knew, he was right. "And this is where you will pay your respects, too, it is where you will see the memorial cairns that remind all travelers of the many Sherpa peoples who have died on the mountain."

I remembered Jack's words. One of the most dangerous jobs in the world, and they did it because they didn't have any other choices. And they died. "It's surprising," I said softly, "that they can even bear to look at us, that they can stand being around us, when we're the reason for all that death."

He looked shocked. "Oh, no, Miss Abigail! The children can go to school, become doctors, become businesspeople, become lawyers and statesmen and chefs, because of the expeditions. At Supreme Summits, we know of many, many such peoples. It is good for the Sherpas."

"Not for the ones under the cairns."

He looked shocked. "They are not buried there, Miss Abigail. It is a memorial."

"I suppose they'd want to be buried in their own villages," I said, thinking it over.

"There is often not a body," he said soberly. "Many stay on the mountain. The spirit is released to be born again, but the body—it is one with the goddess. And it is impossible to find them, most of the time: they are in a deep crevasse, or if an avalanche has come—but no! We do not speak of these things! Now you are close! Because it is the next day that you will arrive at Everest Base Camp!" He made a graceful gesture, a little in the manner of a prestidigitator, and I had to laugh and enter into it. Everest Base Camp.

It was suddenly all feeling very real.

Excerpt from the journal of George Mallory

Bernese Alps, 1909: And so here I am finding myself once more in the mountains. Perhaps in the end there is no separating us.

Geoffrey Young's taken me under his wing. Last year he included me in his rather famous climbing holiday in Wales, where far too many people inhabit an inn and attack the mountains. It's all a little much.

But he's an excellent climber, though he said I have nothing to learn from him. He put me, even now, in the first class of British mountaineers, which has to be a kindness, for I haven't spent enough time at it to really be called anything. And now here I am, lazing in the sun, overlooking Europe's largest glacier...

Young is acutely aware, as am I, that all the Alps' major peaks have already been climbed; for him, the challenge is to find new routes, more difficult and challenging routes, deploying the rock-climbing skills we acquired at home.

I am thrilled to be here. Climbing, searching for holds, stretching oneself physically and mentally, pushing to one's very limits, and doing it in an outrageously beautiful environment—there is nothing more attractive than that.

We lost a day to bad weather but on August fourth we attempted the first ascent of the southeast ridge of the Nesthorn, a fearsomely jagged peak. It was windy and snowing when we left, but around seven o'clock we emerged above the clouds. It took us three hours to work our way along the ridge to a col where the ascent of the southeast ridge began. I'd gone ahead and was just trying to find a foothold above the overhang—this involves, of course, launching oneself both outward and upward—and didn't make it; I plummeted down past Young, but the rope held and so all was well in the end. We did make it to the summit in time for a glorious sunset, and then came back down. We were out twenty-one hours and were altogether rather pleased with ourselves.

We made a good attempt at Chamonix, but the weather was against us, and I was concerned that we'd heard of so many climbers' deaths after the first day, that I was easily convinced to accompany Young to the Weisshorn, which he planned to climb with an American, and for me to meanwhile sit by the fire and enjoy myself.

And so here I am.

Chapter Five

Laxsmi was a lot happier once she had Jack in her clutches, and was clearly pleased when he showed up on time for dinner. I never really then or later figured out exactly what the relationship between them was, but there was just the tiniest whiff of predation on her part when he was around her. I cheerfully and silently wished her well.

I was actually too exhausted to give it much thought. After leaving Anish, I'd spent the day exploring Kathmandu, and found myself more than a little dazed. Exotic, check. Unlike anything else I'd ever experienced, check. A little overwhelming, double-check. The city was ancient and modern all at once, small winding unpaved streets where the buildings seemed to lean over toward each other as though sharing secrets, connected to wider thoroughfares where cars and buses and bicycles jostled for limited space. Everywhere there was clearly new construction, the city having reinvented itself after the deadly earthquake of 2015 showed how desperately building codes were needed.

The same cast of characters was at dinner, and I was way too obviously interrupting something intense. A dead silence fell the moment I entered the dining room, and I hesitated. "I'm sorry. I should have knocked—"

"It's all right," Jack said. "Come in, come in, Andie, that's it, right? Angela?" Then and later I was astonished how someone with such an eye and ear for detail never grasped my name. I didn't correct him; he was still talking. "You're very welcome. To be fair, we could use a different point of view around here. Tell us about your day. Did Anish take care of you?"

"He did, thank you." I was still hesitant. "Really, I can get a tray in my room—"

"Don't be silly," said Mark. He was drinking, with two empty bottles already by his elbow. "Good to have someone here who's normal." He was looking at Richard as he spoke.

"Not sure I qualify, but I'll do my best," I promised, and took the same seat I'd been in the night before. I hoped that the menu would be a repeat performance, too. It would take me a very long time to get tired of chatamari.

As though reading my mind, Richard said, "Chicken tonight. Might as well enjoy it while we still can."

"Why, is something happening to it?" I watched as Laxsmi put more steaming dishes in the middle of the table and retreated again. "Not that I mind; I like chicken."

"We don't eat much meat up on the mountain," Jack said, dishing out steaming bowls of the stew-like substance. He handed me a bowl and I passed it along to Richard, then another for Mark, and finally mine. By then I'd been able to smell it—and that was something else: the smells here were sharper, tangier than back in Boston. Spices, some of which I could identify, most of which I couldn't, warm and sweet, and I was suddenly famished.

Jack was still talking "Anywhere above Lukla, meat's either taken up by yak, or helicoptered in when there are members who want to pay extra for it."

"Ah," I said. "I see your point."

"Let me get you a beer," said Mark to me. He'd stood up and had both his empty bottles in one hand.

"You've maybe had enough," said Jack, without looking up.

"Or maybe not. Let me see: am I climbing tomorrow? Nope. Don't think I'm climbing tomorrow," Mark said. "And that's all *you* have to worry about."

To break the tension as much as to be polite, I said, "Sure, why not? I'd love one. Is it Nepali beer?"

"It's called Khumbu Kolsch Sherpa," said Jack. He glanced up as Mark walked away, and then his eyes were back on his dinner. "There are a few breweries here in Nepal. This is from a craft brewery owned and operated by Sherpas."

Khumbu... I tried to remember where I'd heard the name, then realized it was more than once. The Khumbu Icefall, the most dangerous part of the ascent of Everest; Jack had told me that. And, this morning, Anish had mentioned that we'd be traversing part of the Khumbu Glacier.

"You probably won't want to drink a lot of alcohol on your trek," Richard said to me, playing the polite guide. "It dehydrates you, just when you need as much hydration as you can get."

Mark came back in and set a bottle next to my glass before sliding back into his seat, clutching his own. "So," he said, but didn't follow it up. He was watching Richard.

No one said anything, and the tension—surely I wasn't imagining it—seemed, like the dust, to shimmer in the air.

I cleared my throat. Time to provide whatever distraction they seemed to need. "I didn't know what Hanuman Dhoka was," I said, "so I went to see it today. Anish gave me a pass. It was—pretty amazing."

An overused word, but nothing else would have described where I'd spent the afternoon. Following the guidebook I'd bought as soon as I left the Supreme Summits office, I'd headed to the center of the city and found Durbar Square, which truly *was* impressive: extraordinarily large after the narrow passageways of the old Silk Road, paved with enormous stone slabs, and with at least two dozen colorful religious shrines scattered all through the square. On the sides. In the middle. Different sizes, shapes, heights. Different gods.

The shrines were way, way over the top. Religion in my experience was pretty staid, Gothic cathedrals and stained glass notwithstanding; religion, here, was loud and colorful and very integrated into everything else. Everywhere you looked there were prayer flags, flapping their messages in the wind, and the shrines themselves were painted with the same riotous bright colors. Towering above the square on tremendous stone foundations, most of them were topped by elaborately carved wooden structures in which you could barely discern the figure of a god or goddess, the bright ubiquitous prayer flags fluttering everywhere.

It was, Google had assured me, one of the most important religious centers in Nepal. That was all well and good, but you didn't just come here to pray: mixed in with all the surrounding religion was a world of commerce. At the bases of all the shrines were stands that offered—well, just about everything. Lamps, cashmere, rugs, bells, books, clothing, food, spices, small appliances... everything anyone could possibly wish to buy was laid out on the ground, on small carts, on the very steps of the shrines, being offered for sale by merchants who called out in loud, enticing, unintelligible voices. The secular (and even commercial) jostling with the sacred; total integration.

I knew the square had been significantly damaged in the earthquake; I'd assumed that, as a UNESCO site, rebuilding would have happened quickly, and was a little surprised to see some of the shrines still propped up, as it were, with thick timbers. It gave a feeling of impermanence to the area, which was probably a great theological point for Buddhism, but was also sad—these shrines had been here for hundreds and hundreds of years, the first ones dated from the third century, and then in a flash, in a horrible moment of death and destruction, one earthquake had been enough to wreak havoc.

And that was before you even counted the lives lost.

I recalled myself to the room and the conversation. "I read that people come there from all over, like a pilgrimage," I said, trying for a lighter tone, "It didn't feel like Lourdes or Mecca, though!"

"Respect is shown in different cultures in different ways," said Jack, considering the idea. "Here, it's everywhere. You don't have to trap the gods in churches; they're all around us."

"Especially on the mountain," said Richard.

"Yes," I said. I'd read about this, too. "It's a sacred mountain, isn't it?"

"They're all sacred," Richard said. "But the Sherpa call Everest *Chomolungma*—the goddess of the sky."

I could see it, then: the mountain as the goddess of the sky, stretching out to touch the firmament, the infinite, soaring above all earthly concerns, leading to heaven, inspiring dreams and prayers, anchoring people's lives to the magical, the holy, the beautiful.

Beauty being comparative, of course. "Then the Sherpas must hate all the tourists, trampling all over Everest," I said. I suspected that Mark might have something to say, with his concerns about overcrowding and hapless amateurs on the mountain. I wasn't disappointed.

"Wouldn't you think so?" Mark said. He was well into his third beer by now. He planted both elbows on the table and leaned in, his dark eyes holding mine, intense and focused, nearly black. "Every year they have to send up additional expeditions to clean it up," he said. "It's an ecological disaster. The garbage that people just drop, it's tons of stuff. Clothing, O2 bottles, tents, tools, food wrappers, cans—you name it, it's up there. Not to mention mountains of human feces, sixty thousand pounds of it last year alone."

"Nice dinner conversation," said Richard. "Abbie doesn't need to hear that."

Mark didn't spare him a glance. The air crackled with tension between them; I imagined I could see it, a fizzing bolt of blue electric energy, bright as my hair. I wondered what had been going on all day that made them so bad-tempered—and wondered how they managed up on the mountain, when they were putting their lives in each other's hands.

I cleared my throat. "Anish was very helpful," I told Jack. "It looks like he's worked out our whole itinerary."

"We take a lot of people trekking up to Base Camp," he said. "Not everybody is just here to summit. And trekkers tend to be more…"

"Manageable?" suggested Mark.

"… friendly," finished Jack. He, too, was avoiding eye contact with his guides, seemed relieved to have me to talk to. "They're not as competitive as the climbers are."

I decided to risk another tricky subject. "Did you find out anything more about your friend?" I asked. "Ang Pemba Sherpa?"

Mark pushed his plate away, stood up, and left the room.

There was a long moment of silence in his wake.

"Sorry about Mark," said Richard. "He and Ang Pemba were close. Don't let it bother you, Abbie."

"I'm the one who's sorry," I said. "I shouldn't have brought it up. It's none of my business, really."

Jack said, "I've been looking into it. I spoke with an inspector. The police force is treating it as an accident."

"It might even be one," said Richard. I had a feeling these two had already had this same conversation more than once. "You know that, Jack. He could have had a heart attack, or a stroke, or a seizure. Anything that would make him black out and fall."

"Fine," said Jack.

"Just because we—"

Jack interrupted him. "Then you tell me, mate, what the hell he was doing in Lukla," he said. "He's supposed to be at Base Camp. Mingma Tenzi and Sejun Tej arrived three days ago. They've already been setting up the camp, and the icefall doctors are meant to be there laying ropes right now. Today. What the *hell* was he doing at Lukla?"

Richard didn't have an answer, or at least not one he cared to share. He was turning his empty beer bottle around and around in circles on the tablecloth, studiously paying attention to it and not to his employer. I tried to make myself as invisible as possible. Probably not the best time for a bright remark about the weather.

But it was a good question, for all of that. I hadn't known the Sherpa, but already I felt some allegiance to Supreme Summits Expeditions and its people, and it was a curious set of circumstances.

Right, I told myself. *Which are you—Nancy Drew, or Miss Marple? If a police inspector had said there was no foul play, there was no foul play. And you, my girl, had best stick to your historical research and your mad hiking skills, because it's all about to be put to the test.*

Before I went to bed, though, I did pull up a browser window and typed "Lukla" into the query field, selecting "images" and peering at the results. It was quaint. It was lovely.

For one Sherpa, it had been deadly.

I sighed, closed the laptop, and got ready to go to sleep. I was a research assistant and traveling companion, not a detective. And definitely not someone who wanted to climb the mountain.

But that night I dreamed of Ang Pemba Sherpa all the same.

***

Emma arrived the next day in time for lunch, and if attending a romance writers' conference was as exhausting as she'd claimed, it certainly didn't show; she was briskness personified. "Well, and here you are, dear," she said to me. "Like Nepal?"

"So far," I said cautiously. I was in the dormitory-style bedroom, trying on a kurta I'd bought the day before at Durbar Square, and wondering whether I'd gone a little too far with the riotous colors. I didn't exactly see it being a hit back in Boston; we tend to be a little more staid in our wardrobes.

"Hmm," she said, eyeing my outfit. She herself was wearing linen slacks and a t-shirt that had definitely seen better days. "You'll want to wear trekking pants on the trails," she warned. "Did Jack send you the list of what to pack? I asked him, but he probably forgot."

"He forgot," I agreed, sitting down on the edge of my bed. "But I got it all, anyway. Three cheers for Google."

"Indeed." She looked at me a moment longer, as though considering whether or not to say something, then abruptly changed her mind. She settled a backpack onto one of the other beds, sat down beside it, and poked around inside it a little aimlessly for a moment. "Is Laxsmi here?"

"Should be," I said. I actually hadn't seen her since breakfast. Obviously the house—and I still didn't quite understand whether it was a hotel or Supreme Summits' residence or something else altogether—followed Western culture's embrace of three meals a day; I'd already learned that wasn't the way most people here dined. In a typical Nepali breakfast there's no morning bacon or eggs, no bowls of muesli, and there is definitely *no* peanut butter on toast, my own preferred way to start the day; here, rather, a cup of tea takes priority. Classically the first meal of the day is in mid-morning; the earlier morning ritual revolves around freshly boiled and brewed *chiya*, with or without milk, with enough sugar to kick-start anyone's heart.

But here at the Supreme Summits Inn, Western needs were clearly catered to.

I'd eaten alone; Richard was swallowing the last of his coffee when I made it to the dining room, and neither Mark nor Jack had made an appearance. I drank the tea and Laxsmi silently served me a blend of spiced brown chickpeas and potato curry mixed through with chili and onions and topped off with a hard-boiled egg. The shards of raw onion and chilies ensured I was given a good wake-up call… and a severe case of really bad breath. These small plates of curried vegetables, I'd learned from yet another Google search, were called *tarkari* and had no fixed ingredients. They can range from very simple, with just one or two elements, to extremely elaborate, though the latter is generally reserved for the tourists in Kathmandu. The mountains tended more toward simplicity.

Not that Laxsmi had told me anything about that. There was no helpful patter to accompany the meal, the kind of thing wait-staff in the West might have provided: *Here's your tarkari, here's what's in it.* I was leaning heavily instead on hasty searches performed on my phone.

Laxsmi, for her part, seemed to want to speak only to Jack. I imagined that might become a problem once the other "members" of the Supreme Summits expedition arrived. There's just so far you can go to ignore a roomful of people accustomed to privilege and out for adventure. I'd been a reluctant part of such groups before; people with wealth tend to seek out other people with wealth.

Emma grinned. "Well," she said, "then we'll just have to see how she feels about having *me* stay here."

I raised my eyebrows. "Why? Is there a problem?"

"Only insofar as Jack is concerned," she said cheerfully. "Laxsmi's smitten with him."

"I *had* noticed as much," I said, and added again, "Is it a problem?"

"Not for us," she said. "Maybe for her." She stretched, her arms arcing toward the ceiling. "God, it's good to be here. Even the air feels different, don't you think?"

"Have you been before?" I'd never asked her that, in the months when we were planning the trip and I'd been trying to get into shape; it hadn't come up. But she and Jack appeared to have a shared history of some kind, and he seemed pretty rooted in Nepal.

"Yes," Emma said. "A lot of years ago." There was something in her voice that sounded a lot like a slammed door, with the key turning in it afterward for good measure.

I looked at her speculatively. I'd known her for over six weeks, now, and I knew almost as little now as I had that first cold February night when she'd interrupted my dinner—and my life.

Phillip, when consulted, hadn't been very helpful. "She taught here," he said when I grabbed him and made him take me out for Chinese food. "Here," in Cambridge, was a relative thing; there are at least ten colleges and four universities in the city. Probably more.

"Harvard?" I asked. It was where my brother taught, after all; he'd been able to snag a lecturer position that he didn't even care to wrangle into tenure-track—he just liked teaching, and obviously didn't need the financial security of tenure. We'd long ago together made a pact to never apply for it; there were too many others who legitimately needed the positions.

Phillip was navigating a dumpling and his eyes were watering from the heat. He nodded, swallowed, and grabbed some rice with his chopsticks. "Yeah," he said. "But it was back in the day, I'd think about twenty years ago. At least. Probably more."

"Literature?" I guessed. "Has to be either that or human sexuality, the way some of those romances are explicitly racy." I paused. "Or so I've been told."

"So you've been *told*?" he echoed, the light in his eyes dancing in amusement. "Come on, Abbie, you've never succumbed?"

I sighed. I'd already decided I was far too young to become a curmudgeon, so I'd bought one of Emma's books and read it—I have to admit—in just two sittings. Justine had been right: it wasn't what I'd expected. From now on I would confine my sneering to Hallmark Christmas movies. "I did, I did," I admitted. "And?"

I shrugged. "What do you want me to say? She's good," I said. "Characters with depth, no gratuitous sex, an interesting plot, accurate historical detail. I stand corrected."

Phillip nodded. "You going to finish that cabbage?" He wasn't one to rub anything in.

I pushed the dish across the table to him. The room seemed suddenly too hot, too oppressive, too filled with too many MIT students talking about graphics interfaces and materials processing "What else do you know about her?"

"She has a Wikipedia page, didn't you read that?"

I shook my head. "I thought I'd ask you first. Get it from the horse's mouth, so to speak. Especially since you're the one roped me into this whole adventure."

"See? You're already thinking of it as an adventure!" He was grinning. "All right, all right. She taught comparative lit. Not for very long; must have started writing novels pretty much when she started teaching."

They'd have been a nice break from the rigors of academia, for sure. "No history?" I asked. "She does historical romances."

"Seems history was more of an avocation than a vocation," said my brother, casually picking up the last of the dun-dun noodles with his chopsticks. "But she quit before she got tenure, when one of her books won some big literary prize or other." Phillip reads sparingly outside his own discipline, and never fiction. His relaxation reading involved home décor magazines. *Architectural Digest* was more his cup of tea.

Thus mentally reminded, I poured out the last of the tepid teapot contents into our cups. "How about marriage?" I demanded.

"No, thank you. We're related, remember?"

"Funny man. I meant Emma."

"First-name basis. That's a good sign." He leaned back and sighed appreciatively. "Damn, I always eat too much here. So yeah, there was a Mr. Caulfield sometime in the past, but I only know that because someone told me she'd had a rough time recently and this trip is supposed to put a lot of things behind her, and when I asked if whatever it was would affect you adversely, they said no, it had to do with an anniversary of her husband's death. So as you see, sister dear, I'm always looking out for you."

Back in the Kathmandu here-and-now, Emma was making it clear she didn't want to be asked questions about her past—okay, fine, I could understand that; I'm never comfortable being asked about my past, either. That would mean explaining my mother to people, and I'd spent far too much of my adolescence trying to do that.

And it wasn't as though I was all that anxious for us to become besties: I've spent enough time with people whose boundaries—or lack thereof—included apparently feeling they had the right to entrée to every aspect of my life and thoughts, and wasn't anxious to be That Person vis-à-vis Emma.

But while curiosity may have killed the cat, it was tugging at my imagination, too, and the thought of my employer having a deep, dark secret was intriguing.

Almost like a story from a romance novel.

"Well," I said, "you don't have to see much of her. We're leaving tomorrow. Oh, and Anish—that's Supreme Summits' Man in Kathmandu—has a special surprise for you: our guide's grandfather is from the other side of the mountain, literally, and he was part of the supply team for some of the English expeditions in Tibet. Anish says he has some stories."

Emma's interest sharpened. "Did he meet Mallory?"

"Don't know," I said. "But maybe the luck of Chomolungma will be with us."

"Hmmm." She leaned back and stretched luxuriously. "You've done well, Abbie," she said. "What do you suppose is for lunch? I'm famished."

"If you're lucky, chatamari, which I could eat every day for a year."

She nodded, obviously acquainted with the dish. "Hopefully some protein, too," she said. "Have to eat it while we can. Did you and your Man in Kathmandu go through the stuff we'll need? Got the permits and the packing?"

"Already done," I said cheerfully. "Apparently all peoples trust Supreme Summits Expeditions to never put a foot wrong with paperwork. And he's assigned us a guide named Dawa Sherpa, he's the one with the Tibetan ancestor, and a porter named—I kid you not—Rocky, and they'll have all the supplies we need. We just have to pack clothes and personal items." I hesitated. "If you wanted to bring a laptop or a tablet, he said there are charging stations all the way up, in the teahouses where we'll be staying. So you can work on the novel as we go."

"Yes, yes." For a writer, she seemed remarkably uninterested in that news, and I gave a mental shrug. Her problem, not mine. My MacBook was coming, anyway, even if it meant I had to wash out my socks at night to make room for it.

Jack wasn't around, and nor was Mark, but Richard joined us and with him were three other people, two men and a woman, all three in their forties and obviously in good shape. In at least one case, very good shape.

I notice these things. For someone who doesn't take romance novels seriously, I'm never averse to acting them out in real life.

Richard waved a hand over their heads. "Expedition members," he said, as though that were the only introduction necessary. They stopped eating to shake hands with us across the table.

Emma got right down to it. "Why d'you want to climb?" she asked them, planting her elbows firmly on the table and leaning into them.

"Because it's there," said one of the men with a smile. He was the sexy one, with a voice to go with it: Paolo, from Italy. "As George Mallory said."

"Ha!" It came out as a snort. "Now *there's* a quote that's been taken out of context only about a thousand times," said Emma.

"I have no idea why no one's ever wanted to grant Mallory a sense of humor. You two others on board with that idea?"

The woman, Sylvia, said, "It is an accomplishment, climbing the highest mountain, is it not?" She smiled, fluttered a hand gracefully before putting it on top of Paolo's, which was resting on the table. So they were a couple.

She was Italian, too. "Me, I'd like to go into outer space, on a rocket, but that, that is not happening. So I will go to the top of the world instead."

Emma was nodding, but didn't say anything; maybe she was trying to figure out how to fit space travel into her book about Mallory. Apparently not being able to, she turned to the third man. "And you?"

He shrugged, made a languid gesture. "I have climbed the others," he said. "This completes the set."

"The others?" I asked.

Richard cleared his throat. "There's a collection of fourteen mountain peaks that together make up a set that people want to summit," he said. "There's some prestige attached to it. They're all in the Himalayas or the Karakorams, and they're all above eight thousand meters." I gave him a grateful smile; Richard was the most helpful person I'd ever met.

Except for Anish, of course. But *his* friendliness was exhausting.

"It is an élite club," the third man, a German, was acknowledging. "And I will belong to it."

"Only if you make it to the summit this spring, Jurgen," Paolo said to him. "It is not yet in the bag. Remember what happened at Manaslu."

There was a long pause. "What happened at Manaslu?" I asked.

Jurgen shrugged. "I did not summit on the first attempt," he said. "It does not matter. I made it to the top the following year."

"Some of the summits are tricky," Richard said to me. "Believe it or not, Everest isn't even the most technically difficult. And the question of whether or not someone has actually summited is largely left to the honor system, though in Nepal they require a photo for it to be official."

"I have honor," said Jurgen with dignity.

"Yes, yes, we all know who you are," said Paolo irritably. "We all know—"

He was interrupted by the arrival of Laxsmi, who pushed a cart into the room, leaving it closest to where Richard was sitting. The look she gave Emma could have set a forest on fire. "Here is meal," she announced and flounced out, none of the usual namaste and bowing anywhere to be seen. Emma smiled faintly.

Richard sighed. "I'll just pass things around, family-style," he suggested. "Laxsmi isn't herself today."

Sylvia said, "It is our fault! We arrived early. We emailed last week from Rome…" Her voice trailed off uncertainly.

"No doubt," said Richard, passing bowls around. "But if Jack's the one who read the email—and he probably was, even though Anish tries his best to out-click him—then who knows what he told Laxsmi. Probably nothing, to be fair. No panic."

It was lamb curry, which was just fine with me. I took a few bites and got back to the conversation. "But it can't just be the honor system," I said to Richard. "People must see you when you're at the top, right? And people take pictures? Selfies?" I'd seen a whole lot of those on YouTube. "Plus, isn't there some kind of GPS positioning that would prove it?"

Richard nodded, drank some water, swallowed. "Nepal's mountaineering association requires photo evidence for it to be official," he conceded. "And GPS is inexact."

"And sometimes no one else is there," said Paolo.

"Not so much on Everest," said Richard. "It'd be pretty damned unusual to be the only one up there, unless you're a fool who's left the descent too long or who's up there in bad weather."

"Let me guess," I said with a smile. "That doesn't apply to Supreme Summits Expeditions."

He laughed. "You're catching on," he said, still smiling. "No; we pretty much make sure no one does that. And Paolo's right, sometimes one expedition will snag a weather window the others don't see, or don't want, and there *can* only be one or two people up there. You never know." His eyes were on Jurgen, and they were suddenly watchful. "And listen—Ed Viesturs, he's a famous mountaineer, he's always said it's called climbing, not summiting. We like to think that the *process* is the point."

"The achievement is the point," contradicted Jurgen, his eyes meeting Richard's. He was looking for a confrontation, and when Richard didn't respond, he smiled, slightly, as though scoring a point, then transferred his gaze to me. "You have to understand, Miss—um—you have to understand, the summit is the one yes-or-no proposition there is in all of life," he said. "The summit is what turns humans into heroes. It is everything. Not achieving it is a failure. It can bring fame and it can forge reputations." He looked at Emma. "And that, dear lady, is why I climb—no, I mis-speak. That is why I *summit*."

Paolo said, "It is not just that, though, is it? It has meaning, the summit. It is the ultimate metaphor for achievement, yes? A vertical finish line that tells you—you, yourself, not the world, not anybody else—that you have gone as far as possible, because there is nowhere higher to go."

"Except for space," said Sylvia, a little dreamily.

He smiled at her. "Except for space," he said in agreement, reaching across and caressing her cheek. "But we must not only think of the summit. It is very Western thinking."

"I am from the West," said Jurgen.

Paolo ignored him. "Westerners have a linear view of life and how we are in it," he said to Emma. "We celebrate the end of an effort: it is the paycheck, it is the promotion, it is the highest score. It is the summit."

Sylvia was nodding. "And we miss the point," she agreed. "The more mountains you climb, the more you understand this."

"Every mountain carries unique summit challenges," summarized Richard, his eyes now on his food. He was being polite, I thought, but his heart wasn't in what he was saying. Something in the conversation had distracted him.

"Give us an example," urged Emma. "Besides Everest."

"Okay." He might be bored, but he was a guide, after all, and Emma was a client. He thought for a moment. "Right. So— there's Kangchenjunga. It's the world's third-highest mountain, behind Everest and K2. And on Kangchenjunga there's a long-standing tradition of not touching the top. The local Nepali, *and* the Sherpa, they've always asked climbers not to disturb the home of the gods, which is the actual summit. So in respect to their wishes, we stop a few feet away."

"I touched the summit," said Jurgen.

"To the surprise of exactly no one," said Paolo.

There was a moment of embarrassed silence as we all discovered a sudden interest in our food, except for Emma, who was looking around the table with something like fascination. "Well," she said brightly, "what *would* George Mallory say?"

Excerpt from the journal of George Mallory

Roquebrune, Provence, 1910: What I've been saying is that I need to find work.

I applied twice to Charterhouse, and they wouldn't have me, saying my mathematics aren't quite up to snuff. I have no idea what else I'm qualified for. But I also just received a small family legacy, so I needn't worry... for a couple of months, anyway.

I welcome the break. I still need to finish this blessed essay on Boswell; it's gone completely out of control and is approaching the length of a book manuscript. And perhaps I can pick up some small change as a travel writer whilst I'm here.

My ankle's been playing up again and even hiking is painful, so I'm spending a great deal of time reading, practicing my French, and swimming. And thinking. I draw a parallel between the mountaineering that I love so much, and having that same courage, become willing to take risks, in other areas of life as well. One must commit oneself to a course and stay that course.

And now I find myself in a very pleasant land of sunshine. The Maritime Alps are only about twenty miles away and they must be the most enchanting peaks... so I am testing myself, day after day, to become stronger, to become worthy of peaks such as those. I even have started climbing some of the nearby hills—well, mountains I should call them, for they are real mountain shapes with fine precipices and as high as Ben Nevis.

I don't suppose I shall ever be fully myself if I am far from the peaks.

Chapter Six

We left Kathmandu early the next morning.

We'd returned to our room after dinner, both of us meaning to stock up on sleep, and it was Emma who'd noticed it first. "Someone's been here," she said.

I looked up from my MacBook. "What d'you mean?"

"My backpack. Things aren't right." She straightened up. "I'm a little obsessive about it," she said. "Where I keep my meds, what order the pens are in, which pocket for my phone. Someone's messed it up."

I put my laptop down and picked up my toiletries case, the thing that was closest to hand. There was some mascara missing, something I'd probably not notice unless I was looking. I'd just assume I'd misplaced it.

Emma was watching me. "Check your suitcase," she said. I hadn't heard that voice from her before.

I flipped it on its side and snapped it open. I'm not the world's neatest person, but it was clear that even I wouldn't have left it quite that messy. My toothbrush was inside a t-shirt; the bookmark in one of the paperbacks I'd brought had been moved.

"Someone's searched our things," I said, stating the obvious.

She nodded. "And they don't care whether we know it or not," she said. "That's interesting."

"Is it?" The only other time I could remember someone rearranging my luggage was when I'd been invited to a weird retro country-house weekend in the Cotswolds and a maid had unpacked my stuff.

"Something to think about," Emma said. And that had, interestingly, been that. I personally thought it deserved a lot more speculation, but I was still getting to know her, and by the time I came in from a walk through the garden I'd almost convinced myself that it was our imaginations.

Almost.

Everyone, it seemed, came out to see us on our way, a sort of modern version of the send-offs in Victorian England where the entire staff from butler to kitchen apprentice lined up to bid travelers adieu. In our case, it was Laxsmi, Richard, Mark, Paolo, and Sylvia. Jurgen was conspicuous by his absence. But at the last minute Jack breezed in, grabbed Emma around the waist, and kissed her full on the lips—and while I'm not an expert on things romantic, that was no we're-just-friends kiss.

Laxsmi glowered, Emma giggled—giggled!—and the taxi driver tooted his horn impatiently. "Ladies! The airport!"

"Yes, yes, we must go," said Emma, disengaging herself from Jack's clutches. Since he was a good twenty years her junior (and I was being generous here), and in far better physical shape, this took a minute. It was stiflingly hot, there were horns blasting from the street beyond the wall, and the courtyard seemed suddenly small and oppressive. No matter what else happened, we were heading for the mountains, and I could almost feel my heart lifting in response. Maybe my brother Phillip was right: everyone needs a little adventure in their lives.

I helped the driver get our luggage on board, and with prolonged promises to meet again at Base Camp, we finally were on our way.

Emma settled back into her seat with a sigh of contentment. "There! That wasn't too bad," she said.

I was flipping through the folder Anish had given me. "You have your papers, right?" I asked her. I'd already checked twice. Okay, so I'm slightly obsessive-compulsive.

"Right here, dear." Emma patted her daypack. "I didn't have you down as a worrier," she added.

"I'm not." Okay, maybe more than slightly obsessive-compulsive.

"Hmm." She looked out the window, the street scenes tumbling past as our driver set himself to try out for some invisible Formula One course in the middle of the city. "How far along are you with George?" she asked suddenly.

"George?"

"Mallory," she said, bringing her attention back inside the car. "Remember?"

"Bloomsbury, the Battle of the Somme, and beyond," I said.

"And what do you think?"

My turn to look out the window. Those colors, flashing by in saris and kurtas and shop awnings; strings of bright prayer flags fluttering everywhere, buildings painted in blues and oranges. "I think he spent most of his life looking for something," I said slowly. "His tragedy isn't that he never found it; his tragedy is that he never knew exactly what it was he was looking for."

Her focus had sharpened. "Is that what you think? That's interesting." She clung to the seat as we rounded a corner particularly viciously. "But I don't know, Abbie—I never thought of that. He was actually the perfect man of his times, wasn't he? What was he missing? He was clever, popular, handsome, an officer and a gentleman, an explorer… I think a lot of men wished they were George Mallory."

I shrugged. "Maybe Mallory wished they were, too, instead of him."

She wasn't letting me off the hook that easily. "How do you figure?"

"He was so conscious of being in the spotlight, all the time," I said, grabbing the seat in front of me as we went around another tight corner. "There wasn't ever a time when he didn't feel somebody's eyes on him, you know? And he played into it, of course he did. Who wouldn't?" I hesitated. "But all those letters to Ruth? He recycled them into articles. He was constantly recording his life, constantly reporting on himself, constantly fascinated by the person he was becoming, constantly standing back and observing the great George Mallory. He did it well, of course—hell, he did it brilliantly, I don't have to tell *you* his writing was gorgeous." Like everything else about him, I thought. "And the camera he took with him on his expeditions, and his diaries. He knew the world was watching. And there's part of me that feels a little sorry for him, for that. It's not comfortable at the top, whether it's literally or metaphorically."

"He *wanted* the world to be watching," Emma countered.

"Maybe." It wasn't really that simple, I thought. It had stopped being that simple when he found himself in the mud of Flanders with snipers waiting for an inch of skull to show above the trench line to blast him to Kingdom Come. It had stopped being that simple when he left the hothouse atmosphere of the Bloomsbury set and the intellectual pleasures of Cambridge and tried to settle down to domestic bliss in a "cottage with roses 'round the door" and three children to care for. It had stopped being that simple when he started running—first figuratively, and then literally—from the screaming nightmares of an undiagnosed post-traumatic stress disorder.

Maybe, for Mallory, it had never been that simple.

Emma's eyes had narrowed. "What are you thinking?"

"It's just these climbers, they're all running, aren't they? Either from something or to something." I paused as we screamed to a belated stop at a red light. "Listen, that guy Jurgen, you heard him. Summiting is everything to him. To summit the fourteen peaks. It's like a drug. And what's he going to do after Everest? Do it all again with no oxygen? That's what a climber's like. They're obsessed. When they're not climbing, they're thinking about climbing, reading about climbing, talking about climbing. But Mallory... he had a *life*. His children might have bewildered him, but he loved them. And he seemed genuinely crazy about Ruth. Didn't love teaching, but didn't hate it, either. The point is, he had something to go home to. It wasn't just about the summit."

"Maybe that's all irrelevant. A lot of people think he didn't."

I met her eyes. I had a sudden insight, was seized by a sudden certitude. "But *we* do," I said. "Isn't that what you've been thinking all along? Isn't that what you're going to say, in your book? That he died on the way *down* from the top, not on the way up? That he was the first to summit Everest?"

"What makes you think that?"

"Because it makes for a better story," I said, "and you know it as well as I do. Don't play the ingénue, it doesn't suit you. Isn't that the real reason we're here?"

Emma shook her head. "Of course not," she said. "I can't prove anything. And besides, if I were trying to, we'd be in Tibet now, not Nepal. The evidence is somewhere on the North Approach." She paused. "But yes, I think that's how I'm going to write it." Her voice, suddenly, faraway.

I said, softly, "If you can write the stories for a society, it doesn't matter who writes the laws."

"What's that?"

"Just a quote I heard in graduate school," I said.

"Hmm. They must have fanciful ways of looking at history, over at Boston College, dear."

"Must make you glad you taught at Harvard," I snapped.

There was a long silence, during which I nearly bit my tongue. Feisty the old girl might be, but there was such a thing as overstepping, especially for a lowly research assistant and general dogsbody.

"Well," Emma said at last, "we shall have to see."

And then we were at the airport, and I didn't think about George Mallory again for a very long time.

***

Anish was waiting when the taxi decanted us in front of the domestic terminal at Tribhuvan Airport. I'd come into Nepal through the international terminal—just as chaotic as this one—and while it had only been a few days earlier, I felt like a great deal of time had passed.

I couldn't even see the dust dancing in the air anymore; I'd become that acclimatized.

Anish and Emma bowed to each other and exchanged namastes as I looked around. The international terminal catered to travelers of all sorts; the domestic terminal served only trekkers and climbers, and the large central hall was filled with just as many colors as the shops along Thamel Street—except that here they were Gore-Tex rather than silk. "All peoples are happy to fly into mountains," said Anish encouragingly.

"One trusts he doesn't mean that literally," Emma said, *sotto voce*, as I shrugged into my backpack.

"Don't be so sure. He never said that all peoples actually return." My stomach was doing something unpleasant.

We'd packed only what we absolutely needed for the next month; Laxsmi was presumably looking after the rest of our belongings back in Kathmandu. And even the bare necessities were pretty heavy; I was mentally thanking my trainer back at the gym in Boston. "But you are not to worry!" Anish exclaimed when I mentioned it to him. "You will meet Rocky, your porter, at Lukla. He will help you."

"Isn't he carrying all our gear, though? The tents, all that?"

He nodded. "Very, very strong, Rocky," he said. "All Sherpas, very strong. He can carry the side of a house, Rocky. All Supreme Summits Expeditions porters, very strong."

Emma and I exchanged glances. "It still feels like an imposition," I said, a little uncertainly.

"It is how he feeds his family," said Anish simply, and effectively put an end to that train of thought. We followed him as he pushed resolutely through clumps of travelers, about two-thirds of whom were Caucasian—loud, energetic westerners.

We'd been warned that the usual airline weight requirements were super-strictly enforced here, which made sense: no one wants to be unexpectedly overweight when flying, as Anish said, into the mountains.

Clearly, though, not everyone had gotten the message. The floor was littered with bags and backpacks and people—most of them young—frantically emptying out their contents, offering stuff to other people, re-packing.

Anish was deep in conversation with a uniformed person at the one counter. He came back to us, beaming. "The airplane will be on time!" he exclaimed. "This is a good omen for the esteemed ladies!"

He seemed to be waiting for applause. "That's lovely. Is it often late?" I asked obligingly.

He nodded vigorously. "It has to be clear on both ends, the weather," he said. "Your pilot, he needs to see, yes? To not fly into the side of the mountain?"

"No," I agreed fervently. "We don't want to fly into the side of the mountain."

"Then we go now, please."

Our bags and bodies were duly weighed, and Anish shepherded us onto a small bus. "Here we say good-bye," he said. "At Lukla, Dawa Sherpa who is your guide will be waiting for you. You will like him. All peoples like Supreme Summits Expeditions staff."

It sounded more like an order than an observation, and we nodded meekly, gave the requisite bows, and clambered onto the bus. "Well, all I can say is, I'm glad you were the one to deal with him, dear," said Emma. "I'd get railroaded into doing all sorts of things."

"What makes you think I haven't?"

Seven o'clock in the morning, and already the air was shimmering with heat rising, the smells of curry and something else pungent in the bus. It was a far more utilitarian model than the ones I'd seen in Kathmandu itself, which were all painted bright blues and oranges and yellows and bedecked with bells and prayer flags; this was a straightforward vehicle, with seats made of tough canvas and—as everywhere—no glass to speak of in the windows; just a small statue on the dashboard to remind the driver and passengers that here we were living at the whims of the gods.

Well, we were about to ascend into their home turf; it made sense.

We duly arrived at the plane, a Dornier flown by Tara Air, which had, I was glad to see, twin engines. Belts and braces, as my father, who traveled incessantly, liked to say. The fourteen of us trooped obediently from the bus and climbed into the plane. Backpacks were stored aft in the fuselage, and there was even a uniformed smiling flight attendant to give us safety instructions.

Emma was fiddling with her camera; I listened to the safety spiel with particular attention, drinking in every word.

I should note here that I've never been good in confined spaces, and a small airplane absolutely qualifies. Add to that the fact of it being airborne, and heading for the world's most dangerous airport, and I was fervently wishing that I'd thought to bring serious drugs with me. Or a whole lot of alcohol. Or both.

On this flight, everyone got a window seat; that's all there were. Two pre-teen boys were in the seats ahead of me and were certainly not at all concerned about anything other than their beeping smartphones. The flight attendant gave us all cotton wool for our ears and ginger candy (presumably for our stomachs), the engines roared reassuringly, and off we went.

I wish I could record that I am the sort of person who enjoyed the adventure of that flight. I wish I could note that I admired the scenery as we flew up into the Himalayas, but I can't do it; I think I spent most of the flight in the brace position, rediscovering words to desperate prayers I'd assumed were long forgotten.

Emma certainly seemed to be enjoying herself, peering out the plane's port side (those were, we'd been told, the best views) and snapping pictures, though she must have gotten some blurriness as we dropped suddenly or swayed dangerously (I assumed) from side to side. "Look, Abbie, down there! Eagles!"

We're flying above the eagles. I tried another Hail Mary.

In the final minutes of the flight it seemed the pilot was indeed going to fly us straight into the side of the mountain after all, but we banked to the right at the last moment and Lukla's tiny runway, curving up in a steep incline (to help airplanes stop, presumably) came into view. I won't say my past flashed in front of my eyes, but I did resolve to live a far better life from this day forward if I could only please please please live to tell the tale.

When we got off the plane (I wondered, briefly, if Emma was going to have to peel my fingers from where they'd to all intents and purposes been soldered to the armrests), the Englishwoman who'd sat behind me said, kindly, "Don't worry, it won't be as bad going back. The worst is when you're taking off, and that is just at the beginning, you can relax after that."

I stared at her. "Relax?"

"Yes, well, it's not as bad as landing," she said. "You're airborne as soon as the runway ends, after all."

I somehow found that less than reassuring.

What else was less than reassuring was the fact that I was having problems breathing. *Yeah, Abbie, that's sort of the point of being in the mountains, isn't it?* But it had still taken me by surprise and there was a fleeting moment of panic when it seemed I couldn't get enough air into my lungs.

I couldn't imagine why people did this for fun.

We all retrieved our bags and trooped into the terminal building, which was little more than one room, with everything painted a bright blue. A sign outside the structure read, "Heartly welcome to ladies and gentlemen in Everest region!"

Yep: not even in the same hemisphere as Kansas.

There was a bit of confusion as different groups sorted themselves out and heavy backpacks were hoisted onto backs, and through the moving clumps of bodies I spotted a sign with our names on it. Misspelled, but close enough. I grabbed Emma and dragged her over to the man holding it. "We're Emma Caulfield and Abigail Bradford," I told him.

He smiled, teeth—missing quite a few of them—flashing quicksilver in his dark face, and gave us a bow and a namaste. "I am Dawa Sherpa," he said. "I am your guide. These are your luggages?"

Two very large backpacks and two smaller daypacks; I assumed they'd count as "luggages."

"Yes," I said, shifting my grip on the smaller bag and reaching for the other. "We're all set. Shall we follow you?"

"But no!" He seemed genuinely horrified. "Ladies must not carry such luggages!"

Emma and I exchanged glances. "It's fine," she started to say, but I put a hand on her arm. I'd already gotten the cultural gaffe.

"Thank you," I said gravely, and we watched as he gracefully hefted both big backpacks. "This way, ladies, please to follow."

He led; we followed. Out of the gaily painted terminal building to a series of reasonably steep pathways that switchbacked up to an even higher elevation; it was a very good thing that Dawa had taken our backpacks, because both of us were having problems following. "What's the altitude here, anyway?"

Emma shook her head. "I can't remember. Catch the name of the airport?"

"Tenzing-Hillary," I managed to puff out.

She nodded. "Supposedly the first people to reach the top," she said.

"What... we're going to... change... all that?" It would look really bad, I thought, if I had to ask our little procession to stop for a moment, but I was winded enough to consider it.

I focused instead on her comment. It was indeed Nepali Tenzing Norgay Sherpa and New Zealander Sir Edmund Hillary who had officially been the first to summit Everest in 1953, climbing the South Approach through Nepal. There had been other expeditions before that, of course, but no one else had documented a summit before them.

When a 1999 expedition found Mallory's body on the north side, questions were raised—and not for the first time, by a long shot—as to whether he and his young and inexperienced climbing companion, Andrew "Sandy" Irvine, were on their way up or back down when they died. Hillary famously reacted to the question with anger—which, I supposed, was natural, as proof of Mallory's ascent would have eradicated him from the record-books; but it had still seemed churlish to me.

Okay, in another moment I really was going to have to make us stop. I was breathing as hard as if I'd just sprinted from one end of Boston's Public Garden to the other, and my chest actually hurt.

Dawa saved me by stopping of his own accord at a promontory on the path and pointing out the sights. "Here is view of mountains," he announced, sweeping his arm around and inviting us to... experience? Certainly one didn't just *look* at the mountains: I was feeling that we, anyone, people, were dwarfed by the white snowy peaks that seemed to enclose the village. I could imagine what it must feel like to those who lived up here, those who thought these were the seats of the gods: the mountains seemed to protect the village as well as enclose it. Like a parent's arms around a child.

Lukla itself was exactly as promised: teahouses, hotels, some goats moving about with casual indifference. The buildings were mostly white, but their roofs took up the Nepali color swatches with joyful abandon, a chorus of greens and blues and oranges and yellows all clamoring for attention.

We could see the roofs because Lukla was a village essentially clinging to the side of a mountain—no roads, no cars, the occasional yak. And many of the paths that snaked among the buildings and up the hillside weren't paved. The main street where all the shopping happened had paving stones, but up here it was about pathways rather than full-on streets.

Rested—though not nearly long enough—we started up again. A stone wall ran along the uphill side of our trail and alongside it was a long series of prayer wheels, canister-like and inscribed, that Dawa flicked as he passed; as the wheels turned, prayers were still kept in motion. I wondered if every religion had something similar; Catholics, after all, light candles to keep their own prayers going. No one really likes the impermanence of life, after all. Maybe this was a way to keep prayer and hope and dreams alive, even after one has passed through.

And then, just when my lungs were getting set to rip themselves out of my chest, *Alien*-style, we arrived.

We were staying for our two nights of acclimatization at the Himalaya Lodge in what we were to learn was standard fare: one room, twin beds, and—luxury of luxuries!—our own bathroom, complete with hot water. I'd rarely stayed anywhere hot water was considered an extra, but Anish had been particularly proud of these accommodations for that very reason. "The esteemed ladies will have privacy," he said.

Our room, predictably it seemed, had a wonderful view of the mountains opposite—and of the airstrip just beneath us, which I could have done without: if anyone was going to crash while we were there, I didn't particularly want to be watching.

"You know," Emma said pensively, gazing now at the runway. "Maybe we can employ our time here usefully."

My plan had been to employ my time in Lukla *breathing*, but I supposed I could fit in one or two other activities. "What do you have in mind?"

She turned. "We could find out what happened to Ang Pemba," she said.

I must have looked as startled as I felt. Emma hadn't shown much of a reaction when she learned of the Sherpa's death; now I could see a glint in her eye I was beginning to recognize.

"Did you know him?" The name had come to her easily, and she hadn't appended the tribal part.

"Never met," she said, but there was something about the way she said it that didn't ring true. She'd told me, that snowy night in Boston, that she'd never been to Nepal; she'd even made that one of the reasons she needed a traveling companion. But when she arrived back in Kathmandu, she hadn't remembered saying that, admitting instead to having been here years ago.

What else was she keeping from me?

I let it go; it doesn't do to accuse your employer of lying. "What makes you think we can discover anything? We don't even speak Nepali."

"No," she acknowledged. "But at least we're here on the ground, and we can use Dawa as an interpreter. I'm sure Jack wants to find out, but he won't, will he? He can't come and make inquiries, he's busy organizing the expedition. He has a whole lot on his plate anyway, and they're leaving Kathmandu tonight."

I knew that was true; I'd learned that expeditions up Everest have a very narrow window of opportunity. Every year is a little different, but aiming for mid-May is the usual course of action; the season is over by the thirtieth, and the ladders are all removed from the icefall by the end of the month. I had a focus of precise understanding, having discovered both the blog and the YouTube channel belonging to Alan Arnette, a mountaineer who in his retirement followed annual Everest activities to the minute and shared them with the world.

The best conditions occur when the monsoons start up in the Bay of Bengal, forcing the jet stream farther north and allowing for a few days of possible if not great weather on the mountain; it's the jet stream that's the worst offender at altitude, with hurricane-force winds and whiteout conditions. Richard—or was it Mark? probably Richard, he was nicer—had told me the wind can sound like a freight train.

With you in its path.

So it made sense that all of Supreme Summits was focused on the expedition; there was no way anyone was going to be here at Lukla, sleuthing. People prepared for this one event for years. They threw everything they had at it: money, time, family, relationships. Resulting in divorces, bankruptcy, failure. It wasn't the most important thing; it was the *only* thing.

I could understand that. I know a little about obsessions.

My family's fortune was made in the opium trade: we were among the first Boston Brahmins, the upper-class élite, along with the Cabots and the Lowells and the Endicotts. And all the generations after that hadn't really known what to do with themselves, so they developed what you might call *interests*.

My grandfather had managed to not serve in Vietnam, but once the war was over, he couldn't let it go. He believed President Nixon had written off scores of American prisoners of war held in Vietnam and Cambodia, and he spent over forty years financing and running an operation that went looking for them, hiring mercenaries and retired Army Intelligence and God only knew who else to act as his spies, to scour the wilderness, to follow spurious leads deep into the hidden kingdoms of drug lieges and through the overgrown pathways of forgotten ruins.

When I was a kid, all I remember hearing from him were cryptic updates about mysterious sightings of Caucasian men somewhere in the jungle, excitement that this time, *this time* his people were finally close to the truth. One more trip into the jungle; one more rumor from an obscure village or a neglected temple or a retired drunkard, and he'd be able to find the Marine still held in a prison compound somewhere.

He never found anyone.

So that was my grandfather. My own father's obsessions didn't keep him any closer to home: his boyhood hobby of stargazing turned into a fixation that took him as an adult all over the world, where he stayed in nice hotels and occasionally sent postcards; when he was at home, he rarely came out of the study, where he spent his days and half his nights consulting maps to plan his next trip. Astronomers chase after elusive targets; they live to discover (even if only for themselves) objects that can only be seen with increasingly bigger and better equipment. Whether it's splitting hairline double stars, the faintest of the dim deep-space objects, or whatever—astronomy almost demands obsession and my father was just the man to take it on. For him, perfection would never be obtained until all unanswered questions about the Universe were resolved, until there were no more secrets to be mined.

So—yeah—I know a thing or two about obsessions. And I could see how Everest could become a fixation. And Emma was probably right—people could possibly let their guards down when talking to an amiable romance novelist.

I still didn't quite see the two of us as Sherlock Holmes and Watson.

Dawa appeared shortly before lunch to see if "esteemed ladies would like to see picturesque village." He had his tourist patter down perfectly.

"As long as we do it slowly," I said. Emma gave me an amused look, and, not for the first time, I was annoyed that her lungs seemed to be adapting faster than mine. The woman had at least twenty, twenty-five years on me, damn it. Had she spent all of them in the Alps?

As it turned out, Lukla was, indeed, picturesque. The name, Dawa explained, meant "place of many goats and sheep," though we didn't actually see a lot of them while we were there. Tourism paying better these days?

Dawa, consulted, agreed. "Since airport," he said, nodding vigorously. "Now all peoples help with trekking." And indeed it seemed that, after residential teahouses, Lukla's main offering was shopping: yak hair gloves, North Face knockoffs, batteries for the lamps climbers attached to their helmets.

And, inevitably it seemed, a Starbucks.

Emma wanted to do some shopping, enchanted by the colorful wool hats and scarves, but Dawa stopped her. "Later, later," he said. We exchanged shrugs and followed him to yet another teahouse, this one apparently owned by a cousin. "Here we rest!" he proclaimed, before heading back to the kitchen to order a special tea "all peoples like."

Sitting at one of the tables that all seemed to flank the walls— another common teahouse trait—I said to Emma, "So let's make a plan. Where do you want to start sleuthing? Ask Dawa?"

"I'm beginning to think Dawa won't tell us anything," she responded absently. "Oh, we'll get some stories from him about his grandfather over in Tibet, and I want to hear those for sure. But he won't be helpful about Ang Pemba." She broke off her train of thought. "Oh, look, Abbie, that's the hat I wanted to buy."

"Later, later," I mimicked Dawa. "*Why* won't he tell us anything?"

"He works for Jack," she said. "They're intensely loyal, Jack's people. He'll translate whatever he has to, but he won't help otherwise. It would be like telling tales out of school. He might even think what happened to Ang Pemba reflects badly on Supreme Summits Expeditions."

"That's nonsense," I said stoutly. "Ang Pemba Sherpa wasn't even where he was supposed to be."

Her eyes drifted back to my face. "Right," she said. "Good memory. And tell me, now that we're here in Lukla, have you seen anyplace at all that anyone—much less a Sherpa—could slip and fall to their death?"

We both knew the answer.

Dawa returned to the table and, bowing, asked permission to sit with us. "Of course, Dawa, you are our guest wherever we go," said Emma.

Emma might not think much of our chances of getting information from the guide, but nothing ventured, nothing gained, right? I waited until he was seated—and then another few minutes as we were served tea with yak's milk—before I could start. That was the sourness I'd tasted in Kathmandu with the tea served by both Laxsmi and Anish; odd to my Western palate, but not unpleasant, and I was actually acquiring a taste for it.

Finally I was able to get to the point. "Dawa, do you know where Ang Pemba Sherpa was when he fell?"

Emma drew in her breath sharply, but I was looking at the guide and didn't allow her to catch my eye. She was the one who'd wanted to investigate, anyway.

But what interested me was that someone else in the room had also gasped when I asked the question.

Most of the tables were occupied by westerners, overwhelmingly Caucasian, but there was a group of four or five Nepalis sitting back in the corner closest to the kitchen. None of them was looking at us. In fact, I couldn't see anyone paying us the slightest bit of attention.

But I knew I hadn't imagined that reaction.

Dawa's expression didn't give anything away. "It is not good to speak of him," he said uncomfortably. "We have not yet had funeral. There is still a chance he returns."

"Returns?" Emma and I exchanged startled glances. "Returns—how?" I asked. "As what—a ghost?"

He nodded unhappily. "The soul must wait to be reborn," he said. "It is a process. Sometimes, between one life and the next, there is... I do not know to say in English."

I didn't know how to say it in English, either, but it was pretty clear what he was getting at. The idea of a specter flitted across my consciousness, shimmering bright, its movement glimpsed out of the corner of my eye, just out of reach. "When is the funeral,

Dawa?" I asked instead; then, catching sight of his expression, I quickly added, "We're not inviting ourselves, don't worry."

Emma kicked me under the table. I glanced at her; her expression was serene and she didn't show a flicker of anything other than benign interest. Wait—she *wanted* to go to the funeral? I felt I was getting mixed messages flung at me whenever I opened my mouth. Was this more literary research, or was it she who was taking the Sherlock Holmes act a little too far?

Dawa's dark eyes had pain in them, and I reminded myself that while this might be an amusing way for us to pass the time as Western tourists, it was only too real for him. This was a brother who had died, a colleague, undoubtedly a friend. Treading gently would be the least we could do.

"We're very sorry for your loss," I finally said, more out of a desire to show some kind of empathy than any expectation my words would be the least bit helpful. They never are. At least I didn't offer the famous "thoughts and prayers."

"It is tomorrow," he said unexpectedly. "The family will care for things. It is not for esteemed ladies to worry themselves about."

Emma said, "Jack Bailey and I have known each other for many years, Dawa. He feels the loss very much. If there is anything that I can do, then I want to do it. I understand Ang Pemba Sherpa's family wouldn't welcome strangers at the funeral, but I would be grateful if you could convey my deep sympathy to them. Jack has spoken often and well of Ang Pemba. He was a great man and a great icefall doctor. His loss will be felt everywhere."

Not bad, I found myself thinking. The woman did have a way with words.

Dawa said, unexpectedly, "His wife stay here in Lukla today. You want to tell her, maybe? She is glad all peoples care for her husband. Things will not go so well for her now. It is difficult to be a widow in Nepal."

"Financially, you mean? Isn't there some sort of insurance?" I asked.

Dawa shook his head. "No insurance," he said—although later I did hear of The Juniper Fund, which supports and empowers people and communities impacted by the loss of Himalayan high-altitude workers.

I resolved to make it a major part of my own charitable giving going forward.

"It is very bad for her, for making a living once her husband is dead. Mr. Jack, the Boss-Man, he will help out. But it is not the money that is the worry. Besides that, widows here..." He was floundering a little, searching for a word. "They are considered inauspicious. Very bad luck. I think you would say outcast? They cannot live their lives as they did before. Many peoples will not want them to come near."

He glanced around him, and I wondered how uncomfortable this conversation must be. "Ehani, she will be okay. Boss-Man will make sure. But it is still hard." He paused. "Maybe it changes. There are new widows, younger widows, you understand? They go to Khumbu Climbing Center, they learn to be mountaineers, guides, cooks for members. Before, only men. But the mountains are changing. Maybe Ehani will do this, too. But before that, I will ask her to speak with esteemed ladies."

"If we would not be intruding," said Emma softly, "I'd like that very much."

"After lunch," he said. "You go to Himalaya Lodge, after I come to find you, bring you to see her. Widow of Ang Pemba, Ehani, she has no English. I translate." He nodded. "Good you can tell Boss-Man everything okay."

"I'm sure he'll be reassured," said Emma, catching my eye. I shrugged. It felt a little like we were treading where angels might fear to go, but hell, we were nearly at their altitude. Why not?

Lunch was *gundruk*, a pickled dish of mustard, radishes, cauliflower, and a few other things I couldn't identify, spicy and slightly fermented, into which we dipped flatbread. "Not the best place to be a widow," I commented, thinking of Dawa's words.

"Not the best place to be a woman, period," said Emma. She caught my eye. "And not just for the Sherpa."

"Western women?" I made a face. It seemed to me that we'd been positively cosseted since we'd arrived.

She took a long swallow of tea. "Imagine," she said, "that you're somewhere with a man who has power over you, and he says things that are uncomfortable."

"Not difficult to imagine," I agreed.

"Now imagine you're both halfway up a mountain and your getting back down, your *survival*, depends completely on him."

I must have looked as startled as I felt. I hadn't seen that one coming. "Oh, God."

She nodded. "Oh, God, indeed," she said briskly, and stood up. "Come on, dear, we have a widow to see."

I thought of Sylvia, protected by climbing with her partner. And of all the other Sylvias, who weren't.

"Oh, God," I said again.

***

Ehani Sherpa, widow of Ang Pemba Sherpa, was staying with relatives in town. Theirs was one of the few homes in Lukla still with a couple of goats tethered in the front garden. The house was at a small distance from the closest cluster of buildings, and her family did some subsistence farming, relying for their survival in large part on Ang Pemba's considerable earnings as an icefall doctor. Extended families benefited from tourism as well.

Ehani Sherpa was small and graceful, dressed in the Nepali version of widow's weeds, bright white cotton flecked with gold. She sat on a tiny leatherette couch that looked like a refugee from 1950s America, her eyes down, her voice a murmur. We presented our apologies for trespassing on her grief. She inclined her head, but didn't look at us directly; in fact, as it turned out, she never once met our eyes at all.

It was entirely possible my blue hair scared the hell out of her. I was going to have to rethink my color preferences when I got back to Boston.

Emma had started out interested in this endeavor but now seemed to want to take a backseat. Dawa watched me, ready to translate and—should it become necessary—no doubt apologize for and explain any cultural *faux pas* we might make.

The room was small but bright, with painted furniture and rich colors in the wall hangings that no doubt helped with insulation. Ehani was not alone to meet with us; two men whose names I never did catch were introduced as her uncle and cousin. They didn't say a word beyond the first formal greeting, but watched us closely as though we might be ready to take off with the silver.

Had there been silver, of course.

"There was a letter," Dawa was translating. "Ang Pemba get this letter, very unusual. She does not know what it said, but after he read it, Ang Pemba tell her he must first go to Lukla before he went to Khumbu Icefall, and that he would meet other peoples at Base Camp."

"Does she know who it was from?" I asked.

No; she didn't, only that it was written in English and thus was from a westerner. A letter in Nepali would have been passed around the family and talked about; this one, Ang Pemba had not shared.

"Does she still have the letter?"

No, she didn't, Ang Pemba had kept it on his person, in a pocket. He had folded it and placed it there as soon as he had read it.

"Forgive me—it was in English? And he read it?" I had assumed that as an expedition sherpa Ang Pemba would probably speak English... but he might not. Many of them, I gathered, didn't; they relied on the head expedition sherpa to organize their work. Still, as an icefall doctor and, it seemed, Jack's right-hand man on the mountain, Ang Pemba would probably need to speak excellent English.

Consulted, Ehani thought perhaps he had shown the letter to one other person. No, she did not know who that was. She hadn't attached any importance to the whole affair, just reminding her husband that he was due to be working at the Khumbu Icefall and that he needed to take his red jacket, the one with the tear she had repaired for him. He had assured her he would be on time, but the trip to Lukla had to happen first.

I looked at Dawa. "Was the letter there—I mean, um, on his body, when they found him?"

He didn't have to consult with the widow. There had been no papers at all in Ang Pemba's possession, either on his person or at the couple's home in Namche Bazaar. Dawa knew this; everyone at Supreme Summits Expeditions knew this. The Boss-Man had said so.

For the first time, I felt a prick of curiosity about Jack. And the tight hold he had over his company, the loyalty of his employees, the passion of his devotion to them. Was it a little... too perfect? I stole a glance at Emma, who knew far more than she was saying, but she was gazing at Ehani, her thoughts far from mine.

"So," she said, once we'd regained the path and were heading back to the teahouse lodge, "he got a letter that sent him to Lukla. From a westerner."

"Sounds like a set-up to me," I said, telling my lungs that we could indeed breathe, walk, and speak at the same time. "Sending him... out on a wild goose chase... to isolate him? But why? Why would anyone... want to hurt... an icefall doctor?" Emma didn't say anything, so I grabbed what breath I could and pushed a little harder. "Come on, you're the author. What would the motive be?"

"I don't write mysteries," she said, her voice a little brittle. She clearly held mysteries in the same contempt I reserved for romances.

"Neither do I," I pointed out reasonably. "But I can't help... but see one... here."

Emma stopped and looked at me. "You should have spent another week at the gym, dear," she said austerely.

"You're telling me."

Jeannette de Beauvoir

Excerpt from the journal of George Mallory

Charterhouse, Godalming, Surrey, 1910: All last year I applied for position after position, only in order to be turned down for each and every one. It doesn't do to be discouraged, of course, but one has to find a way to make a living... and now I have been offered the position of master of history, maths, French, and Latin at Charterhouse. I'll also be able to teach history to candidates for Oxford and Cambridge, so there will be some intellectual stimulation as well.

I don't start until the fall, so there is still time to join old Benson—who's been rather poorly from a psychological point of view—hiking in the Lake District, and then on to the Alps again, as I've undertaken to give an introduction to Alpine climbing to a fifteen-year-old who apparently wants nothing to do with it; I suspect his parents merely want to give him something difficult, in order to perhaps change his disposition from arrogance to accommodation. I don't know how well that will go.

I do know that my friend Cottie, whom I met at Pen y Pass, will be climbing at the same time. She's a lovely girl and I treasured our walks and conversation together; I hope I can look forward to more of the same.

In the autumn we shall see what else there is to see.

Chapter Seven

I was still thinking about Ang Pemba Sherpa and his mysterious letter when we finished a leisurely dinner of *dal bhat*, the lentil-and-rice concoction that seemed ubiquitous throughout Nepal. We'd followed the warnings against eating meat at altitude—not that it was bad for you, but because it was brought up from the valley to all the trekking teahouses by yak, and there was little refrigeration in the mountains—and I was taking it seriously. Some stomachs could handle it; Emma and I had agreed that we weren't rolling the dice on whether ours might be among them.

Besides, these vegetarian concoctions were delicious.

Emma went off to read in bed and I attempted a short walk down to the airstrip and back. I was really going to have to push myself a little more: we only had one more day of acclimatization in Lukla, and then the fun would really begin. My current goal was to get a single sentence out without gasping.

I had it on reliable information that many three-year-olds are able to do so; I should be, too.

I was sitting on a wall, my back resolutely to the airstrip and watching the Himalayas above the town shimmering in the sunset when a voice behind me said, "Nothing like it, is there?"

The voice was male, the accent maybe Australian. Or maybe not; not as broad as Jack's, for sure. Maybe from New Zealand? I couldn't parse the subtleties of Down Under speech.

I turned and found myself looking into the bluest eyes I could ever recall seeing. And the rest wasn't bad, either: a guy about my age, with tanned skin and dirty-blonde hair, a little designer stubble on the chin, and an easy smile. He wore a braided cord necklace, with a couple more on his wrist, trekking pants, and a t-shirt under a short-sleeved unbuttoned shirt. "It's gorgeous," I said in agreement. I could surely manage two words at a time, right?

"Seat of the gods, they say. Mind if I join you?"

I gestured for him to take a seat. "My wall is your wall," I said lightly.

He grinned and hopped over. "Sweet as," he said. "I'm Myles."

I did the automatic namaste greeting, palms together, a quick touch to my nose. "Abbie," I said.

"Nice hair. Been in Lukla long, have you?"

"Just flew in this morning." I swallowed. "It was—exciting."

"Uh-huh." He nodded, the knowing grin never leaving his face. "That's an understatement, I'd guess."

I looked at him curiously. "You'd guess? What did *you* do, teleport in?" *And if so, please please please show me how.* I wasn't forgetting that at some point in my future I was going to have to fly off that small airstrip.

He laughed, his head back, delight from the belly up. I liked that; I couldn't help but smile in response. "Nah. Trekked up from Jiri. Helps you adjust to the altitude."

"I *had* noticed," I said, "that your breathing is going well. I'm jealous."

"You'll get it back. You're staying two days?"

I nodded. "And then up to—what is it called? Namche Bazaar? Have you been there before?"

"That's it," he confirmed. "Sure, I've been there. You'll like the trek. No worries: on Day Two you'll see Everest itself, and once you do that, everything will be worth it. You'll never want to leave."

"If I have to fly out from Lukla, I may never leave anyway," I said grimly.

The bright blue-jay eyes were watching me. "What you need," he said, not unsympathetically, "is a little more of a spirit of adventure."

"Hey, I'm in Nepal, aren't I?"

He seemed to find that amusing. "First time," he guessed.

I smiled. "What gave me away?"

"Oh, I don't know. Maybe that look of sheer terror. But I get it. It's one thing to climb, to have one foot at least on the old *terra firma*. Trusting yourself to the air currents, that's something else."

"You're telling me," I said fervently.

"But really: no panic. Once you're on the mountain, you'll forget Lukla, you'll see. You'll be too busy thinking of other ways to die."

"You really are a fount of optimism," I said admiringly. "And I'm not climbing. I'm only going as far as Base Camp."

He raised his eyebrows. "Didn't anyone tell you? *Everest* Base Camp? It's—um—on Mount Everest?"

I smacked a palm against my forehead in mock dismay. "Holy cow! I should have read the fine print on my contract, I knew it!" I waited until he finished laughing. "What about you? Is that what you're here for?"

"The Lady Chomo? Yeah." He looked up at the peaks soaring above us; only the very tops were now on fire from the sunset. "I tried for it last year. Didn't make it."

"Didn't make it to Base Camp? Now there's encouragement. Thanks a lot."

"Didn't make it to the summit," he said.

"Oh." I sat with that for a moment. So that was who he was. One of them. "You're all insane, you know, you climbers," I said. "Wanting to be at the top of the world." I looked at him speculatively. "Why? Why do you do it?" *And where the hell do you get the money?* Not everybody had the financial advantage I shared with my brother; I had no idea how people who weren't born rich became rich. I put up a hand, forestalling his response. "And don't even think of saying because it's there. Don't even think of it."

The smile was back. "Nah, yeah. The Pacific Ocean's there, too, but I've never thought of swimming across it."

"See? A sensible response," I said. "So... why, then? Really?"

"Really?" He waited for my nod, then leaned back, propped a foot on the wall, encircled one of his knees with his arms, gave it a moment of thought. "Okay, really. Because I wanted stuff I couldn't get anywhere else. Not just like an adrenaline junkie, though to be fair that's probably true, but it's more than that. To understand people in an accelerated environment. An alternative to the day-to-day world, where nothing really matters that much; I want my days to matter." He paused. "And … okay, I guess that's it, too: to see if you can do it. To spend time with yourself and see if you are really who you think you are. To discover your limits. Take your pick."

"It all sounds better than anything I've heard so far," I confessed.

"And that George Mallory quote, that thing about climbing the mountain because it's there? That's actually heaps more complex than it sounds. Most people take it at face value and just see the arrogance."

Emma had hinted at something like that, back in Kathmandu, when she said that no one seemed to think Mallory had a sense of humor. And the other expedition members, they'd mentioned it, too. It tallied with my understanding, at least so far, of the man. "Really? What do *you* see when you look at Mallory?"

"Someone who wanted to capture something—some allure, some mystery." He glanced at me, and then away, his eyes on the valley, his mind concentrating. "But maybe our reasons are more prosaic. I mean, there's the peacefulness of being high on a mountain watching the sun peek around the Earth. Then there's the camaraderie of friends being roped together as they work up a mountain—not as individuals but as a team. Working together, depending on each other, everyone with the same goal. And, I don't know, there's the challenge of taking a step on a steep slope while you know that a mistake could be deadly… but that the next step will be heaps rewarding beyond anything you've ever experienced before." He paused. "Every time, I swear I'm not going again."

"And how long does it take you to change your mind?"

He looked at me then. "Hell," he said, a sort of wonder in his voice. "You *get* it."

"I'm beginning to."

We smiled together for a moment, knowing we each found the other attractive, not knowing yet if that meant anything.

"I'll tell you something about last year," he said. "I came up with the expedition and we did a lot of acclimatization. Six weeks. I'd been climbing really well, too, feeling fit and liking the other members, everything going just so. Over the icefall, even on the last rotation up the Lhotse Face." He could see that didn't mean anything to me. "That's a passage that's close to vertical, just under the Death Zone," he explained. "Difficult climbing. Challenging climbing. And it was all good. So on summit day—well, night, actually, we left camp at midnight—I started up and then one misstep and I felt my knee go. It wasn't bad, just a twinge, but suddenly I was nauseated. All I could see in the headlamp looking down was the snow and my bright yellow boot, and I kept gagging. I turned the O's up, but even with the oxygen and my thought that this was probably just a sprain, I could still make it... until I realized I couldn't. I turned around and went back to the South Col and Camp Four. I was pretty gutted, I can tell you. All that preparation and one second, just *one second*, of inattention undid it all. No summit for me." He hesitated, and then added, "And I still don't know if that was a test of my body or my mind."

"Probably," I said, "a little of both. And now you're going to test it again."

He nodded. "Why I'm trekking in. Not taking chances with altitude sickness or seeing if my knee's back to normal." He slanted a look at me. "You know about altitude sickness, right? You can get it at Base Camp."

"Yeah, so I hear," I said. "Because Base Camp *is* on Mount Everest, after all." I couldn't help but giggle a little.

Giggle? Steady on, Abbie. What you don't want to do is step into one of Emma Caulfield's steamy romances.

Well, maybe not. Or maybe ....

Myles was still trying to sell me on the idea, which wasn't really necessary, but I liked listening to him. "I once heard," he said, a little diffidently, "that adventure is defined as when you are doing it, you pray to God to get you out alive, and once it's over, you pray to God to do it again."

I laughed. "Yeah, but that's when there's danger, isn't it?"

He stretched. "Same idea, ay," he said. "Danger's what drives the adrenaline that keeps us going. Like I said, maybe a commentary on the lack of excitement in our everyday lives. And the thing about climbing, you know—well, it's all the stuff you've already heard, you have to be fit, you have to really want it, you have to have a mental space where you're in control, you have to be patient, you have to be a team player, all that—but especially you have to be okay with failing. It's not a box you tick automatically. A lot of people don't get that, and anyone who doesn't believe it, doesn't belong on the mountain."

"That sounds familiar." I was remembering the conversations back in Kathmandu. The ones with Jurgen, who thought summiting was everything. And Mark and Richard, their disdain for some of the other climbing outfits. "I met some guides a few days back—they said half the people going up, shouldn't be. That people want to summit no matter what."

"Sounds about right." He cocked a look at me. "What guides? From which expedition?"

"Supreme Summits," I said. No reason not to.

"Richard," he said, nodding. "Good bloke."

"I'm glad to hear it. Mark was complaining about people signing on for trips who didn't know how to use their crampons."

Myles laughed. "That's Mark," he said, nodding. He paused. "He's not wrong, either."

"If they can't put on crampons," I said, knowing full well that I couldn't put on crampons, "then they're probably not going to do too well with your theory about being accepting of failure."

"Too right." He paused, now looking up at the peaks as though finding an answer there. As, perhaps, he was. "It's not about not *wanting* it," he said. "Hell, everybody wants it, ay. It's about knowing the odds, knowing yourself. And knowing there will be another day. And anything can turn you back—weather, equipment failure, getting sick, getting tired—your own inadequacies, a teammate's inadequacies. And this after prepping for the ascent for months, maybe even years."

I wasn't sure I'd ever try anything with that kind of possible failure ratio. "What happens to people who don't accept failure?" I asked.

"There's something they call summit fever," Myles said, seemingly on a tangent. "Sometimes it's associated with cerebral edema; sometimes it's just about being stubborn. In the military they call it target fascination. But to answer your question? There's no way *that* person is breaking off an attempt. They're *determined*. I've seen members lying in the snow saying they'll get up in a minute but still not getting up. *Refusing* to get up. No sense of the passage of time. I've seen guides and climbing sherpas standing still for an hour or more trying to talk an expedition member down."

"They can't leave them?"

He grimaced. "Sometimes they have to," he said. "Good on you, you're hitting all the ethical roadblocks in one conversation. The thing is, no one can carry someone down the mountain, especially someone who won't or can't help. Rescues on Everest are unusual; it's just too much risk for everyone else, plus sometimes it's physically impossible. The only rescue that's possible is for someone who's able to walk, to move. There's bodies on all the high mountains. There's hundreds of them here on Everest."

"So I gather," I said carefully. "Do people know who they are?" *Like, do you say hello, or rest in peace, as you go by?*

"Not all of them, ay." He glanced at me as though to gauge my reaction. "Some are just body parts, caught up in the glacier, pulled under, coming back to the surface. That sort of thing. Some are famous. For a long time there was a corpse everyone had to pass, he was nicknamed Green Boots, for obvious reasons. He's been identified, finally—and moved. And there's a woman they call Sleeping Beauty."

"And there's George Mallory," I said.

He grinned. "You know your history."

"Maybe the first man to summit," I said.

"Shh! Don't let my native son hear you say that." So: he wasn't Australian. "We're all pretty proud of him. If you grow up Kiwi, you either want to be an All Black or you want to climb mountains. Or both."

"An All Black?"

"Rugby, woman." He said it reverentially.

I didn't want to talk about rugby. "Anyway, even if Hillary *was*, he wasn't the first by himself," I said, taking off my glasses and polishing them on my shirt. "Tenzing Norgay Sherpa should have just as much credit."

"Doesn't it strike you," said Myles after a moment, "that the Sherpa lived up here for a whole lot of centuries, and in all that time, *none* of them ever felt the need to climb the mountain? Generation after generation, living perfectly good lives in its shadow. That should tell you something about how daft the idea is. It's not part of their culture. These people, it's a whole process for them. They have to spend literally days ahead of time, and hours every single one of those days, just asking to be absolved of the spiritual damage summiting involves for them. They're paying an immense spiritual price, doing this."

I shivered. "That sounds dark."

He glanced at me sharply. "It *is* dark," he said. "Mountaineering has a dark colonial past. It's always been about white people staking the lives of others so they can collect glory, plant a damned flag. Climbing's a form of greed, always has been. The disparity of risk is..."

He seemed to be searching for a word. "Troubling?" I suggested.

He made a face. "At the very least, troubling," he said. Yet still here he was. "It's only westerners that feel a need to conquer. And people who've been long exposed to Western culture. One of my mates, he's Māori, he climbs. But by and large it's just the conquerors who don't know when to stop."

"I don't know," I said. "I hear there's a decent number of climbers on the other side of the mountain, too. People climbing from Tibet. I read that a lot of them are Asians, not westerners."

Before he could answer, I went on. "Which brings us back to George Mallory." I took a breath. "So, okay, he's actually why I'm here. Why I took my life in my hands to fly in to someplace I may never fly out of—and I can assure you, the jury's still out on that one."

My aviation woes didn't concern Myles anymore. "You're here for George Mallory?" He looked at me quizzically. "You're about a century or so too late."

"Yeah, I've heard rumors to that effect."

"And you know he went up the north side, through Tibet, right?"

I nodded. "But Supreme Summits Expeditions doesn't." I paused. "I mean, Supreme Summits doesn't go up the north side, not that Supreme Summits doesn't know Mallory went that way. I'm working for an author, a historical romance writer, who's doing a novel about him. Well, based on him. We're up here getting the atmosphere." Or something; the truth was, I was less and less sure why we were there.

"Who's the author?"

I wrinkled my nose. "You've probably never heard of her."

"I have three sisters, ay; try me."

I laughed. "Okay. Emma Caulfield. I told you—"

Myles held up a hand. "Emma *Caulfield*? She's up here? Holy shit. Yeah, I know who she is. Hey, can I get an autograph? My sister Brittany will go heaps wild."

"Yeah, sure," I said, bemused.

"Emma Caulfield's writing about George Mallory. Now there's a thing!"

I was starting to feel slightly irritated. Um, hadn't we been... well, *flirting*? Emma'd hijacked the conversation without even being present. Impressive. "Well, it's a story that *includes* him," I said cautiously. "There's more to it than just him."

"No doubt." We sat for a few minutes without talking, the silence comfortable, the shadows lengthening. Then he seemed to shake himself out of some reverie. "Well, Abbie, it's been interesting, ay." He pushed himself up off the wall, stretched. "You coming? I'll walk you back wherever you're staying, if you'd like. It'll be dark soon, and you don't want to wander around Lukla at night."

Startled, I said, "Why? Is it dangerous?"

I laughed. "Not in the way you're probably thinking," he said. "I'm talking about twisting your ankle. Some of the streets are pretty steep. It's easy to fall."

Without thinking, I said, "Even for a Sherpa?"

He stopped. "Ang Pemba Sherpa," he said slowly. "Of course. You're with Supreme Summits. Did you know him?"

So apparently there was no secret about the death. "I didn't," I said. "But I spoke with his widow today. It just seems… odd… that he'd fall. In a place like this."

"The mountains can be deceiving," said Myles. "Especially this time of year."

"For a Sherpa? In Lukla?" With my newfound expertise came attitude. My voice had to be dripping with skepticism. Without my even noticing it, everyone else's concerns seemed to have become mine as well. "Mark thinks he was killed. I mean, killed deliberately. Murdered."

Myles didn't immediately refute it, which both scared me and made me like him. "I do think there's more there than we know," he said.

"Are the police looking into it?"

He shrugged. "Who knows? We're only westerners, Abbie. They wouldn't tell us. We're never going to be anything but tourists on these mountains. Come on, it really is starting to get dark."

And we didn't talk about the Sherpa again.

I tiptoed into the room I was sharing with Emma; the light was out, so presumably she was doing the intelligent thing and getting plenty of sleep. I stubbed my toe—twice—and swore under my breath—more than twice—before finally using the flashlight app on my phone to orient myself and find my way to the bathroom.

I needn't have bothered. The covers on her bed were rumpled, but Emma herself was nowhere to be seen.

Excerpt from the journal of George Mallory

Charterhouse, Surrey, and Pen-y-Pass, Wales, 1911: I've been trying to treat my classes in a friendly way, which appears to both puzzle and offend them at once. I'm trying to get them to stretch in the ways Benson has done with me, encouraging them to try something new, to read whatever interests them, but instead of appreciating the freedom I'm offering they seem to see my technique as a challenge.

I am increasingly seeing climbing as a metaphor for what education could achieve. I want the spirit of man to exercise itself as freely and fearlessly and joyously as a climber on a hill.

During the winter I met up with Cottie at Pen-y-Pass, a week before the actual gathering, so we could do some climbing on our own; and she oddly became frightened, begging us to find an easier route to the peak. I found that quite incomprehensible: what does that sort of fear feel like? I don't even know. Is that something that's lacking in me?

Pen-y-Pass this year is wild and big and filled with a party spirit such as I haven't seen at the event before. We're spending our days out on the crags and hills, and return, exhilarated, to evenings filled with talk and music: sea shanties and boat songs, German Lieder and duets from Mendelssohn. The only way the proprietor can entreat us to go to bed is by turning off the power!

I am struggling to make sense of my friendship with Cottie. My experiences of friendship are all with members of my own sex; if she were a man, I would know what to do. To confess the truth, I don't much understand women and they make me feel like a mouse. But I suppose one may be friends with a lady.

Mountains are far easier than women.

Chapter Eight

Emma was at breakfast, and remarkably cheerful. "Eggs!" she exclaimed, reading off the blackboard at the end of the room. "How perfect! Who would have thought?"

I looked around the room. It was long and broad, a door at one end, a kitchen and the stairway to the rooms on the other, and in between tables were lined up against the two long walls; some small, others clearly meant for eating family-style. I was surprised to see it was almost full, everyone in the room climbers or trekkers, the bright colors of their North Face and Eddie Bauer jackets jarring slightly with the brightly painted walls. Languages swirled around me—English, French, Italian, Russian... even a little Nepali, from a group sitting with a Nepali guide near the small table I'd scored.

My own breakfast was a compromise between East and West: lots of milky tea, yellow lentils and *saag*... with toast. "They'll cook whatever you want," I said, moving my book—a guide to Nepal—out of Emma's way so she could sit down.

"Eggs, then," she said positively, and when the server was gone she turned her bonhomie on me. "You're breathing well, dear," she said. "That's splendid. Lukla's fine, but I'll be happy when we can start on the trek."

I sipped my tea. "I'm surprised you're so eager," I said. "You didn't get much sleep last night." She had, in fact, come in just after midnight. I'd pretended to be asleep and in fact couldn't have stayed awake long anyway—the mountain air was having its way with me.

She wasn't the least bit discomfited. "No, I didn't, did I?" she said brightly. "Sorry if I woke you up."

"I wasn't awake for long." I paused, waiting for her to fill me in on her nocturnal activities, but instead she pulled out a map. "Show me where we're going today," she said.

99

I oriented myself on it—I'm an Internet girl, this was possibly the first time I'd handled paper maps, at least of the current century—and pointed out the trek route. "Here. We're staying at a place called Phakding tonight. It's just five miles, and believe it or not, it's partly downhill, it's the lowest point on the trek. So today's our easiest day." I was surprised that I sounded so much like I knew what I was talking about; Dawa had in fact issued me the map and the schedule minutes before Emma had arrived in the dining hall. But Anish and I had talked about it back in Kathmandu.

Emma was studying it. "And we reach Base Camp when?" she asked.

"Day Nine," I replied. *Let's ditch the itinerary; might as well get right down to it.* "So what's at Base Camp, Emma?" I asked. "Is there something you want to find out about Mallory there?"

"It's a matter of getting a feel for the environment," she said, with a casual wave of her hand.

I'd looked up photos of Everest Base Camp these days—bustling and filled with high-tech gear—and others, the old black-and-white shots of Base Camp on the Tibetan side, the place where for three years Mallory had based his attempts to summit. They had, as far as I could tell, absolutely nothing in common. *Atmosphere?*

The young woman who worked the teahouse brought Emma's breakfast then, and before she could even settle in to eat, the flap of embroidered fabric that substituted for a front door flopped open and Myles and another guy came in. Myles narrowed his eyes to the comparative darkness and then caught sight of me, and, saying something over his shoulder to his companion, he came over to the table. "Namaste, ladies, g'day. Any chance we can join you?"

Emma looked at me expectantly. I cleared my throat and made the introductions. "Emma Caulfield, one of your fans from Down Under, this is Myles—I'm sorry, I don't know your last name."

He was smiling at her. "Myles Walker," he said easily, putting out a hand to shake.

"Please," said Emma. "Pull up some chairs." She shot me a look, and I shrugged. I didn't know quite what to make of him, either.

"Ned Rafter," said Myles's companion, shaking hands with us in turn while Myles borrowed two chairs from a nearby table. He wasn't white; this must be Myles's climbing "mate." Māori? "G'day. Glad to meet you."

"And you," I said. "We're actually leaving soon, but—"

"Heading to Namche Bazaar?" asked Myles, sitting down. He unzipped his orange down jacket and turned to the server, ordering something in halting but obviously comprehensible Nepali.

"Phakding," I said. "My kind of climbing: downhill all the way. Namche Bazaar is for tomorrow."

He nodded, noncommittal. "My sister's read all your books," he said to Emma. "Sweet as, she says."

She smiled. "Happy to hear it," she said. "Are you trekking?"

"On our way to Everest," Myles said. "We're meeting the rest of the expedition at Base Camp."

"Really? Which one?"

"Top Ascent Enterprises," he said easily.

Emma shook her head. "Really? I haven't heard of it."

Why would you? I thought. If she was such an apparent expert on the various climbing outfits, why did she need me with her? I was accumulating more and more questions about what Emma was really doing in Nepal.

Ned, inexplicably not hearing my thoughts, answered her. "It's a boutique operator," he said. "Don't be bothered, no-one's heard of it. We've been climbing with them for years, Myles and me. And what about you ladies?"

"Just trekking," Emma said. She seemed content to carry the conversation. I tried to catch Myles's eye, but he was scanning the room as if committing everyone in it to memory.

The server appeared at that moment and put heaping plates of food in front of the two men. Ned grinned and rubbed his hands in anticipation; up until then, I hadn't thought anyone actually did that outside of fiction. "Dal bhat power, twenty-four hour," he said. He glanced at me. "It sounds better when you say it with a Nepali accent, ay," he admitted.

"I imagine it does." I drank the last of my tea and stood up. As pleasant as the opportunity might be for a little light flirtation, my job was to facilitate whatever it was we were actually doing there. "Emma, I'm going to go find Dawa. Can you meet us out front in—say, half an hour?"

"Of course." She was watching the New Zealanders dig into their food with something close to amusement.

I said to Myles, "Are you leaving today as well?"

He nodded, swallowed, washed the food down with a swig of tea. "Heading straight up to Namche, ay," he said. "Might run into you on the trail, but we're doing it faster than you should." A shadow of a smile. "You're stopping a couple of days on the way for acclimatization, yeah?"

I nodded. "At Namche Bazaar and—Dingboche, is that how it's pronounced?" I said.

"Right on. You'll be fine, you'll see."

"Yes. Thanks." Maybe it sounded sharp; had part of me been hoping he'd want to continue our conversation from the night before? *And don't I sound a little too much like one of Emma's heroines?*

I went upstairs, not sure who exactly I was annoyed with and finally concluding it was myself. I packed my clothes, made sure my snacks were easily accessible in an outside pocket of my day-pack, and headed down to meet Dawa. He held up a pair of ski poles. "Sure, Miss Abigail?"

"It's just Abbie." I'd said it half a dozen times already. Apparently the "esteemed ladies" were deserving of a full name. "And yeah, I'm sure." I might be short of breath, but I wasn't hiking with ski poles in my hands. With my luck, I'd manage to take out an eye with one of them. If not mine, somebody else's. There was more than one way to be dangerous on the slopes. "Hey, you ever hear of Top Ascent Enterprises, Dawa?"

He was tightening the ties on one of the bundles of mysterious stuff he and Rocky the porter would be carrying for us. "Of course." He nodded emphatically. "Very good expeditions.

Always small, not many peoples, very quick." He glanced up at me, a knowing smile flashing quicksilver across his dark face. "No hand-holding with Top Ascent," he said. "Very strict."

"I thought that's what Supreme Summits Expeditions was supposed to be."

He shrugged. "Different," was all he said.

An hour later we were on the trail. We were far from alone; this was a prime trekking season, Anish had told me, with the added presence of real climbers passing most of us on the way, heading purposefully up the trail, their hearts already among the peaks in more ways than one. I'd read that some climbers didn't bother with the trek, getting helicoptered into Base Camp, but I assumed they'd already done some acclimatization wherever they came from. The Everest climbing window wasn't wide, and you had to be ready for anything up there, as soon as you arrived—it made sense to start the way you planned to carry on.

I was reassured to find that I could follow the trail without too much exertion and with decent breathing—until I remembered that we were descending into Phakding, not climbing. Yet.

Not thinking about breathing, of course, left me free to think about everything else. The sudden, razor-clear beauty of this place absorbed all the senses; the lush greenness of the trees, Himalayan balsams and firs, scenting the air with sharpness and raising the gaze to the mountains above us. Lukla had been all orange marigolds; now the flowers that crowded each other were wilder and sweeter, a profusion of colors, tumbling in brilliant arrays down the slopes.

Strings of prayer flags greeted us as we entered Phakding, fluttering in a breeze that seemed to gather strength as it moved down into the valley. Dawa had arranged for us to stay at the Shangri-La Guest House, another of the teahouses that had sprung up in the last fifty or sixty years to cater to foreign visitors, either climbers or trekkers.

This one was truly lovely, built of stone with a patio and café tables, and all the woodwork a brilliant passionate blue; you could almost imagine that you were indeed in Hilton's fictional earthly mystical paradise, isolated from the rest of the world, the Himalayan utopia of Western imagination. The place where you never grow old.

Of course, in non-utopian style, what I hadn't known before was that the farther up we climbed, the more rustic the teahouses became. Electricity in the mountains was an errant and unpredictable thing; it was all solar and hydro, which was wonderful for the planet, and was an "extra" everywhere above Namche Bazaar: bathroom, extra; electricity, extra; charging station, extra; Wi-Fi, extra. The Shangri-La was to be our last taste of luxury.

Dawa deposited us at the door. "Go on," he urged, nodding. "The staff talks in English."

"Now there's a recommendation," said Emma as she moved past me, out of the sunlight and through the door. I'd tried twice to engage her, but she was having none of it, diverting all my questions into exclamations about the beauty of the trail or observations made to Dawa, who was happy enough to answer despite carrying what looked like a ridiculous amount of gear on his back. The porter, Rocky, was also carrying the load; he, apparently, did not "talk in English," and so we smiled a lot at each other and left it at that.

There was something about the Shangri-La, despite all the modern gear piled beside the front door, the bright padded jackets and trekking pants, the Yeti bottles for water; the teahouse seemed to be a backdrop more than a participant in the scene. I stood looking at it for a moment and then took off my glasses, allowing the whole scene to shift out of focus and carry me back in time.

James Hilton was, after all, a contemporary of Mallory. Even though he wrote *Lost Horizon* a handful of years after Mallory disappeared, they were of the same generation, the same Empire.

Mallory had come out here as the Empire was still expanding, still stretching out into continents and across oceans without a single sunset in mind. In 1924, when he set out for his final attempt to scale Everest, it was a world Great Britain still dominated; it was, after all, the same year Forster published *A Passage to India*, the same year Douglas Fairbanks starred in the Orientalist

104

film *The Thief of Bagdad*, the same year the British Imperial Airways began operations. It would take another world war and the middle of the twentieth century before that sun did finally set, and by then Mallory's body had long since found its resting place on the north col of Everest.

He was a part of the beginning of the end. Another adventurer from another empire was realizing at about the same time that a window was closing fast. In 1939 Antoine de Saint-Exupéry had lamented, "The horizons of our journeys have faded out one after another." He'd sought to conquer the skies even as Mallory wanted to conquer the mountain. To be the first to do anything.

And it really led you to ask the question: What happened to these people once they ran out of firsts?

Neither of them had had to answer the question, Saint-Exupéry disappearing on a reconnaissance mission during World War Two, and Mallory, of course, dead on the slopes of his obsession. Who would they have become, had they lived? How do you square the need to be first with a world that doesn't offer any more of them?

We were shown again to a double room with two twin beds, standard teahouse fare. "You will like a view from your window," said the girl who'd carried our personal packs up for us; it was as usual lost in translation, unclear whether a suggestion or an order. When spoken with a Nepali accent, everything sounded like a command.

I opened the curtains, and she was right: the expanse of the Himalayas reached heavenward all around us. We weren't even halfway there and it was clear, already, how this was considered the seat of the gods.

Emma came and stood next to me, uncannily echoing my thoughts. "You can see why the goddess chose to live here," she said dreamily, her eyes on the snow-capped peaks.

"She has good taste," I said, a little flippantly, before sitting on my bed and easing my feet out of the hiking boots I'd worked so hard to break in, back in Boston. I was grateful for that now;

even after the relatively easy five miles we'd trekked from Lukla, my feet were feeling it.

Emma was still communing with the peaks when I left. I put on a pair of Keds (slim and light, easy to pack) and headed down to explore the village. Smaller than Lukla, just as picturesque, with a beautiful wooden arch and children rolling marbles on the pavers.

I walked around it enough to consider my muscles sufficiently stretched and then returned to the Shangri-La, sitting at one of the patio tables and ordering a Nepali beer, something called Gorkha. It would be my last alcohol for a while—Richard had warned me that they don't really mix; I didn't need anything that would make me more thirsty. So this was my last treat for myself. Sitting in the sun in someone's version of Paradise with a cold beer in my hand. You really couldn't beat it.

Dawa appeared and I waved him over to join me. "Can I get you a drink?"

He eyed the bottle in front of me. "I see you find Nepal premium beers," he said, smiling. "Yes, I will happily join you in this moment of merriment."

I ordered another bottle and sat back in my chair. The sun was low but still warm, and I took off my glasses and closed my eyes in contentment. Without opening them, I said, "Dawa, where do you live?"

He didn't say anything, and I opened my eyes again. "Dawa?"

He pulled his attention away from a conversation at a nearby table carried out in—I thought—Mandarin. "I live in Lhotse," he said. "Many Sherpa mountaineers lives in Lhotse. Guides, porters, cooks. Is nice place. There is monastery there, very nice, monks pray for us on the mountain. This time of year, this whole town waits and prays that no Sherpa deaths on the mountain."

"It's a hard way to live."

His face was impassive. "It is how we live," he said, with dignity.

I was suddenly very glad that I wasn't a climber, only a trekker. With any luck, my engaging Dawa and Rocky wouldn't entail them dying for the dubious pleasure of dragging my body up to the summit, taking my money because they had no other choice. Trekking paid a lot less, Anish had told me, but the men were sure at least to go home at the end of the trip.

Struck by that thought, I said, "Dawa, why are all the climbing sherpas men? You mentioned that some of the widows are training. What's that about?"

He gave me a half-smile. "It is the way," he said. "Our culture is that a man does the work outside of the home, and the woman keeps the house, she farms, cares for children and animals, all that important work. But it is changing." He paused. "You have not heard the name Pasang Llamu Sherpa, I think," he said.

"No," I agreed.

"She was the first Nepali woman to climb Mount Everest," he said. "This is a long time before already, this was in 1993. She was the first. But there was a storm on the way down from the summit, and she died. But even so, she is big influence on Sherpa girls. They are called the Sherpani, you see, we now even have a word for them. Some climb when they are widows and must care for their children somehow. Others are not widows, but they want to make the money, they want the respect. It is new, but it is not bad." He paused. "There are companies now, they have all-women guides, porters, cooks, they have all-women members. Many womens, they feel more comfortable with other womens."

"Does Supreme Summits employ any of these women guides?"

Dawa smiled. "Boss-Man think it a good idea."

"A good idea, but...?"

"All his guides, men. All his climbing sherpas, men." He looked out over the mountain panorama stretched out in front of us, almost achingly beautiful, almost impossibly magical. He seemed to be thinking about it. "Not everything change," Dawa said.

"Not everything change" seemed as good an assessment of women's place in the world-at-large as any other. I wished them well, the Sherpani. I couldn't imagine anything was made particularly easy for them.

"Tomorrow," Dawa said, "you see the mountain. And then you understand."

"Understand what?"

"Why they climb." He caught my eye. "Miss Emma, she likes mountains. But you, Miss Abigail, I think, have not the same feelings."

"If you mean, would I ever want to climb one, then you're right," I said fervently. "Where I live, in Boston, there are no mountains." Though Beacon Hill in the past had sometimes felt like one. "But they're beautiful," I added. I made a sweeping gesture at our surroundings. "How could anyone think they're not beautiful? You live in paradise, Dawa."

He nodded gravely. "But to understand this man, this Mallory, you must also love the mountain," he said.

Why had he brought up George Mallory? Did he know about Emma's book? I narrowed my eyes. "Most people assume he climbed for the *adventure* of it," I said. "I don't know if that's the same as loving it." But maybe it was. "You know, they called Everest the Third Pole, once men had been to the North Pole and the South Pole." I found I was ticking them off on my fingers. "It was the only big thing left to conquer." Belatedly I heard my own words, and remembered the conversation with Myles in Lukla. *The Sherpa lived up here for a whole lot of centuries and in all that time, none of them ever felt the need to climb the mountain.*

I cleared my throat and added, "Well, white men, anyway, westerners. Do you think Mallory was different? That he was closer to the mountain than other explorers?" It was a novel and attractive thought. "Dawa," I said suddenly, remembering. "Wasn't your grandfather a guide, over in Tibet? Forgive me asking, but Jack Bailey told us about him." Had his grandfather been part of any of the expeditions Mallory was on? I couldn't do the math quickly enough to fit it into the conversation. Probably not.

Dawa was unperturbed. "He organize porters," he said easily. "And, Miss Abigail, you see, I know this mountain. It is not the most difficult to climb, you understand? K2 much harder mountain to climb, is called Killer Mountain. Much more technique. Other mountains, harder. But this mountain... special."

"Special because it's the highest? It's all about being on the top of the world?"

"It is the highest," he admitted. "But it is more than that. It is holy. You will see it tomorrow, you will understand."

I took a long swig of beer. "Well," I said consideringly, "I *have* seen photos of Everest, you know."

Dawa shook his head. "No, no, Miss Abigail. There are no photographs show the goddess's true face. That, you can only see for yourself. She only speak to peoples who are here to be patient, to listen to her words."

This was starting to sound as mystical as Shangri-La itself. "I'll look forward to it, then," I said politely, and we left it at that.

Later, though, I found myself wondering. I had this impression that somehow Everest was at the center of something else, something darker even than ambitions willing to die, willing to kill, willing to risk family and fortune and life itself, willing to do anything for that one moment of glory at the summit.

And although I couldn't say why, this felt like a Moment. With a capital M. I remembered one of Agatha Christie's lesser-known mysteries, *They Came to Baghdad*, and I had the same impression now, a sense of disparate people from all over the globe called separately, converging on one place for... what? Something was there, I was sure of it. Just beyond reach. Just beyond perception. But there.

And then Emma came back to the teahouse and blew all my musings out of the water.

Excerpt from the journal of George Mallory

Graian Alps, 1912: This is where I belong.

I finished the year at Charterhouse somewhat better than I'd begun it; the boys have settled down, and I've settled in. But truth be told, I couldn't wait to get out of the classroom and back into the mountains.

I'm here with Irving and Tyndale, and the years have changed us; where I was content enough in the past to merely follow their plans, perhaps it's the challenges of teaching that empowered me to make plans of my own. The easy routes have all been done countless times; the thing is to find more difficult routes, to go where others thought it would be impossible to go.

I'm out in front of them all these days, cutting steps into the ice with my axe, smoothing the way for the others, and with every breath feeling surer and more... what should I say? At one with the slopes? Tyndale is impressed; he says my economy of movement should be a model for every mountaineer. High praise indeed.

I've discovered a hunger within myself to do what others couldn't. If I cannot be the first up a mountain, then I will be the first to try it from a different angle, the first to take the dangerous routes—I've only ever fallen once, so I expect that some of this attitude can be put down to bravado.

And then, I have to confess, I paid the price for my pride. We'd planned to attack Mont Maudit along the difficult east ridge. I'd drunk some sour Chianti the night before, but thought nothing of it; it found its way into my stomach and by the time we'd reached the crest of the ridge I fainted altogether... and then did so again when I was meant to be paying out Irving's rope.

What to do? We could descend, of course... My legs were feeling as though they were made of lead, and I struggled hard to keep going—but, even then, there was no question in my mind.

To be this close and to deny oneself the opportunity seemed the greatest waste I could imagine, and by six-thirty we were standing on the highest summit in Europe, a sense that we were higher than other men, and that it was where we ought to be. We felt delighted... but also sober. It was no small thing.

Vanquishing ourselves and our limitations is as powerful as vanquishing any enemy without.

Chapter Nine

Emma hadn't been at dinner, and I'd ended up sitting with a group of trekkers from Scotland who'd honed their hiking skills following an odd pastime they called "Munro bagging"—climbing a list of Scottish mountains put together by some fellow called Munro in the 1800s and rising up to three thousand feet—and were all excited about applying those skills to the Himalayas. They were very hospitable and kept me well entertained, at least when I could follow their accents, but when I finally went up to our room, I found Emma there, seething. "Where did you put them?" she demanded.

I looked at her blankly. "Put what?"

"You know! Where are they?" She was practically spitting the words out.

I was gobsmacked. "Emma, I have no idea what you're talking about."

"My notes!" She grabbed her backpack in one hand and shook it in the air. "My notes! They were here. Where did you put them?"

"Emma," I said, forcing my voice to be calm, "I have no idea what you're talking about. I don't have your notes. I didn't touch your things."

"You must have! Who else would?" The question was clearly rhetorical. "All my work! All my research!"

If she were carrying all her research with her, she'd have needed two yaks at least for transporting the paper. And, well, seriously? Carrying your intellectual property around on a trek? Who does that? The beer I'd drunk with Dawa was starting to turn nasty on me. "You're talking about a flash drive?"

"Of course I'm talking about a flash drive! You've seen it, you've seen me working with it."

Probably so, but I hadn't particularly noticed anything. She had her laptop out a fair bit; of course I'd seen her writing, but

I'm really not as observant as she was giving me credit for. "Okay. But I still didn't touch it. I didn't touch your bag, or anything that's yours. In fact, I haven't been in this room all evening."

We stared at each other, her anger dissolving slowly and almost visually in the air between us, leaving the room feeling somehow smaller. "Maybe you misplaced it?" I finally ventured. "I can help you look if you want."

She shook her head, still looking at me, but her stare was vacant, as though she were somewhere else. As though she was doing sums in her mind. "It's gone," she said blankly. "Someone took it."

"Who?" The question was out before I had time to think. "Who'd want your notes?"

Her gaze was still vacant. "No one. Of course, no one."

"But someone took them? You're sure?"

She looked at me, but I felt her mind somewhere else altogether, plunging down obscure pathways, consulting strange specters. As though she'd checked out and wasn't seeing me at all. I was once in the presence of someone having a mini-stroke, and that's exactly what this looked like.

My brain finally engaged. "Someone searched our room in Kathmandu," I said loudly, trying to rein her in. "Remember? Okay, so maybe someone stole your notes here. They go together." I took a deep breath. "That isn't normal, Emma. And neither are you, to be fair. You're out half the night and you lie to me about it. Weird things happen to our stuff." I hesitated, but really, what did I have to lose here? "Emma, enough's enough. You have to tell me what's going on."

She came back to reality with a click that could almost be heard. "Nothing," she said briskly. "Nothing's going on. You're right, of course. I must have misplaced the flash drive. I'll look through my pockets." But she didn't move.

"Emma," I said. "You're paying me to be your assistant. I'm here because of you. I want to help you, I really do, I'm totally on your side. But you have to be honest with me."

"No," she said, and I got the cold professorial voice, the one that says *no, you may not make up your midterm.* "I don't have to be anything with you, Abbie. As you said, I'm paying you. You're my assistant. I'll tell you what you need to know."

Oh, for heaven's sake. "You're not paying me so much that I won't walk out if you're doing something illegal, or something immoral!"

"Immoral?"

We stared at each other for a moment. At some level, it was so absurd, I could feel bubbles of laughter rising up inside me. "Well—um, okay, what is it? Okay, unethical, okay? Illegal or unethical!"

"*Immoral?*" she repeated again, and finally really caught my eye, and then we were both laughing at the absurdity of it all, laughing with a release of tension, laughing... but with the shadow of something darker inside. "Oh, God, that's too funny! Seriously! You did everything but stamp your foot, Abbie!"

"I did consider it," I admitted, wiping tears from my eyes.

"I'll bet you did!"

And then, slowly, the laughter, too, dissipated, just as had her anger, and it left us standing facing each other in an empty barren room.

With no answers at all.

Morning came far too early, accompanied by a serious hangover, which at sea level would have happened after five drinks; up here, one had done the trick. As I rinsed my teeth I was grateful that last night's "moment of merriment" on the terrace with Dawa marked the end of my alcohol consumption for the balance of the trek. The guys back in Kathmandu were right: altitude and booze don't mix.

Headache notwithstanding, I was—to my surprise—breathing pretty well. We'd see what the day would bring; today was supposed to be one of the tougher sections of trail, combining as it did a reasonably long distance—just under seven miles—with a massive change in elevation. At Namche Bazaar, our next stop, we'd stay over two nights to allow our bodies to acclimate; the biggest risk for developing altitude sickness is increasing your elevation too rapidly. I'd read about it in some detail on the Internet. Theoretically, you shouldn't do more than one thousand feet a day, though today would be nearly twice that—hence the extra day in Namche, a bigger village than Phakding, and a hub for trekkers and climbers alike.

Dawa and Rocky were waiting when we emerged from the Shangri-La, and Dawa made sure we had enough water and snacks for the trail. "Esteemed ladies ready!"

I hadn't had a chance to talk to Emma at breakfast; the Scots had engulfed me again, urging me to eat their porridge ("Aye, it's just the thing for the climb!"), which I washed down with plenty of milky tea. Wherever we were going, I was going to need a couple of bathroom breaks for sure.

We were shrugging into our backpacks as the Scottish climbers set out just ahead of us. "Now is when the fun really begins!" one of them told me happily.

I waved gaily back, but I had a feeling that, whatever was ahead, it wasn't going to fall into any category of fun I could imagine. Something had shifted. There was a shadow here, dark, unsettling, just over one's shoulder, just beyond the corner of one's eye. Whether we'd brought it with us or it had been waiting up here for us didn't really matter. It was here.

The first highlight of the day's trek—or most terrifying moment, take your pick—was crossing the Tensing-Hillary (yeah, there he was again) suspension bridge, which was oh-my-God high up over a ravine and swayed alarmingly. The hundreds of fluttering prayer flags affixed to it did nothing to reassure me. There was no prayer I could summon that would make this any easier, but I did have the brilliant idea of removing my glasses and putting them into my pocket. *What you don't see can't hurt you.*

After this, I promised myself, I was never leaving *terra firma* again.

But even I could appreciate the stark beauty of the mountains. The valley below still had threads of mist clinging to the tops of the trees, but up here the air was clear and sharp and the sky an impossible blue. The prayer flags adorning the bridge snapped purposefully in the wind, and I could almost see the prayers they stood in for, the pleas and the remembrances, the needs and the gratitude, all flicked out from the stiff cloth into the mountainside, riding the wind currents, ghostly and ephemeral.

But Myles—and what had happened to Myles, anyway?—had been right: by midmorning we were following the tributary of a river whose name I never quite got, rounded Namche Hill—a corner on the trail—and, suddenly and magnificently, there she was: Chomolungma, Everest, the sacred mountain, the seat of the goddess.

My exhaustion melted off me as though it had never been there.

There was no experience I'd ever had that could have prepared me for that moment. A few months ago, I hadn't given the slightest thought to mountain-climbing; now I found myself inhaling the sight of Everest like a drug.

The oddest thing was that we were at quite a significant distance away, yet it felt like you could almost reach out and touch her. Dawa and Rocky had both stopped to say prayers, facing the mountain; I was too entranced by the optical illusion presented.

Emma, too, was transfixed. There were tears in her eyes. "There it is," she breathed, and then, singing under her breath, "I see the mountain, the mountain comes to me..."

"Is that a Buddhist prayer?" I asked.

She glanced at me, and laughed. "American folk song by Dave Carter," she said.

"Dawa said once we saw it, we'd understand," I said. I had a feeling I was coming late to this party, and was just grateful I'd been invited at all.

We duly arrived (if stumbling can be characterized as a suitable gait for arrival) in Namche Bazaar, a bustling mountain town offering climbers their last chance to buy necessary gear, souvenirs, and Western snacks.

Dawa had booked us into the grandly named Garden Palace Hotel, a little off the beaten path, with the beautiful woodwork and swirling vivid colors I'd come to anticipate in Nepal. But he wasn't done with us: we still had to hike some more before dinner. "Climb high, sleep low," Dawa said encouragingly, echoing Anish's advice back in Kathmandu. Certainly neither he nor Rocky seemed the least bit tired, and Rocky was carrying about half a building on his back.

"I don't even know what that means," I complained. I was ready for a shower. I wanted time to adjust. I was feeling things I couldn't remember ever having felt before. I needed them to sink in, to become part of me.

He wasn't having any of it. "Altitude sickness," Dawa said, nodding energetically. "Always climb higher than you sleep. Climb up, walk down, sleep safe. Come along, esteemed ladies!"

I was surprised—and, okay, yes, a little bit glad—to see that Emma was finally feeling the exertion. Well, it wasn't exactly cause for satisfaction or celebration: she had, after all, quite some years on me. She said she felt a little dizzy on the extra six hundred feet Dawa imposed, but the dizziness abated as soon as she stopped, and he finally pronounced us fit enough to carry on.

Namche Bazaar might have had the nightlife of Paris (spoiler alert: it didn't) and I *still* wouldn't have been around for it. I was asleep by eight o'clock, having taken some ibuprofen and drunk a quart of water and wondered, for about the hundredth time, why I was there. It was gorgeous. It was an experience I'd treasure for the rest of my life. But... why?

Emma needed me as much as she needed a dead fish. She hadn't asked me any more questions about my research. She hadn't given me any research assignments for teahouse evenings. My "companion" role so far had only included showing her the map and being accused of stealing intellectual property.

But the trek had accomplished one thing: sleep was easy and immediate.

Morning brought the droning sound of unison horns, almost like thousands of bees flying past, interrupted occasionally by a single clash of a cymbal—a thin whisper of sound weaving its way through a surprising early-morning mist. I lifted the drape from the window beside my bed and looked out at a vague white world. The horns were oddly both muffled and magnified by the moisture, and sounded very close at hand.

I drank milky tea and ordered dal bhat for breakfast, not just following the adage to do as the Romans when in Rome, but also because it surprisingly did seem to offer more energy than my usual buttered toast. Decades of Nepali mountaineers couldn't be wrong.

Emma, of course, was nowhere to be seen. I was starting to get used to her odd absences, and the morning had brought clarity: I wasn't going to allow them to bother me anymore. She was right: what she did was her business. I was there to assist, whether it was providing historical research or ordering tea. I'd already spent far too much time wondering what it was she was up to.

So of course I was still wondering what she was up to.

Anyway, today was acclimatization day, and I was spending it in a beautiful place, with the bonus that it was Saturday and that meant—or so my guidebook assured me—that the must-see Chinese market would be open, with traders from Tibet selling their wares in exchange for Nepali and Indian food and goods brought up from Lukla by lowland porters.

Namche, my book informed me, was the place to stock up on essentials, and I'd already seen proof of that: shops and stalls lined the cobbled streets—most of the traders were Sherpas, many of them Tibetans—and I'd also scoped out some cafés and bakeries that looked promising.

Dawa had asked us, the night before, about our teeth.

"Teeth?" I asked blankly. "What's wrong with our teeth?"

"Nothing, I am hoping," Dawa said. "It is very bad to have problems with teeth on mountains. Here in Namche, is dental clinic. It is the last one."

Last exit before the highway, I thought. Last chance to get a toothache. *Beyond this be dental dragons.*

Emma was typically no-nonsense. "Our teeth are fine, Dawa," she said. "I'm interested in the market; can you take us there?"

He looked bemused. Teeth were important in his world, the Chinese market less so. "Of course," he said.

The market was open-air—no stalls per se, no awnings, just wares spread out on blankets. And a whole lot of haggling going on around us, primarily in Nepali and Tibetan, both of which were softer than the Mandarin and Cantonese I'd heard elsewhere, but still sounding abrupt to my Western ear, sentences sounding almost like accusations.

"Cooee! Finding anything to your liking?" It was a familiar accent, and I turned quickly, hoping it was Myles—but it was Jack Bailey who stood there, the fitful spring sunlight that had nudged out the morning mist encircling his head like a halo. I was going to have to sort through my understanding of Australian and New Zealand accents.

I looked around for Emma, but she and Dawa were nowhere to be seen. "Fancy meeting you here," I said.

He grinned, his glance taking in the area, not particularly interested in me. "Just passing through. Like everybody in Namche."

"It does seem to be a crossroads," I agreed.

His attention swung back to me. "*Seems* to be a crossroads?" he echoed. "You're looking at the Silk Road itself, Allie." He hesitated. "Um, it *is* Allie, right?"

"Abbie," I said automatically. I knew he had a lot going on, organizing an expedition, but we'd spent a couple of days together in Kathmandu, he'd picked me up at the airport… and he was having problems remembering my *name*? What was that about? "Abbie Bradford," I added for good measure.

He nodded. "Abbie. Right. Abbie. These people you see here, they've been doing this for generations. The Silk Road came through Tibet and over the mountains into Nepal—right here where you're standing, at Namche—and then down into the valley where it hit Kathmandu. Some of the winding streets you saw in the city? They might not have felt like they had any rhyme or reason, but if you'd looked at them from above, from the air, you'd be able to trace the road, running right through the old city. And then from there on to Afghanistan, Turkmenistan... and Europe."

"Really?" I might have sounded doubtful; the Chinese market was colorful and interesting, of course, but it didn't seem all that important in a grand-schemes kind of way. The Silk Road sounded magical and distant; this felt a little more everyday.

But Anish had pointed it out, too.

Jack nodded, now seemingly interested in a bottle of dubious-looking liquid he'd picked up from the merchant in front of us. I wondered if he had some kind of ADD. Again, maybe not an ideal trait for someone leading other people up a perilous mountain, but what did I know? "This is it, the route of all marvels," he said. "They didn't just bring goods back and forth, either. The Silk Road's steeped in tradition and ideas, religion, and culture."

There was movement beside me. "Don't tell me Jack's giving you his Silk Road lecture," said Emma. I hadn't seen her approach.

Jack put the bottle down and turned to face her. "Emma. How's the trek going?" he asked politely.

There was a mischievous glint in Emma's eyes. "Very well, thank you," she said. "How's your school field trip going?"

He waved a hand back behind us. "They're all busy making sure they have enough Snickers bars for the duration," he said, then turned and reached over to move a wisp of hair off her forehead, the gesture intimate. "And you didn't tell Amy about the road, so someone had to."

"It's Abbie, not Amy. And tell me what, exactly?" And why did I feel like I was interrupting something here? What was going on between these two?

"The history," said Emma to me. "You're a historian; you must know some of it."

"Okay," I conceded. I did, of course. Parts of the Silk Road history leaked into my own period of study, but I'd also taken some time online since February to investigate Nepal's past. Even though the name derives from the popularity of Chinese silk among tradesmen in the Roman Empire, it sure as hell wasn't the only important export from the East to the West. The rich spices of the East quickly changed cuisines across much of Europe. And gunpowder did the same with geopolitics.

Trade along the economic belt included fruits and vegetables, livestock, grain, leather and hides, tools, religious objects, artwork, precious stones and metals and—perhaps more importantly—language, culture, religious beliefs, philosophy, and science. Commodities like paper and gunpowder, both invented by the Chinese during the Han Dynasty, had obvious and lasting impacts on culture and history in the West. The paper part was truly world-changing: paper's arrival in Europe fostered significant industrial change, with the written word becoming a key form of mass communication for the first time.

The eventual development of Gutenberg's printing press allowed for the mass production of books and, later, newspaper, which enabled a wider exchange of news and information; the real change came first, with paper.

"But it's all history," I said dismissively, which had to be a first for me. "There's no Silk Road anymore."

If I hadn't been watching for it, I wouldn't have seen the quick look that passed between Emma and Jack, swift and knowing. I had no idea what that was about. There was something there—Laxsmi's jealousy back in Kathmandu had indicated as much; I wondered how this tied in. Had they been romantically involved in the past? In the present? And what attachment did they have to the Silk Road?

Or was I reading a lot more into it than was actually there? For some people, the thin air of the mountains encourages hallucinations. *Keep yours in check, Abbie*, I reminded myself.

It was none of my business, of course. But since for now my life seemed to be inextricably intertwined with theirs, I still wondered.

I passed on lunch at the teahouse and instead tried the outdoor patio at Café Basecamp, which prided itself on yak steaks; I remembered how far we were from Lukla, and ordered the vegetarian version of my beloved chatamari instead. It was a lovely day, really, and I sat nodding over my tea for a while, ostensibly reading more of Mallory's book on my e-reader, in actuality dozing. I'd promised Dawa I'd retrace our steps from the evening before—hike high, sleep low—but there was plenty of time for that, surely, and the sun had become soporific…

A shadow came between me and the sun and an unmistakably English voice said, "Still eating chatamari? Did we create a monster?"

I didn't even open my eyes. "Richard," I said.

"Out late partying? Mind if I join you?"

I opened my eyes, put my glasses back on, and peered at him. He was balancing a plate of dal bhat and a tin cup of—what else— milky tea. "Partying? After climbing miles and miles and crossing a bridge destined to give you nightmares for the rest of your life? Hardly," I said. "Yeah, sure, sit down. Did Jack mention you have your expedition clients with you? Members, you call them, right? Are you all stopping here, too?"

"It's for team-building," Richard said agreeably, sliding into the chair across from me. "We're trekking up fast, but we're trekking together. Jack insists on it. No shortcuts with Supreme Summits Expeditions." He glanced around. "You found the right place for lunch, by the way. It's where all the Nepalis eat. Are all your instincts this good, or did Dawa tell you about this place?"

"I have terrific instincts," I said with dignity. "*And* Dawa told me about this place."

"We thought we might run into you here," he said, digging into his food. "Pretty much everybody does. I've been in Namche sometimes and seen blokes I hadn't seen since school. You'd be surprised who you might run into, sometimes the most unexpected people."

"You must have made good time, anyway," I said, and then stopped myself. "I have no idea why I just said that; I've lost all sense of it," I confessed.

He swallowed and shook his head. "We try and move pretty fast through the trekking section," he said. "Leaving in about an hour or so, actually. The members—" he gave me a wicked grin—

"are all in good shape, they've been doing low-oxygen training for months. They acclimatize quickly. We keep them moving."

"They're all here?" I asked. "Your whole team?"

"Somewhere in Namche," he said, waving a hand in unconscious imitation of Jack's earlier gesture.

"Loading up on Snickers bars?"

He laughed. "Pretty much," he admitted. "Last chance at that sort of thing, don't you know. We'll spend tonight in Tengboche, then press on for Base Camp after that."

"We have another acclimatization day," I said, frowning. "At—"

"—Dingboche," Richard supplied, nodding. "If you're going to get altitude sickness, that's where it's most likely to strike. Take your time, drink plenty of fluids, and you'll be fine."

"I plan to," I said fervently.

"For now, just enjoy the view," he said.

The truth was, I was breathing far better than I'd anticipated. Maybe my lungs were getting used to the thinner air. Certainly no one I saw at Namche Bazaar seemed to be having troubles with *their* breath. I wandered around the shopping area, bought a few Snickers bars for myself (*when in Rome…*), and nodded at a whole lot of people I had already seen at other teahouses and on the trails, starting to recognize faces (and in some cases, outfits). More of them seemed to be recognizing me: the bright blue hair attracts attention, if nothing else. I blended in nicely with the riotous colors of Nepal, the bright climbing gear.

And Richard was clearly right, this was a hub of the trek to Everest.

Dawa collected me and Emma before dinner and we dutifully followed him up about eight hundred feet, following twisting paths that did again, from time to time, afford us a glimpse of Everest itself, each time inexplicably breathtaking in its simultaneous familiarity and foreignness. There were more of the familiar marigolds here, and rhododendrons, colorful and bursting with life, but they were already thinning out; soon it would be just trees, and after that, rocks and the Khumbu Glacier.

I shivered even thinking of the name, and blessed the people at Urban Outfitters in Cambridge who'd made sure my clothes were mountain-warm.

We finally found ourselves sitting with our backs against a scree, enjoying some of the lowering rays of the sun, while Dawa told us a story about a yeti said to live in the region. "But he is not abominable, as the westerners all say." His voice was earnest. "The yeti here in the mountains, he is a gentle creature, an omen, a sign of good luck if you cross his pathway." He nodded energetically. "There are many stories of lost climbers who have been guided back to safety by the yeti, and of climbers who feel his presence in their tents on the coldest of nights. He has rescued many climbers." He paused, then added, "… and he has sat with others so they do not die alone." He perked up. "Perhaps the esteemed ladies will be so fortunate to encounter the yeti!"

"Not if he only shows up if you're in trouble," I said. My back muscles were starting to tighten, and I stood up. "I am walking over there for a moment alone," I announced, the code we'd agreed upon for using a nonexistent toilet, and Dawa said, "and I go and fetch backpacks for esteemed ladies, then we return to Namche perhaps?"

"You two go," said Emma, leaning back and closing her eyes. "Pick me up when you're ready to leave."

I hadn't even gotten to the place I'd scoped out as protected and semi-private when the ground started to shake and an immense, senses-assaulting roar engulfed me. Someone was screaming.

I whirled around. It looked as if half the hillside behind our bench was on the move, big boulders and smaller stones tumbling down fast, dust rising and blotting out the light with a roar like a tornado.

"Emma!" I screamed, running without thought, ridiculously trying to get to her before the rocks did.

She was quick—amazingly quick. It was a thought in my mind, even barely that, before I realized she wasn't sitting where we'd left her, that she had screamed and moved simultaneously, flinging herself down the hill to her left and out of the way of the rockslide.

I reached her in seconds, grabbing her shoulder, gasping for breath. "Emma! Are you all right?"

She nodded, not looking at me, fighting for breath, looking at where the bench was no more, covered with rocks. We clutched at each other, hearts pounding; I could feel myself shaking. "Are you all right?"

"Yeah." She pulled away from me. "Where's Dawa? Is he all right?"

"He went that way." I pointed up the slope; he wasn't in sight.

A moment later he came trotting out from a spinney of trees. "Esteemed ladies! You are not injured? Is everything all right?"

I've always thought that an odd question even under normal circumstances, since it's usually asked when everything is clearly *not* all right; here it sounded simply absurd. "Everything's great," Emma said ironically.

"We *are* alive," I reminded her, though for Emma it had been damned close.

She didn't say anything; I could sense as much as feel her trembling.

"What happened, Dawa?" I demanded. "Is that—a thing? Landslides?"

He was looking soberly up at the hill. "Not here," he said.

Not here.

Ang Pemba Sherpa dies at Lukla: icefall doctors don't die there. A landslide had almost killed Emma, possibly even me, too, at a place where they didn't happen. Some might say our trip was jinxed.

Or, perhaps, that a kindly Nepali yeti had grabbed my middle-aged companion at the very last moment and pulled her to safety.

It wasn't until much later, just as I was dropping off to sleep, that the unwelcome thought surfaced. Dawa had been out of sight when the rocks started tumbling down.

He couldn't have had anything to do with it, I told myself.

Couldn't he?

Excerpt from the journal of George Mallory

Charterhouse, Surrey, 1912/1913: The challenges of public school life are not to be with the actual learning, it seems, but rather with fitting in.

I take solace in living a life as rich as I can manage within the constraints of my position. I secured a publisher for my Boswell biography, after a couple of resounding refusals. Of course the whole thing needed rewriting; I have, it seems, a ponderous style that detracts from the reader's understanding of what I'm saying. I tended to bristle a bit at this suggestion, but old Lytton stopped by: he claims my sentences are overloaded and my point of view vague.

The book, once finished, garnered some most excellent reviews; I never imagined that anyone would care a scrap about it except Boswell students, so it's all the more pleasing to hear that people like it.

I've been asked to write an article for the Climber's Club Journal, which is of course a thundering great honor, but I'm unsure of what tone to take. The point, of course, is to discuss the element of risk in climbing, the knowledge when one sets out that one might not return, a sober truth as three of our fellow climbers have died on mountains this year alone.

I am among those who do take terrible risks. I am, more often than not, liable to cross "the line," that yardstick we all use to judge whether we are in control of the risk we run every time we set foot upon the mountain.

I do it; many of us do it; but from time to time one must take a step back and reflect on whether such risks are justifiable.

The more I think about it, the more I see climbing and its inherent risks as a sort of spiritual journey best captured as a symphony: there is a beginning, intermediary passages, and an ending. One could describe both the experience of climbing and the experience of creating a symphony as having themes and variations, climaxes and gentle passages, and—God willing—moments of a supremely harmonious experience.

I am offering "The Mountaineer as Artist" as a title for the piece, and we shall see how it sits with the public.

Chapter Ten

"Someone," I said to Emma as we were getting ready to set out the next day, "is trying to tell us something."

She didn't answer, focused on lacing her boots.

"Or maybe you knew that already," I added.

She finished, put her foot down, straightened, and looked at me. "What are you trying to say?"

I was ready for just that sort of question. And determined to elicit some answers. "Okay," I said, holding up my fingers as I ticked off the instances. "In Kathmandu, someone went through our luggage. In Phakding, someone stole your flash drive. Here in Namche, someone tried to kill one or both of us."

"The police don't think so," she said. "Landslides happen."

"Add to that," I said, ignoring her, "the fact of you being connected to Supreme Summits Expeditions, which lost its icefall expert prematurely and under questionable circumstances that might even be murder, and you'll forgive me for thinking that maybe you're not telling me everything. And don't for a moment say this is normal. I've talked with dozens of trekkers since we left Lukla, and no one talked about any of this stuff happening to them. The teahouses are safe. Most trekkers don't even bother locking their doors. And the trails are safe, too, all the way up until Base Camp. Rockslides don't happen here unless they've been sent on their way on purpose."

"It could have been accidental, dear, and now whoever caused it doesn't want to come forward," she said.

She would have to eliminate the "dear" at some point, or I was seriously going to do her a violence. "Oh, really? Did that same someone break into our rooms? Is that the same someone you've been going out at night to meet? This sort of thing doesn't just happen, Emma, unless somehow *you're* making it happen."

She sighed. "Abbie, I don't know what to say. I'm a famous person. People look for souvenirs."

"By breaking into your room?"

She shrugged. "You never know. Listen, I want to talk about Mallory."

"Yes, but—"

She held up her hand. "I'm not doing this, Abbie."

Great. A standoff. She wouldn't talk about this mysterious interest in us, and I perversely decided I wouldn't talk about Mallory. So there.

We were barely speaking at all by the time we set off. First, a stop in town to start the big prayer wheel cylinders moving, Dawa and Rocky chanting as they did it. I followed suit with a prayer to my own guardian angel; I had a feeling he or she might be working overtime on my behalf, if not now, then probably very soon.

And then we were off.

What can I say about that day? The air was clean, if thin; the sun was bright and hot; the path steep, but every moment you looked around there was something exceptional to see. The mountains; the streams, the—*gulp*—suspension bridges, even. It was, by anyone's reckoning, a spectacular day. White fluffy clouds in a sky so blue you could lose yourself in it. Mountain peaks straining to touch it. Everywhere you looked was postcard-perfect, pristine, glacial.

Yet there was a little cold claw of fear right at the base of my spine that wouldn't leave me alone.

We met people on the way, trekkers coming down from Base Camp, climbers heading up to it. I wondered where Jack and Richard and Mark with the Supreme Summits crowd were by now; probably halfway up Everest carrying three climbing sherpas each (okay, so I exaggerate, but they did all seem a little *relentlessly* athletic).

We spoke little. Emma stopped frequently to snap photos; I stopped frequently to get my breath. Dawa pointed out various peaks around us and told little amusing anecdotes of other, prior visitors to the mountains; I wondered what he'd tell future trek-kers about us.

Probably that the odd Western ladies, esteemed or not, never spoke to each other.

I was exhausted by the time we reached Tengboche. I'd drunk all the water I carried and most of what Dawa carried, my muscles were all ready to go on strike, and I was beginning to seriously wonder whether my traveling companion was a romance writer or a spy.

There was no rest here for the weary: the purpose of stopping in Tengboche, it seemed, was a visit to the monastery to have our venture blessed. Dawa was insistent. "You can see the monks practicing the Buddhism and the beautiful paintings on the walls," he promised, ever the helpful tour guide. I was more in the mood for a hot shower and a soft bed than for watching monks practice the Buddhism, but Dawa didn't seem to think it was optional.

I'd gotten used by that time to seeing stupas in Nepal; they were everywhere, even in Kathmandu, bell-shaped structures that contain something sacred—no one really was clear in explaining exactly what that was—and beside or around which one did puja, which (to my utter confusion) was a *Hindu* ritual of cleansing and devotion. There seemed to be quite a bit of cross-religion compo-nents to Nepali culture. I'd been seeing stupas all along the trail and there were a number of them surrounding the monastery; but Dawa was insistent that this time, we had to go in.

"Tengboche Monastery is a bridge between the religious life of the Sherpas and the rest of the world. Blessings and compas-sion flow out of monastery, while we make sure goodwill and dol-lars flow in. Monastery is destroyed twice, been able to rise from the ashes time and again. Is very holy place, very special."

No doubt, I realized belatedly, we would be expected to help with the goodwill and dollars part. I didn't mind; Anish had helped me change quite a lot of American money into Nepali rupees for just this reason, though it felt as if I'd gotten back more than I gave—a hundred dollars is roughly equal to thirteen thousand rupees; it was just a matter of finding which pocket I'd zipped them into.

It was a vast place, the oldest monastery in Nepal, with rooms three stories high and everything lit by thousands of candles. The chanting of the monks made a droning sound that vibrated in the air around us, and the incense and wax made me feel more than a little nauseated. Plus it was hot, the heat of thousands of lit candles, flames everywhere.

"The monastery is home for sixty monks," Dawa informed us. "Every year many visitors and trekkers visit monastery to get blessed by holy man Lama." He shook his head mournfully. "It used to be, many boys in village join to be monks. Now not as much. Sherpa boys want to work in mountaineering or trekking activities."

We stayed well behind Dawa and stood silently when he gestured for us to do so. The heat was almost overwhelming. The droning chant was almost overwhelming. My lenses misted over twice before I got them under control. I finally pulled my eyes away from the flames of the hundreds of candles in time to see someone, a man, in Western gear, just to the side of one of the massive pillars, staring at us.

As soon as our eyes met, he turned and slipped into the shadows.

I don't think I hesitated. I crept away from Emma and Dawa—probably neither of them noticed—and followed.

Outside, the air was sharp and cold; I'd quickly gotten accustomed to the heat in the monastery, and when the sun goes down in the mountains the drop in temperature is dramatic. I looked around, a little wildly. Where had he gone? And who was he? Why was he watching us?

Was I imagining things?

I looked around, skirting stupas and watching my step on the loose rocks. What was the mystery here? Who could possibly care about us? We weren't engaged in investigative reporting—Emma was writing a *romance novel*, for heaven's sake. It didn't get much more innocuous than that. Dawa and Rocky were part of a well-known, well-regarded, professional organization that, at the end of the day, was about tourism.

All in all, it was difficult to think of anybody less likely to be followed—and even possibly killed, if that landslide back in Namche was intentional and meaningful in any way—than the four of us.

But this wasn't my imagination, either. I've never been one for flights of fancy; as much as I teased Emma about what she did, I couldn't do it in a million years. My own academic work had been solid and plodding and based completely in as much reality as one can glean from primary historical sources. I didn't imagine things. I didn't even have particularly vivid dreams. I read nonfiction for pleasure. I didn't wish I'd been born an actor, or an explorer, or a circus performer. I just didn't do any of that.

And yet it was clear to me that someone was very interested in us indeed.

While these thoughts were drifting through my brain, I kept looking around. Who had been there? Away from the surreal atmosphere of the monastery, away from the smoke and candlelight and droning chanting, I wasn't sure anymore what it was I'd seen. Could I have imagined him? A male; the person was large enough for me to make that assumption, even in an area where people tended to be shorter than I was used to in the States. Not wearing the orange robes of a monk, but wearing what? Around here, the uniform of trekking pants and insulated jackets was pretty ubiquitous, and very distinctive; all you'd have to do was lose the brightly colored padded jacket to change your entire profile.

There was no one around slinking into the background, removing their coat, or otherwise acting suspicious, and I stopped. There were a million places to hide among the stupas. If he didn't want to be seen, I wasn't going to see him.

This was getting a little ridiculous.

Emma was, for once, present at dinner. We were staying in yet another teahouse, the now-familiar long dining hall filled with people, most of them trekkers, a few accompanied by monks, here for a retreat perhaps. There were other people at our table, and the shared conversation was all about the mountains and the monastery; but I caught her on her way out. "Emma. I need to ask you something."

"Yes, dear?" Her voice and face were bland, innocent.

I hated it when she reverted to that auntie-speak. I had to wonder if it were some sort of defense mechanism.

I grabbed her wrist and led her—maybe a little forcefully—to a bench outside the teahouse. We had, of course, another spectacular view of the mountains, with Everest itself seemingly stretching up hopefully to catch the last rays of sunlight on its summit. "Sit down a minute. We have to talk."

"Yes?" Again, all innocence, with even a trace of amusement running behind the bland exterior.

Now it was going to sound stupid. I took a deep breath. "There was someone in the monastery today, watching us."

"Oh yes?"

"He left when he saw me looking at him. Never mind if you don't believe me. But it just got me thinking. All these things— our luggage searched, and your flash drive missing, and that horrific rockslide, and this guy tonight—tell me I'm wrong, but this isn't normal tourist stuff, Emma, and I know you know something. And I'm ready to quit right here and right now if you don't tell me what it is. I'll go back to Kathmandu and take the first flight home."

"You saw this person at the monastery? That explains it. I wondered where you'd disappeared to."

I let out a sigh of exasperation and tried a different tack. "Emma. You hired me as a research assistant. So far I've read Mallory's letters and his book. Besides that, I've read more about him than I've read about any other twentieth-century figure, and you haven't asked me anything, except before when you were trying to change the subject. I've learned about climbing mountains and about people who like to climb mountains, and you haven't said anything about checking your writing for accuracy or authenticity. Aside from acting as the tour guide's assistant, it's become really unclear to me why I'm here."

She looked completely relaxed, sitting there, which was all the more annoying. One leg crossed over the other, her hiking boots showing a little comfortable wear, a wool hat pulled over her gray hair against the chill of the evening, her hands clasped loosely in her lap. We could have been talking about politics, gardening, a favorite movie. And I'd had enough. "Okay," I said suddenly. "Tell me the truth. Are you a spy?"

Her eyes widened at that and she burst out laughing. "A—spy?" She could scarcely contain her merriment. "Oh, that's wonderful, Abbie. I love it!" The laughter transitioned into coughing—we were, after all, at well over twelve thousand feet now—and I waited until she had it under control. But she was still enormously amused. Wiping tears from her eyes, she regarded me with pleasure. "I've written about spies," she said at length, "but I never thought I'd be taken for one. You've made my week!"

When you considered everything that had happened over the past week, that was pretty rich.

I didn't say anything, just kept watching her, and she finally shook her head. "No," she said. "I am not a spy. It might have been a more exciting career path than the one I chose, but sad to say, I am definitely not a spy."

"So if you're not," I countered, "tell me what the hell is going on here. Stop looking like that. Why are we really going to Base Camp? Why do all these weird things keep happening to us?" And as she didn't respond right away, I said, angrily, "You owe me an explanation, Emma. It's my life here, too. You have your reasons for wanting me along, but I have a right to know about them."

She sighed, and looked off into the distance. Dusk was falling, and the temperature was dropping with the shadows around us. It didn't seem to be a good portent. "All right," she said. "All right. It's true that I'm writing this novel about George and Ruth Mallory." She sounded irritated.

Ah. So I *had* gotten a little under her skin, after all. "And?"

Another sigh. I didn't know *when* she'd planned to tell me whatever it was she was about to tell me, but it clearly wasn't here and now. "For some years, I've been in correspondence with a colleague in China," she said at last. "He's—a writer, a novelist, and a scholar."

"Okay." I tried to rein in my impatience.

Another sigh. "You have to understand, Abbie, this is still a major controversy. There's an ongoing heated Internet-slash-academic debate between Michael Tracy and Jake Norton—Norton was on the 1999 expedition that found Mallory's body."

I nodded; I'd seen a little of this. Google Mallory and Irvine and all you see is the twenty-first-century argument online; YouTube's fairly alight with maps, photographs, and squabbles. "About whether or not Mallory and Irvine reached the summit," I said impatiently. What did it have to do with a Chinese writer?

"About whether or not Mallory and Irvine had a *camera* with them," she corrected sharply. "There was at least one, there's documentation for that. Irvine had a camera—there are photos he took at camp before he and Mallory set out, though it's not known whether he took it up with him. But why wouldn't he? They were going to the top of the world." She paused. "If that's not enough, though, it's probable Mallory borrowed a Vest Pocket Kodak camera from another climber in the party, Howard Somervell, before they set out. One of Somervell's relatives talks about it, his great-nephew I think, on some PBS special, I've forgotten where. But he seemed certain that Somervell had the camera and was in the habit of passing it to other expedition members."

She paused. "Somervell was actually supposed to summit during that trip, you know. When Mallory and Irvine went up. In 1924. But he'd been on the mountain earlier and in fact was part of a rescue of four Sherpa stuck somewhere on the North Col. He got frostbite in his larynx and nearly died. So Mallory and Irvine went instead. Somervell felt he owed the mountain something. He'd been on the 1922 expedition when all those Sherpa were killed."

I nodded. "Mallory wrote about it," I said.

"Somervell took it to heart. He was a surgeon, you know, and an Evangelical Christian who took his religion seriously. Ended up a medical missionary in India."

It sounded like another of her red herrings. "But he had this camera…" I said encouragingly.

She took a deep breath and nodded. "No camera was found with Mallory's body, of course. Well, and here's the thing, some other important things weren't there, either—the photograph of Ruth he'd brought with him, that he'd promised to leave at the summit, and a letter to her that he was going to leave with it, he'd told people that was what he'd do; but the camera is all that matters, really, isn't it? If there was a camera, it would put the rest of it to bed once and for all. You wouldn't summit Everest with a camera and not take some pictures. Find the camera, find the proof."

"And your Chinese friend's found the camera?" I asked, lightly, teasingly, then caught her expression. "Wait. What? Are you serious?"

She looked at me steadily, her eyes reflecting the lights coming on around us in the street. "Back in the nineteen-seventies, some Chinese climbers saw what they described as an old English body, a white westerner wrapped in a sleeping bag slightly below the Second Step," she said. "I'm not going to go into the geography, that's part of the debate, but if the person they saw was Sandy Irvine—and we know now it wasn't George Mallory, his body was found later—then it might indicate that Mallory and Irvine did take the couloir rather than the step." She waved the words away impatiently as though they were gnats. "That doesn't matter right now. You can read about it. The point is that since then, no one's seen that other body, the one that wasn't Mallory, and in fact there were a number of rumors that the Chinese simply got rid of it."

"Got rid of it?" I was startled. "How?"

"Moved it, buried it, threw it into a crevasse or ravine, anything," she said impatiently. "I don't know where it was supposed to be. It could have ended up anywhere: the glacier's always moving, bits and pieces of climbers are always turning up. It doesn't matter. What matters is that Yuan Bo's found it." She paused. "And the camera was there."

I was excited in spite of myself. "But that's *fantastic*, Emma! It's unbelievable! Were they able to develop the film? I mean—why hasn't this been—"

"They can't develop it," she said. "They can't do anything with it. They were climbing in a prohibited zone; just *being* there's enough to get them sent to re-education camps for life. They're damned lucky they've gotten away with it so far. He's a respected figure, that helps—a climber who's also a scholar, a scholar who's also a novelist, and a novelist who puts out state-prescribed material on demand. It's only because of his toeing the party line that he's been permitted to have any exchanges with the West—and why I was able to meet him. He has a nice house, a good income, he's relatively safe. Well," she hesitated, "safe to an extent, anyway. Like everything else."

I think I knew it then, understood in a moment of crystal clarity what was going on, the whole picture shifting and vibrating and then settling in front of my eyes. "He's bringing you the camera," I said. It was a statement, not a question.

"He's bringing me the camera," she agreed.

"Holy shit," I said reverently. "But…"

Emma's voice was even. "He's going up the north side of Everest in a week. Jack's sending his people up the South Col at the same time. If it works out, once they're summiting, Yuan Bo is planning to defect. With the Somervell camera."

I stared at her. The sheer number of things that could go wrong with this plan was astronomical. The timing had to be perfect. The secrecy of the thing had to be preserved. There had to be a viable weather window on both sides of the mountain. The Chinese writer had to get away from his group. "What happens if it doesn't work?"

"Yuan Bo and the camera disappear forever," she said calmly.

"Holy shit," I said again.

"The Chinese usually send a Party apparatchik with climbing teams," she said. "There are Sherpa on the Tibet side; there's always a concern that one of the climbing sherpas will want to defect to Nepal. It doesn't happen much; it's been a long time since the border was fluid. Nepal was closed to westerners until 1951, and then, after it opened, China isolated Tibet. There's not as much chance now of families wanting to reunite after over a century of separation. But they don't leave a whole lot to chance. The Chinese are prepared, alert, and motivated." She shook her head. "I know how insane it sounds. It probably is exactly that insane. But if it works, Yuan Bo gets his freedom, and the world will know for sure whether Mallory and Irvine were the first westerners to summit Everest."

It seemed a dubious goal on which to risk one's life and future, but to each their obsessions. I knew too much about those already. Maybe that was the only thing that differentiated us from each other, at the end of the day: what we were willing to give our lives over to.

Or die for, if it came to that.

I said, "And you'll be able to write your novel and feature the camera and the truth. Maybe do a book tour with your Chinese friend." I hadn't meant for it to sound unkind—I was still just sifting through my thoughts—though I suppose it did.

"Yes," she said after a moment. "There is that."

"And you didn't think this might be a good thing for your research assistant to know about?" I frowned. "Emma, why am I here?"

"Ah." She drew in a very long, very deep breath and released it. "Well, okay, for one thing, it's a gift, really, Abbie. Yuan Bo won't write about it; if he gets through, he has weightier things on his plate to write. Matters of life and death, literally. And I'm putting all this, what we find out from the film, into my novel about Mallory. But someone's going to have to do the nonfiction part. Telling the world about it. That's where you come in. I've read your dissertation and some of your articles. You're very good. You make the past come alive."

"You need a reporter," I said, shaking my head. "A journalist. *National Geographic*. Something like that. I'm an academic. My stuff reads like a line of computer code."

She shook her head. "No. It doesn't. We need *you*. Don't give me that look, you really think I came to you by accident?"

"Phillip," I said, belatedly understanding. Maybe I really am slow. There had been no ad to be answered on Harvard's Intranet. I had been targeted from the beginning, with my brother's full collusion. "My brother Phillip."

"Yes. I know him, have known him for years. He thought you'd be up to this. You're a historian. You don't belong to an institution, so no one can oversee what you're doing. It isn't your research period, so you bring fresh eyes to the business. You don't have an axe to grind either way—you haven't been part of the endless arguments among climbers and analysts and everybody's Uncle Someone on the Internet. No matter how modest you want me to think you are, you're an excellent writer, and you know it. Face it, all you ever loved about academia was the research and the writing. So here's your chance to get what you've wanted all along. Phillip agrees with me. We think you should write this book."

"If everything goes to plan," I said.

"There's that," she admitted.

"And the odds against are astronomical," I said.

"That, too."

I sighed. The mountains were bewitching, I thought: they made you believe you could do anything. Like touching the past. Climbing summits. Solving mysteries. And I wasn't the one who stood to lose anything here. "All right," I said. "For what it's worth, I'm in." As soon as I said it, I felt a slight electric frisson travel down my spine. *Yes. This is what you're supposed to be doing.* I took a sharp breath. "What's next?"

That night for the first time I lay in my bed at the teahouse and really considered what it must have been like, that last day. June 8, 1924. One of the high camps. George Mallory and Geoffrey Bruce had already tried once to summit, without oxygen, but the weather got worse and the porters rebelled.

Mallory had to know this was his last chance at the mountain, and must have lain awake as I was doing now, seething with impatience. Not despair; he didn't seem one to give in to difficulties. Just impatience: the mountain was there, he was so close to touching it, he could probably come close to tasting it. He'd been defeated before, and he wasn't going to let the rest of the expedition's insistence on climbing *sans* oxygen deprive him of his chance.

That was why he'd chosen Sandy Irvine, of course; the kid was a whiz with the oxygen apparatus.

I turned over, trying not to make noise and wake Emma in the next bed. The amazing thing I'd learned was that even without modern clothing, sophisticated climbing gear—pitons, ascenders, quickdraw wires, harnesses, even crampons—Mallory and Irvine had actually made better time than have modern climbers. Three hours' difference, I'd read. So they were going up that mountain hell for leather, and it wasn't their fault the weather broke. The expedition had begun far too late in the season; monsoon winds were starting.

And then something bad happened.

I really felt I could see it. It's late in the evening on the eighth of June, long after twilight, and the two climbers are still high on the mountain. Exhausted, with failing oxygen supplies, they're desperate to reach safety. As they cross a notoriously treacherous layer of marble and phyllite known as the Yellow Band, one of the two climbers slips.

It may well have been Mallory. If so, his fall is halted by the rope, which dashes him into a rocky outcrop. His ribs are instantly broken and his elbow is dislocated. But he's still held there by the rope connecting him to Irvine, dangling above a void.

And then, perhaps not unexpectedly, the rope snaps and he plunges through the darkness. He lands on a steep shelf of snow, snapping his tibia and fibula. But still he doesn't stop. Gravity drags him down the North Face at tremendous speed.

He's terrified and in appalling pain, but still conscious and trying to save himself. In desperation, he clutches at frozen scree, digging his fingers into the ice. Faster and faster he slides until his forehead smashes into a jagged outcrop of rock. It punctures a hole in his skull. He comes to a standstill at the same time he loses consciousness.

Shock and hypothermia rapidly take over. Within minutes, George Mallory is dead. The beautiful Bloomsbury boy, the fearless soldier, the husband and father, the writer, the expert mountaineer, gone.

But did it happen going up or coming down?

In 1933 Sandy Irvine's ice axe was discovered on the ridge a short distance below the First Step. In 1999 George Mallory's body was discovered a few hundred meters directly below. There was a hole in his skull and a rope, which had snapped, around his waist. His sunglasses—as I'd already learned, absolutely necessary, critical even, to prevent snow-blindness—were in his pocket, suggesting the pair may have been descending in the dark, when Mallory no longer needed to wear them.

The ridge was wider at this point, and no trouble for fresh climbers during daylight hours. For exhausted climbers descending at night, a fall seems more likely. Perhaps it was Irvine, the inexperienced one. Perhaps he dropped his ice axe in the fall and the rope was cut on a rock as the pair plunged down the scree.

Mallory was a man obsessed with "conquering" Everest. He saw it as his destiny, and he knew that after two previous attempts the expedition in 1924 would be his last chance. The money, the support, the interest were all running out. Myles had told me about summit fever, how it takes hold of people even less obsessed than Mallory would have been. With the summit so close, there was no way: I couldn't believe that he of all people would have turned around above the Second Step, especially if he was still moving "with considerable alacrity," as the observer Noel Odell had noted. Once above the Third Step it seems unthinkable, except with the benefit of hindsight, knowing how far there is left to go.

The real issue around summit fever isn't getting there. The real issue around summit fever is ignoring the realization that, at the top, the climb is only halfway done. That going down is harder than going up. That oxygen and strength are both terribly depleted, and while you can cache oxygen bottles on the way up (as Mallory and Irvine are thought to have done), you can't cache strength, and you can't cache good weather.

Even George's own son (along with Sir Edmund Hillary, understandably) said that a summit isn't a summit unless one returns.

His father would have differed, I thought. To be at the top of the world, at the Third Pole, was everything. He kisses the photograph of Ruth and buries it in the snow along with a letter to her, as promised. He takes photographs, the first-ever Everest selfies. He and Sandy Irvine congratulate each other. But it's late, and even in the midst of their celebration, it's clear the light won't linger forever.

So they start down and continue into history.

And now, within a week or two at most, there was a real possibility I was going to see the camera that had taken those selfies.

Excerpt from the journal of George Mallory

Venice, Italy, 1914: Well, the thing is done. I am quite simply mad with love.

Turner asked me to join him and his daughters here in Venice, and as soon as I saw Ruth, I knew. I simply knew. She did feel it, as well! She did fall for me as hard as I'd fallen for her! I think that all along, somewhere deep in my body, I knew, with a certainty that I've only ever felt around mountains.

She is perfectly marvellous. The best way to describe her is Botticellian, with her wistful, innocent beauty, her blue eyes, her luxuriant brown hair... she is an angel, she has stepped out of a storybook to grace mortals with her presence.

We took the train—just Ruth and I—out to Asolo, a romantic town with a medieval castle in the hills northeast of Venice; Robert Browning once lived here. We walked the hills and sat for a time in a meadow thick with alpine flowers. I have never felt so much at ease in the company of another person.

I've never written poetry before; words are to be descriptive, not evocative... and yet I stayed up all night last Tuesday to write a sonnet for her.

I shall probably never give it to her, because events have overtaken me. I arrived back in Godalming only ten days ago, and then today—what a fortuitous day!—I asked her to marry me, and she said yes!

Really, I don't know what's overcome me. I'd thought for some time I might just marry Cottie—after all, we have so much in common, she's a smashing girl and quite a decent climber in her own right—but that was before I knew someone who could rip my world apart as Ruth Turner has done.

Chapter Eleven

The question still remained, of course: who was on to us? Now that I knew the truth behind our own little expedition, it threw the motives of whoever was following us into sharp relief.

And in fact, now that I knew the truth, it made what we were doing painfully obvious. Why would a novelist and her assistant trek to the base of the Khumbu Glacier and hang out with one of the most professional, most famous, most expensive of the Everest expeditions?

Someone else had known what we were doing even before I did.

Okay, search our belongings, even steal Emma's notes—check. That made sense if someone suspected what we were up to, or just wanted to snoop through our stuff in a more general way for clues. Oddly enough, it felt as though that would make more sense if we were on the Tibetan side of the mountain—but perhaps that was my own guilty conscience, now starting to worry about the response of Chinese authorities to this plan.

But the rockslide? What would killing *Emma* achieve for someone?

And who the hell *were* they?

We returned to the monastery at dawn to pray for safe passage, and set off early. None of us talked much. Rocky never spoke, thinking whatever thoughts he engaged in under the weight of our gear; even Dawa was strangely silent. It was turning into a spectacularly beautiful spring day, but I couldn't help but feel something of a cloud settling over us. Emma was allowing her worry to surface, now that she'd unloaded her secret to me; and now that I knew, I too was feeling vulnerable, exposed.

"If esteemed ladies get sick," Dawa had assured us, "it happen at Dingboche."

He was talking about altitude sickness, of course, and even though I don't have a tendency to hypochondria in the course of my normal life, I found myself checking compulsively for symptoms.

We had a rest day at Dingboche, and I spent most of it mooching around. Amazingly, my breathing seemed to have stabilized, and I even made a couple of short forays farther up on my own, following Anish's sage advice. As well as a trip to the Mani walls, thousands of stones engraved with the *om mani padme hum* mantra inscribed over and over and over again; I thought we could use all the prayers we could get. And not just for us—I kept being haunted by the knowledge that, somewhere on the other side of that mountain, a mountaineer and novelist was preparing himself for the climb of his life.

Or of his death.

Was it worth it? The controversy, the mystery, all that—it was a tempest in a teapot to most of the world. Sure, it's fought out in social media feeds and dueling blogs and online videos with a passion that only true aficionados of a narrow niche interest can achieve, but it's not going to cure cancer or alleviate world poverty; it probably won't even help in the rarefied (in more ways than one) air of Everest Base Camp.

Everyone who wants to climb the holy mountain will still do so. Sherpa will die; climbers will die; and the question of who was the first to summit will get lost in the waves of current summiteers. The mountain's body count will continue to rise and the corpses will remain on the mountain, their bright plumage a stark reminder to others on the way, ignored by most.

Camera or no camera, novelists would still write about Mallory—either like Emma with exquisite research or like Jeffrey Archer, apparently with amazingly little—and photographers would still try to capture the ultimate view of the top of the world and wealthy dilettantes would still see it as a personal affront that there was a horizon that still beckoned. At the end of the day, the only person to whom the discovery would make a profound difference was Emma's friend—if he lived to tell the tale.

And the more I thought about it, the more I doubted that would happen.

And now I had a part in it all, because I had to admit that the more I thought about the book that would come out of this trip, the more I wanted it for myself, too. The sense of having skin in the game.

I wanted to tell the story of Mallory and be able to put the ending in place, show that he'd done it, and also honor the man who'd risked everything to get Mallory's proof to the world. Was the family obsession taking hold of me? I hoped not. But there was an excitement now I hadn't felt before. That I had a goal, something to work toward, something meaningful that was mine, not by virtue of my money, but by virtue of myself. The beginnings, perhaps, of something new; I could almost sense myself going through a doorway, leaving something behind.

And yet... the scheme was so absurd. The number of things that could go wrong was as awesome as the peaks these climbers were attempting.

Which made it, perhaps, the most appropriate and logical of Everest stories.

***

In the event, we didn't get sick.

We both got grinding headaches, but they weren't incapacitating and even felt like they were easing when we got going on the hike.

Emma had seemed to be in great shape from the start, and even I had found—somewhat to my surprise—that I was feeling energetic and breathing well, so perhaps all those hours at the gym had paid off. Or maybe it was the mountains.

I could understand, now that I was here, the timelessness of this space, the reverence in which it was held. You looked up at the peaks around you and you could almost feel the Earth forming, feel the movement of oceans as they deposited their fossils and then retreated, the rock staying the same, perfect, for centuries on centuries on centuries, and while I was preoccupied with two men who had been here a mere hundred years ago, the presence of humanity in these mountains was but a speck on a timeline. Everest didn't care for or about people; Everest just was. It had stood here long before humanity crawled out of the sea and would stand here long after the race destroyed itself, and it just didn't care.

But the people did. The people who tended its flanks and removed the garbage from its slopes, the people who erected stupas and did puja, whose voices and gongs and incense were all raised to ask permission and forgiveness of the goddess; the people cared.

I wondered then, for the first time, if perhaps someone didn't care too much. Someone who had had enough of the pollution and the garbage and above all the egos, the egos that took their toll in death and grief and long lonely nights. Someone who didn't want a camera found, a mystery unraveled.

And then there was Ang Pemba Sherpa. What had happened to him at Lukla? Did it have anything to do with this dangerous *rendez-vous*, or was that a separate mystery, someone else's tragedy? Had he been meant to summit with Jack and guide the Chinese climber down the other side of the mountain?

The village of Lobuche was dwarfed by the slopes in which it nestled. This was the terminal moraine of the Khumbu Glacier, where the main glacier on which Base Camp sits ends. We reached there late in the afternoon of Day Eight, and Boston had never felt farther away, more insignificant. I found that in my heart I was feeling part of something bigger than just researching and writing about a historic figure; the camera aside, it would be worthwhile to help this Chinese man, a fellow scholar, start a new life, with the freedom of working uncensored.

Before we reached Lobuche, though, there was the Everest memorial to visit. "All peoples stop here," Dawa told us seriously. "To remember the peoples who die."

It's not one memorial, not really, but a fairly desolate area of wind and scoured earth and rock. You come up a rather steep hill

146

(okay, what was that I said before about breathing better? this was the sting in the tail of a long day) and then, suddenly it seems, you're there: cairns of stone, stupas adorned with prayer flags, big rocks with brass plates screwed into them. Names; names everywhere. All the hopeful. All the obsessed. All the lost.

All the dead.

We stood alone surrounded by stupas and small stone walls marking out the memorial area. It was remote, and solitary. It wipes the smile from your face as you realize where you are now. The explorers who came this way before you are remembered here. Those chasing dreams and paying with their lives. It seemed lonely, a place of recollection for the few who shared the same obsession.

I read the brass plate on one stupa: "May he have accomplished his dreams."

Emma was again absent from dinner at the very rustic Lobuche teahouse, and I crawled into bed—this time, inside my sleeping bag, as our teahouse had for some reason run out of bed linens—and I even slept through her arrival much later in the night.

This time, I didn't ask her where she'd been. It had something to do with planning a defection; the fewer people involved, I thought, the better.

For someone holding such a dramatic secret, Emma seemed calm and composed. I suppose I was, too, to the naked eye; but I felt jumpy and there was a weight gathering in the pit of my stomach that had nothing to do with digestion. I had no idea what the state of play at Base Camp would be when we arrived. I had no idea how to speak to Jack—or any of the other members of his team, or his guides, or his climbing sherpas. How many of them knew?

I came upon Dawa outside the teahouse, squinting up at the sky. "What is it?"

"Weather changing," he said without looking at me.

"It looks fine," I said. In fact, it was cold, but the sun was nearly hot: winter in the shade, summer outside of it. But I knew he wasn't talking about where we were. "Is the Supreme Summits expedition on the mountain now?" I asked.

He nodded. "They do rotation, get used to altitude," he said. "But also watching weather."

I knew this was no small thing. The weather on the mountain can change literally from one moment to the next, from brilliant sunshine to howling winds, the light loose spindrift morphing into white-out conditions in minutes.

Dawa turned to me. "It will change soon," he said. "We must leave now."

Once more with the backpacks, the water bottles, lacing up the hiking boots. After so many days of trekking, the movements came easily and automatically. I was feeling looser and better in my skin than I ever had, and even the prospect of this final six-mile climb wasn't daunting anymore. Besides, tonight we'd sleep at Base Camp.

What would happen after that? Anyone's guess.

It was a fine day, actually, and the trek didn't seem bad. We passed other hikers; still others passed us. A few were coming down from Base Camp and I was again struck by the friendliness of everyone, guides and trekkers alike. I'd read stories about climbers determined to summit, heard Myles talk about summit fever, and wondered if—being such a different breed—their mileage on the friendliness scale might vary. It would be interesting to see.

We stopped for lunch midway, sitting on rocks and eating dal bhat (what else?) from insulated containers. "Snow used to be here," commented Dawa.

It didn't look anything like a snowline to me. "What happened?"

Emma answered before Dawa could. "Global warming," she said. "The glacier's melting, there's rock in plenty of places that used to be snow and ice. Before you know it, they'll be trading ice axes for rock pitons to climb Everest."

We contemplated this gloomy pronouncement in silence and focused on walking the trail after that, and a couple of hours later

I got my first glimpse of Base Camp. Sitting right at the foot of the Khumbu Glacier, encircled by some of the most iconic peaks on Earth, its colors and patterns seeming brave and somehow not diminished against their whiteness and grandeur.

I'm not sure what I'd been expecting; perhaps when I'd heard the term "pop-up city" to describe it I'd expected temporary buildings of some sort; but what I was seeing, instead, was a sea of brightly colored tents of all shapes and sizes, anchored as it were to a large central stupa and with prayer flags flapping madly just about everywhere.

Dawa was as pleased as if he were showing us around his home—which I suppose was true to some extent, as treks came here not just during the climbing season but also in the fall. There were two helipads, he said, mostly used for evacuation of injured or sick climbers, though some people came on helicopter tours, with Base Camp as the pinnacle—no pun intended—of their trips. Tourism was the biggest business in Nepal, and not all aspiring climbers want to trek for a week to arrive at Base Camp. Those willing to pay the high fees can hire a helicopter to reduce travel times between villages.

Base Camp sounds like one place, but in fact it really is exactly like a city, with a myriad of individual neighborhoods.

The Himalayan Rescue Association's Everest emergency room—well, tent—is there to provide walk-in services for basic ailments, though the helicopters are again used for anything serious, including injuries, pulmonary edema, cerebral edema, and blood embolisms. National Geographic has a presence at Base Camp, located beside one of the helipads, and the Sagarmāthā Pollution Control Committee Camp—set up by local people, not the government—was nearby; they had the really fun job, managing solid waste removal from camp and along the trekking trails. They run the bathroom tents, constructed so that waste can be removed in trash bag-lined plastic barrels, to be hauled to lower elevations; and they collect trash and remove it.

Though from what I'd been reading, climbers were now responsible for removing their own poo. Fair enough.

"Sherpas are trying to take away all garbage," said Dawa. "Now, the peoples all know about it. Before, no peoples know about it. Only the mountain. We take better care of her now."

Each expedition, he pointed out, had its own *quartier*, so to speak, with sleeping tents, meeting tents, dining tents, cooking tents, and more. And then of course there was our home away from home, the Supreme Summits neighborhood, with a huge dome tent in the center of camp with clear panels for epic views of the surrounding peaks.

All of Base Camp is at or below 17,500 feet; no one wants to try living any higher than that. A well-provisioned base camp, Richard or Mark or someone had told me, provided mountaineers with a secure place from which they could dash up the mountain for three to five days at a time, and then return to recover in the relative comfort of somewhat thicker air.

For every single foreign climber, there were three to four local workers living at Base Camp as well—either climbing sherpas working on the mountain itself or Base Camp staff—the cooks, dishwashers, servers, and team managers who all look after the guided clients. This small army of service industry workers is overwhelmingly Nepali, though not all ethnic Sherpa, and they are the engine that keeps Base Camp humming.

I'd read somewhere in the distant past that an army fights on its stomach, and it's the same on Everest. Expeditions invest massive amounts of effort and resources to provide their clientele with the best food they can. Most commercial expeditions try to provide three square meals a day, which include a protein, carbohydrate, and some form of fruit or vegetables. Staples like rice, pasta, eggs, canned fruit and vegetables, and flatbreads form the bulk of the ingredients, but I'd already learned a creative chief finds ways to keep the diet interesting.

And no worries about going hungry, Dawa had told me. "In between mealtimes, there is much for esteemed ladies, there is tea, and dried fruit, and candy at Supreme Summits Expedition tent. Also Pringles!" he added with a flourish, as if revealing a *pièce de résistance*.

"Where do all these people stay?" I was a little dazed.

"Some live in villages," Dawa said. "Most local workers stay here, in tents also, and they eat over there—" he gestured toward a long tent that was draped in prayer flags.

"Do they eat Pringles, too?" I asked lightly.

"Dal bhat," he said.

Expedition campsites, I learned, were generally taken on a first-come, first-served basis. Some savvy organizers even send local representatives to stake a claim to prime real estate months in advance, Supreme Summits among them. With hundreds of people camped out in a few square miles, camp organizers face many of the same problems as urban planners in small cities.

While I was looking around, Rocky and Dawa were busy setting up our tents in a reserved area Jack had apparently set aside for the esteemed ladies. Dawa was staying with us, though it was unclear to me for how long; Rocky accepted our tips with multiple nods and beaming smiles and took off downhill to help someone else make the climb. I was pretty amazed at how such a physically slight person could carry so much weight, and I probably over-tipped him by a tremendous amount, and every penny of it was well spent.

Emma and I each had our own bright red tent next to each other in the Supreme Summits neighborhood. And I had to say that Jack really gave value for money, if this was any example of the professionalism—not to mention comforts—of his outfit. There was a tremendous dining tent—big enough to seat twenty-five people, high enough for even the tallest mountaineer to walk in upright. There was the central dome tent, nearly as large as the dining hall, with enormous clear plastic "windows" and squishy pouffes and beanbags on a carpeted floor for relaxation and mountain viewing by day or—for insomniacs dealing with the altitude's sleeplessness curse—by night.

Walk-in box tents with beds, unlimited electricity via gasoline generators, hot showers, strong reliable Wi-Fi through EverestLink, projectors for after-dinner movies, and even dedicated spaces for yoga and stretching.... There wasn't much roughing it, at least not in this portion of the climb.

Of course, Base Camp wasn't even considered a climb by most of the people here.

All in all, it truly was a small city, albeit one made of canvas and nylon rather than concrete and wood and glass. Climbers from various groups and their expedition sherpas—cooks, porters, guides—wandered around, putting in their time, waiting for their bodies to get used to the thin air, waiting for the perfect weather window for the ascent, visiting each other, swapping stories. Most of the climbers seemed to know each other, which made sense: many of these same people climbed not just Everest, but peaks all over the world. Their team spirit was touching.

It was an international city, too: prayer flags weren't the only ones flapping in the wind. Flags I didn't even recognize; flags with bright colors and in interesting shapes; a United Nations of a community perched on the tallest mountain that somehow brought them all together. It was, I have to admit, a little thrilling. Some flags flew on big communal tents; some were stitched onto individual nylon pup tents. Here, at least, it seemed the nations could coexist in peace.

I had, in a moment of silliness—that's really all one could call it—looked up the New Zealand flag at one of the better Internet-accessible teahouses in Namche, and found it combined the Union Jack with the Southern Cross and a big Commonwealth star; but finding one flag in this sea of flags and color and people was disheartening, and I decided that if I ran into Myles it would be fine, and equally fine if I didn't.

Well, almost equally fine. He really *was* attractive.

Dawa had done us proud: our ultra-warm sleeping bags and mattresses were installed in reasonably large (compared to many of those around us) tents with American flags stitched into the nylon. He'd filled them already with our rucksacks, packs holding the necessities that would last us for the projected two to three weeks we'd be spending at Base Camp.

At the end of the season, most guided climbers would beeline it for home as quickly as possible, but there would still be weeks of work left for the Base Camp staff to dismantle everything and see it transported down-valley for safe storage. Some operators, Dawa told me, rent storage space in nearby villages to avoid the long journey back to Kathmandu.

Many large expeditions have their own doctors embedded with the teams, some of whom are also climbers. Otherwise, if you had a serious medical issue, the absolute best thing would be to leave Base Camp and get down to a lower altitude. Everything about life, it seemed, does better at a lower altitude.

I unpacked what I could, hanging up my camping lanterns, arranging my clothes and toiletries and laptop where they made sense to me, drinking a lot of water. We weren't in the Death Zone but we sure as hell were at an altitude I'd never experienced. Suddenly winded, I sat down on my sleeping bag and stared out the front of the tent at the competing colors all blazing bright in the sun.

Now what?

Emma appeared beyond the tent flap. "Knock, knock," she said.

I crawled to the opening and stood up awkwardly. "Hey."

"Let's walk," she said.

We made our way through the camp, me watching the rocky uneven ground in case I twisted an ankle, Emma seemingly already adept. When I got back to Boston I was going to have to learn and follow this woman's regimen. She was the healthiest person I'd ever met, and her sure-footedness on the trails had already put my relative youth to shame.

It took a long time to reach the edge of the camp, where we could talk without feeling that someone was just behind a tent flap, listening. "Jack won't talk on the radio," she said, her voice annoyed.

"Well, that makes sense, doesn't it? Anyone can tune in to the frequency, right?" I had, of course, no idea what I was talking about. I know slightly less about radio frequencies than I do about Polynesian gastronomy or the atmosphere on Mars.

"The only thing the other expeditions care about is knowing when the team will make its summit bid," Emma said. "That's what they're all listening for. And everyone knows Jack has the most sophisticated weather equipment, so if they know we're from Supreme Summits Expeditions, chances are we'll have an eavesdropper or two. It's sacred up here, the weather report. It's always been a problem for Jack, keeping that information under wraps. He frets about it."

I wondered fleetingly—again—how deep Emma and Jack's personal history together went. Another mystery. But not for to-day. "Maybe," I said. "But it might not just be about the weather. If he started talking about someone defecting, you know they'd take some interest."

"Well, of course." She was staring into the distance, up the Khumbu Icefall. "I'm sure he has codes, or something. Jack's been communicating with Yuan Bo for a while, somehow. I didn't ask how. But Jack's resourceful, he's thought of something. I know I can trust him. He's as committed to this as I am."

I shivered. The air was crisp and the sun blindingly hot—I'd learned already on the trek to not take off the dark sunglasses I clipped on over my own glasses for any period of time, so I wouldn't burn my retinas, and here the danger was multiplied, surrounded as we were by snow—but there were clouds obscuring the summit and the icefall itself looked eerie and dangerous. "Does he know when he's going to the summit?"

"Jack doesn't usually summit," she said, almost absently. The mountain was holding us both in thrall; it was as though we couldn't tear our eyes away from it. "No one up in the Death Zone can make good decisions consistently; even some experienced guides died up there. Jack stays at Base Camp, stays on the radio with the guides and climbing sherpas, keeps an eye tracking their positions." She shivered, as though from a sudden wind or a disquieting thought. But there was no wind.

And then her mobile phone's ringtone sounded and she glanced at it. "It's him," she said, surprise in her voice.

"What does he want?"

She was staring at the text. "Here we go," she muttered.

"What?"

"They've found the letter. Ang Pemba Sherpa's letter."

Jeannette de Beauvoir

Excerpt from the journal of George Mallory

Godalming, Surrey, 1914: My father tells me that he is *"very pleased
you have decided to break out into matrimony,"* and my mother is of course
effusive, as is her wont.

I spent some time before the wedding introducing Ruth around—even if
simply via letters—to my many worlds. She knows about the mountain-climbing, of course, and we've been for a great many hikes together. She's no mountaineer, but I think she understands what I see in it all.

Ruth's father's come through in the most smashing way, not only setting
quite a decent allowance on her—he says she cannot be expected to live on a
schoolmaster's income—and also purchasing us a house in the same village.
So everything is set.

I wanted to take Ruth to the Alps for our honeymoon—not to do any
serious climbing, but some smaller peaks could be just up her street, I felt—
but then came the assassination on June 28th and since then Europe's been
well and truly at war.

We settled for Somerset instead.

When we returned to Godalming, it was to the news that my brother
Trafford has already enlisted in the army. I am heartbroken over the declara-
tion of war. I've always taught my pupils that as mankind progresses, problems can be solved through diplomacy, intellectual rigour, and shared morality.
I am gutted to understand I was teaching a lie.

Still, everyone says it will all be over by Christmas, so there's comfort in
that.

Ruth has shown herself to be as sweet and marvellous as I'd thought.
She's volunteered at the hospital, where they're treating casualties shipped back
from France.

More and more of my friends are joining up. Geoffrey Young—an old
man in his forties—went over as a war correspondent and to my astonishment
has ended up running an ambulance service in Dunkirk. Ruth is talking
about going over as well, which is absolutely out of the question; even I am not
to be permitted to do my bit, as schoolmasters are meant to stay at their posts.

Chapter Twelve

Ehani Sherpa had found it.

"He mailed it to her," said Jack.

He wasn't looking happy. He was sitting in the big Supreme Summits dome tent, eschewing the more comfortable pieces of squishy furniture for a camp chair, leaning forward as though ready to spring to his feet at any moment.

"That was clever," said Emma.

Maybe, I thought. But it implied he'd known he was in danger—and that the letter was part of the danger.

"I thought Ehani didn't speak English," I said.

"She doesn't," he said, giving me a fast, hard look. "She doesn't know what it says. She gave it to her cousin."

"Who's her cousin?" asked Emma.

"Lakpa Sherpa," said Jack. "He's one of our blokes."

Of course he was. I took a deep breath. "Okay," I said. *Let's get to the point.* "What's in the letter?"

He had it in his hand. "It says Pasang Dawa Sherpa is in trouble in Lukla," he read, though I suspected he knew it by heart. "It gives an address and urges Ang Pemba to come at once."

"Who's Pasang Dawa Sherpa?"

"Ang Pemba and Ehani's son," said Jack. "He went to school in Kathmandu. Lives there, works there, too. Some sort of import business."

I shook my head. "It doesn't make sense."

"What doesn't?" asked Emma. She was looking a little dazed, as though her thoughts were coming at her too fast.

"For heaven's sake, Ehani *saw* the letter, didn't she?" I demanded. "She might not read English, but you can't tell me she wouldn't recognize her son's name! She'd find someone to translate it for sure."

"Possibly," said Jack. He didn't look like he was conceding anything.

"And do we know where this Pasang—Pasang what?"

"Dawa."

"Okay, this Pasang Dawa, do we know where he is now? If he really was at Lukla? If he really was in trouble?"

"You're thinking he was lured there," Emma said to me. She already thought so, too; I could read it in her eyes.

"Ang Pemba was, yeah," I said. "He'd go anywhere for his son if he were in trouble. Anyone would. Doesn't tell us why, though."

She nodded. "If we find the who, we'll find the why."

Jack scowled at her. "You Miss Marple now, or something? This isn't fun and games, Em. This is someone's life."

"I'm very aware of that." Her voice was cool. "But you know as well as I do that we can't afford anything to go wrong—"

"Yer not kidding. But we can't talk about—"

"Abbie knows," she interrupted him calmly. "You can say whatever you want in front of her. And you can't tell me that this isn't a bad sign for us."

A *bad sign*? That was all? Talk about it being someone's life… or death. I cleared my throat. "What does the son—Pasang Dawa—have to say about it? I take it he didn't write the letter." As soon as the words were out of my mouth I wished I could recall them. *Well, no, Abbie, the letter being in English and all.* Emma was looking at me in astonishment, as well she might. It had to be the altitude; I wasn't generally quite that dense.

Then again, the kid lived in Kathmandu, he worked in some kind of import business, he might be fluent in English. Or any number of other languages as well.

"Pasang Dawa doesn't have a lot to say that makes any sense," said Jack, shaking his head. "I sent Anish to have a conversation with him, but it's fair to say he wasn't ever at Lukla and he never wrote any letter or asked anyone to write one on his behalf. It's not like he was going to come running or anything. He hasn't talked to his parents in—oh, God, who knows how long?" He seemed to consider the question for a moment, then let it go.

"Years, anyway. And in a culture that's based around family, that takes a hell of a lot."

"Why doesn't he talk to them?"

Jack shrugged. "He's a junkie," he said. "Functional drug user, I think the term for it is; he more or less keeps a job, he usually has a place to live. But he's already OD'd twice. Heroin, fentanyl, whatever."

"You know a lot about him."

"I know all my blokes." It was a simple statement of fact, but behind it I could sense something bigger, the warmth, the years of working together, the plans and the dangers and the celebrations. The family. "It was a good ploy, actually—Ang Pemba would for sure believe Pasang was in distress, he misses him like hell, they all do, and he'd probably even buy that the letter was written in English. He could believe it wasn't a Nepali who was trying to get word to him—in Kathmandu, shooting galleries take on an international flavor. Could have been an American junkie who wrote the letter about Pasang, who knows." He shook his head. "Good move, as far as it went."

"But he didn't go to Kathmandu," I objected. "He went to Lukla."

Jack was looking at me as though wondering who'd let the new girl in. "It don't exactly grow in Kathmandu," he said. "It comes in—" He broke off as Mark appeared in the tent doorway. "Yeah, what?"

Mark didn't even glance our way. "One of the Russians," he said. "Yevgeny Something. He's dead."

Jack was halfway out of his chair. "They have people up in Camp One already?" he demanded. "Shit. There wasn't anything on the radio about—"

"He wasn't climbing," Mark said briefly. "Dead here at Base Camp. Yvette says it looks like he was poisoned. In his tent."

An electric current seemed to run through me; I wondered if any of the others felt it. "Who's Yvette?" I asked.

"Base Camp doc," Jack said. He hadn't taken his eyes off Mark. "When?"

"Had to be after nine, they had a team meeting this morning."

"Accidental poisoning?" asked Emma.

Mark flashed her a look. "Yvette says not."

Jack was standing, now, cracking his knuckles. "Okay. Thanks."

Mark hesitated. "We should tell Richard," he said. "They were friends. I haven't seen him all day."

"He's been on the icefall," said Jack absently, then looked up at Mark. "Richard's friends with a Russian climber?"

"Richard's got a lot of friends," said Mark, and shrugged. "Equal opportunity. He don't care, long as they can all talk about mountains. He knows all the lads on the Russian team."

Jack nodded. "Go find him," he said, and waited until Mark had cleared the tent. "What the hell is going on," he said. It wasn't a question.

Emma hissed, "See what I mean? We have to cancel."

Jack turned to her again. "Yer out of yer mind," he said. "There's no canceling now, sunshine."

"But people are dying—"

"And yer friend is already acclimatizing on the other side of the mountain," he said, and grabbed her shoulders. "Babe, listen to me. Listen. He's gonna make a break for it whether we're there to help him or not. Safest thing now is to keep our heads down and just get the job done."

"But—"

"Don't you have some research to do?" he demanded. "The two of yous—go talk to somebody about Mallory, for Chrissakes."

"And the Russian? What about him?" Emma's voice was steady, but I could hear the undercurrent of strain, almost of... panic. I'd thought panicking was my department, but it seemed there was enough to go around.

"Not yer problem, babe." He picked up his puffer jacket from the back of the camp chair. "I'll go find out what's going on. You two, stick to history for now, yeah?"

But whose history, I wondered as I followed Emma, a little blindly, back toward our own tents. We seemed to be getting way too many of them entangled.

***

It was a pristine day, if you liked a magnificent view and didn't care much about breathing.

I'd be okay in the night; the expedition thought of everything. Dawa had left me with oxygen canisters when he departed Base Camp, the same ones the climbers were taking up the mountain, showed me how to work the valves, and counseled me to use them at night. "Keep you safe," he said. "No dying in your sleep!"

I'd laughed when he'd said that, but it wasn't feeling too funny right now.

A perfect day, one would have thought. The sun was hot, though I knew better than to take off my padded jacket; I was, after all, on Everest, and one thing that had been drummed into me was how the weather could change on a dime—and how seductive the sun's heat was up here.

"I'm going for a walk," I told Emma, and didn't wait for a response. I wasn't in the mood to talk about Chinese novelists or Mallory's camera or summit fever. I hadn't ever before spent a lot of time hearing about the violent deaths of people once-removed from myself, and there was a feeling of dread rising that wasn't exactly helping with the breathing. A walk would settle it all, I decided, as long as I didn't stumble into the Russian enclave—or seek out the Base Camp clinic.

The unfortunate murdered Yevgeny could rest in peace as far as my prying eyes were concerned.

It was, truth be told, a prolonged stumble rather than a stroll; Base Camp is pitched on extremely uneven terrain, with small boulders and pockets of snow and loose gravel everywhere. I'd managed to trek all the way from Lukla without breaking a leg, and I was damned if I was going to do it here.

Besides, I wasn't about to find myself in the clinic tent next to a sheeted body. I was wondering what would happen to him now when a voice quite close by—I'd been pretty much ignoring the people who seemed, like me, to be wandering sort of aimlessly among the tents—said, "Well, the romance novelist's assistant, ay. And you still owe me an autograph."

I'd found Myles without even looking for him.

"For your sister," I said, squinting to see him in the sharp sunlight. He was sprawled on a beach chair outside a tent, looking for all the world like a surfer, even down to the shark's-tooth necklace he was wearing. A t-shirt and loose padded pants. Tanned skin and bleached hair. "Brittany, right?"

"Good memory." He held up a bottle. "Beer?" He made it sound like *bee-ah*.

"Bit early for me, thanks." And hadn't he been the one to caution me about alcohol at altitude?

He looked me up and down. "You'll want to put your sunnies on," he observed. "Blind yourself otherwise soon's there's more snow."

"Sunnies?"

He tapped his goggles, which were hanging around his neck. "Protect your eyes. Burn your retinas. Didn't anyone tell you?"

They had, but it hadn't seemed that bright. "Are we expecting more snow?" I asked.

He nodded. "Sure to be, ay. Tonight, maybe."

I looked around and thankfully found a reasonable-looking rock close enough for conversation and sank down onto it. "Have you been up there yet?"

"To the summit?" He looked incredulous. Obviously another of Abbie's Famous Faux-Pas. "Nah. Just came back from Camp Three, though. We'll be going up in a couple of days, when the weather clears."

"You want it clearer than *this*?"

He grinned. "What you see here ain't what you get there. And like I said, snow's coming tonight or tomorrow, even down here." He took a swig of beer. "Here's what you should remember.

You're interested in history, in those blokes in the twenties. There was that photographer fellow—forgot his name—who lost sight of Mallory and Irvine in a storm. Your Mrs. Caulfield probably knows all about that.

I do, too, I thought, but managed not to say it. No need to sound prissy.

Myles was still talking. "Everything was just peachy where the photographer was standing, but he saw the snow squalls through his long-range lens, saw the men disappearing into them. The higher up you get, the more uncertain the weather."

"What are you now—a Mallory expert?" I asked suspiciously.

"One of the gods of climbing," he said easily. "Disregard him at your peril."

"Disregard him? I've been trying to live inside his head for weeks." I stretched my legs out, wiggling to find some comfort on my perch. "Anyway, this whole enterprise seems positively *fraught* with peril," I said. "I don't know how you do it."

"Death wish," he said solemnly.

"Not just you," I said. "Did you know him—Yevgeny?"

"Who's Yevgeny?"

All that did was confirm my feeling that Supreme Summits really did have its finger on the pulse of the mountain. "One of the Russian climbers," I said. "He died this morning. Um—well, I guess he was *killed* this morning. Um—I heard he was poisoned."

"Poisoned?" He stared at me.

I swallowed and nodded. "Mark heard about it. Um, Mark Robinson? From Supreme Summits?" Trust me to take a light conversation and introduce murder into it. "Sorry, I thought you might know. Mark said Richard's friends with the Russians. I guess the ER doctor—Yvette, that's her name, right?—says it's suspicious, anyway."

He shook his head. "Poisoned," he said again, slowly, then glanced up at me.

Another irrelevant idea flitted across my mind. "Who investigates crime on Everest?"

"If it really is a crime, they'll probably fly someone up from Kathmandu, at a guess," Myles said. "But a Russian—Moscow'll send someone, too." He looked like his mind was elsewhere. "A lot of Russians on the mountain this year," he observed, à propos of nothing that I could see. "And most of them ain't exactly socializing with anybody else."

"What are you getting at? Language barrier?"

Myles laughed. "Are you kidding? Their English is probably better than mine. No, they pretty much keep to themselves."

"Richard knew him," I said. "Mark says he knows all the Russians."

"Ah, Richard. He's cracked the code."

"What code?"

"Russians can drink anybody under the table, any day of the week," Myles said. "Richard's pretty good at it, too."

But I was remembering back in Kathmandu, when Mark had been the one pounding back beers and Richard had been counseling him to slow down. Something there wasn't tracking.

"Anyway," Myles said, "I wouldn't know this Yevgeny bloke if I ran into him."

"Small chance of that, now," I said sourly.

His interest seemed to sharpen. "What is it? What are you thinking?"

"That there've been two people killed within a couple of weeks of each other without even climbing the mountain," I said. "Ang Pemba Sherpa in Lukla; this Yevgeny guy at Base Camp. Doesn't that make you suspicious? That can't be normal. They have to be connected." Or not. Coincidences did happen. I took a deep breath. I couldn't tell him about the camera, or the Chinese climber who was defecting; that wasn't mine to tell. I shivered in the sunlight. "But I can't imagine why."

"You want to know why, do you? Turn and face east," he said immediately. "A lot of Nepal's troubles come out of China, ay. And we're right on the edge."

I stared at him. I'd been so busy thinking about defections that I'd forgotten the other border issue—the one that was purely transactional. Capitalism rampant centuries before Marx called it out. "On the Silk Road," I said, something slowly coming back to me. It felt like it had been weeks, not days, since Jack had reminded me about it. And before that, Anish. "But that's ancient history."

"You're kidding, right? Silk Road's alive and well and functioning."

I shook my head. "No way. China doesn't need mountain passes to export anything. They're doing just fine with container ships and—" I stopped, seeing his expression. "What?" And then, as he didn't say anything, I added more sharply, "What aren't I seeing?"

"Drugs," said Myles. "Fentanyl. It's a major export. There are labs in Beijing and—oh, who knows where else? Connecting to Lhasa through Highway 108. The old Silk Road, still at it, still selling dreams to the West, just as it ever did, ay."

"How do you know?"

"How don't I know? How do you think some of these guys can afford their expeditions? How do you think the smaller outfits get through bad seasons?" He gave an exasperated snort. "Don't look at me like that, Abbie, right? It's a rich man's game, climbing."

"But—"

"And don't look around you like that. Nobody's gonna admit to it; the only drugs anyone cares about for themselves up here are Dex and Diamox. And it ain't even everybody here, so get that deer-in-the-headlights look off your face. No one who climbs mountains does any of that stuff. Steroids, maybe, but that's all. None of the climbers are what you might call customers. But Base Camp's a great cover, and not all the porters and guides are Sherpas."

"That would make a difference?"

He nodded. "Sherpas? They're not saints by a long shot, but they're all family. Some of 'em have kids in the city. They're not helping move drugs."

Something clicked. Loudly. "It was Ang Pemba Sherpa's son," I said slowly. "That's how they got him to Lukla." Whoever the shadowy amorphous *they* were. "There was a letter, it was sent to Ang Pemba. Jack has it now. The letter said he was in danger. The son, I mean." Couldn't remember his name. "It said he was in Lukla, but he lives in Kathmandu. Jack calls him a functional user."

"Lot of that around in the city," Myles said, nodding. "Like any city, really. But not on the mountain. They might move drugs through here, but no one's doing them. You got to be heaps crystal-clear here. It's too easy to die at the best of times, you know? With everything on your side? No one needs help doing that. And up there in the Death Zone, it's like you're on drugs anyway, your brain slows down so much." He sighed. "But that don't mean it's not a major industry. Contributes to what they call the South Asian Cocktail."

Fentanyl. Damn. Call me naïve, but that had never occurred to me. I was looking for a clever Agatha Christie-esque drawing-room murder plot ("Murder in the Himalayas," anyone?), and now it seemed it might have been just another drug deal gone bad. Death is death and all that, but it was still—well, disappointing. "What's Dex?" I asked instead, picking my way back through the conversation. "And the other thing you mentioned?"

"Dexamethasone," he said. "And Diamox. They're not illegal; I've got some in my pack, ay. Dex is a steroid that helps with high-altitude edema so your brain don't swell up and start leaking down your spinal cord. Diamox helps you acclimatize faster and better to high altitudes. If you take 'em together, you're significantly lowering your chance of getting sick, or at least if you do get sick, your symptoms will be milder."

"That sounds like a good thing," I said. "Why doesn't everyone take them?"

"Depends on your philosophy. Thing is, it's like O's—a lot of people think you aren't a real climber if you use assists like that."

I nodded. I wasn't entirely sure I understood everything he was talking about, but I also didn't see how any of it could be particularly useful for me. Except that… "That was an issue with Mallory and Irvine," I said suddenly. "George took Sandy along primarily because he was a wizard with oxygen. He'd tried summiting before without it and it didn't work."

"I think anyone who does it without oxygen is mad," said Myles calmly. He finished off his beer in one long swallow. "There's so much that can go wrong up there even if you've got your wits about you, and no one can tell me anyone who can't breathe has their wits about them, ay."

"Do you use the drugs, too? You said you had some."

He grimaced. "Only in emergencies," he said. "If you're trapped somewhere on the mountain, Dex may be the only way you won't develop edema. Maybe the only way you're gonna live. It's an emergency drug, you use it when there's no other way. At least, that's how we use it on my team. Everyone's mileage may vary."

Edema sounded like only one on a list of terrible things that could happen on the mountain, but I didn't pursue it. If there was anything that would make you not want to climb, it was considering that list. Though, now that I stopped to think about it, the risk at Base Camp itself was starting to gather momentum. There had been the earthquake that sent an avalanche through the camp in 2015… and now, murder. "Tell me about your team," I said instead, trying for normalcy. "Where are you from?"

"All Kiwis," he said, comfortably. "The guides, that is. And most of the members, too."

"Jack's Australian," I said. "You Southern Hemisphere guys must really like to climb."

There was amusement in Myles's eyes, as though he were reading my thoughts. "You should come visit sometime," he said, slowly, and again there was that flash of something between us, some potential future that it was too soon to explore.

"Only if I don't have to climb," I said.

"You really are developing some negativity here," he complained. "Seems a little unbecoming for someone sitting at the Base Camp of the highest mountain the world."

"Saves me developing negativity about all the other peaks," I said, smiling. "Go for the top, get it out of the way."

"Not a woman who does things by half."

"A woman," I said, "who says yes a little too quickly."

"Truth? I'll bear that in mind." Yep: the flirtation was back. Good.

"The other drug?" I asked, dragging myself back into mystery-solving mode. "You said there was another—"

Myles nodded. "Diamox. It can prevent a whole bunch of high-altitude sickness symptoms. Some climbers use it instead of taking the time to acclimatize. Speaking of your deceased friend, there—Yevgeny, right?—the Russians use it all the time." His tone left no doubt about what he thought of the practice. And of said climbers.

"But they're not illegal, these drugs, right? That's what you said?" This was feeling more and more like a dead end. It didn't sound like Yevgeny had been killed because he was facilitating a brisk trade in altitude-sickness drugs.

Myles shook his head. "Easily prescribed, easily obtained," he said. "What are you getting at, Abbie?"

Definite jolt of electricity this time when he used my name. I ignored it. "I don't even know," I said, frustrated. There had to be a throughline here somewhere, I just wasn't seeing it. "I'm not seeing the connection."

"A connection about what? Two men dying?"

"Two men getting murdered," I said firmly. "Come on, you have to see that's statistically improbable."

"But not impossible," he countered. "Anyway, the police will investigate. I thought you were here to experience the ambience of Base Camp for your book."

"It's Emma's book," I said, even more firmly. I couldn't talk about the other book yet: the one that really was my book. My contribution. My future.

He shrugged; the surfer-dude persona back in place. "Whatever. Anyway..." His voice trailed off.

"Anyway," I echoed, looking at him. We sounded like middle-schoolers.

"Anyway, we're leaving in a day or so," he said. "Magic weather window opening."

I almost said, "be careful," and then realized how that might sound to someone who'd just spent the last twenty minutes talking about being careful. "Well, good," I said instead.

He grinned and raised his empty bottle. "I'd drink to it, but I'm cutting myself off."

"I have to go," I said. I didn't, not really; I didn't know what Emma was doing, and my notes on Mallory were up to date. I could re-read parts of his book, I supposed; actually being on the mountain now might give me a different perspective on his words. But the more I looked around me, at the flashy modern set-up at Base Camp, at the high-tech gear and colorful down-filled jackets, I felt I was the first to marvel that those guys in the nineteen-twenties could do *anything* up here, much less try to summit.

I'd looked at their clothing in detail. To be fair, I'd be cold wearing their gear on the Boston Common on a windy late-fall day, never mind scaling Everest. "What do I say?" I added. "Is climbing like the theater, where they say break a leg because it's bad luck to say good luck?"

Myles looked startled. "Let's not wish for broken bones, ay," he said.

"Good luck, then, if I don't see you," I said. I pushed myself off the rock and stretched.

"I'll come find you before we leave," he said, his voice amused.

"Good," I said again.

But as I picked my way back through the camp it occurred to me that Myles had done a very neat job of deflecting the conversation away from Ang Pemba Sherpa and onto the drug importation business. Maybe it was an accident.

Maybe it wasn't.

***

Over at Supreme Summits Expeditions, things seemed to be moving into high gear. Richard and several of the sherpa guides were in a meeting inside the dining tent with expedition members, going over the changing out of the all-important oxygen canisters. Something worth my attention, as Sandy Irvine was only selected to go up that mountain with George Mallory because of his mad skills with the O2 canisters—which, back then, weighed in at a very hefty thirty pounds apiece.

Not the same at all. But still, knowing anything about the process was better than knowing nothing.

I sidled into the tent and stood next to Mark, who was watching, his arms folded, looking critically at the different people as they individually demonstrated their prowess at the task. I recognized a couple of them—Sylvia and Paolo—from Kathmandu. The odious Jurgen was nowhere to be seen; I remembered that he didn't want to use oxygen. I wondered if he'd won that particular argument with Jack; somehow, I couldn't see it. Jack struck me as being quite willing to kick anyone off the team who wasn't going to play by his rules.

"They seem to know what they're doing," I said to Mark. At least no one was dropping the canisters, which was what I'd probably be doing in their place.

Like I would ever in a million years be in their place.

Mark snorted. "It's easy to do here, with no pressure on," he said. "This ain't the real test. You have to be able to do it in the dark, and the cold, and high winds. With gloves on. We'll see." But he added, "I'm not worried. We don't do beginners here."

"They've all been up before?"

"Not Everest," he said. "Well, no, I lie: two of this lot have made attempts before. But they're all experienced, they've all used oxygen before, they've done serious climbing on other peaks. They'll probably do all right."

"Are you leaving soon?"

That earned me a quick glance, and I remembered Emma telling me how jealously these outfits guarded their weather information, their climbing strategies, tried to get first in line for the magic window. "Why d'you ask?"

I shrugged. "Just wondered. I was talking to one of the New Zealand climbers, and he says his expedition's going up soon."

"Summiting?"

"I think so."

He shrugged, his eyes back on the oxygen demos. "Lots of 'em haven't done all their acclimatization climbs yet," he said. "It's early days yet, for some of 'em. Not us. We've already taken the members up to Camp Three and back."

"I think they're summiting," I said. I didn't know if I was supposed to say for sure or not.

He nodded, noncommittal. "That's fine," he said. "I'm not worried. Jack's got the best Met software, and he's got a feel for the mountain. Like a sixth sense. And it don't matter if someone else goes up ahead of us, as long as we do it without hitting a bottleneck. Even if that happens, we'll still have the optimum opportunity for success, based not just on what's happening but on what's going to happen. That's what Jack says, anyway, in pretty much those words. I've always trusted him; he hasn't been wrong yet. We'll know first."

I looked around, thus reminded. "Where is he?"

"He doesn't do this part," he said, and paused. "But..."

"But what?"

He glanced at me quickly, then looked away again. "Jack's going up," he said.

I had rather thought that was the point. "Isn't he supposed to? Lead the expedition, all that?"

"That's *our* job," he said. "Me and Richard, and the other Supreme Summits guides. Us and the climbing sherpas. We're the guides, we take the members up, keep them out of trouble, get them out of trouble if they get into it... it's our job. Jack stays down here, at Base Camp. He keeps an eye on the weather, stays in touch on the radio, does real-time tracking so he knows where everybody is. He's the hard-working spider at the center of our web, don't you know. But not this time."

"Why?"

Another shrug. "Boss-Man knows best," he said. "Richard's going up with him. I'm gonna replace him, stay down here in the comms tent, keep an eye on the weather, stay in touch with the expedition. Jack's never wanted anyone to do that part, so I've never done it before, but never say never."

"Maybe he just wants to keep his hand in," I suggested, my voice as casual as I could make it. Of course it made sense that Jack was summiting—he wouldn't trust a high-altitude defection to anyone else. I'd nearly forgotten the Chinese novelist-climber. The one with The Camera. I didn't know what Mark knew, or didn't know, and I couldn't guess if there were anything behind his words.

He didn't even spare me a glance. "Jack spends more time climbing than he does sleeping," he said. "But ours is not to reason why…"

He fell silent after that, and I crept away, belatedly remembering the line that followed that one.

Ours but to do and die.

Excerpt from the journal of George Mallory

Godalming, Surrey, 1915: Rupert Brooke has died of blood poisoning; what a nightmare this war is turning into. Trafford is a second lieutenant with an infantry division, and for a time was writing almost daily of the horrors—especially of the gas attacks they're suffering. "You have an alternative of putting your head down in the trench and being asphyxiated or putting it up over the trench into rapid fire," he wrote recently.

His division attacked the German trenches, and he got a leg wound, and I believe he's in hospital in Oxford now.

The real news is, of course, the birth of our first child, Frances Clare. I am unsure what kind of parent I shall be, and I cannot claim any great interest in this baby at present, but Ruth is delighted and that is, after all, what matters in such things. We've hired a nursemaid and she's taken her place alongside our cook, housemaid, and gardener, all of which eases my mind considerably about my climbing trips... Ruth need never be alone, even when I'm off in the mountains.

Some of my pupils have made their way to France to join the fighting, and as I'd been feeling despondent over the regulations that kept me in my teaching position rather than allowing me to follow them, I am happy to report that I finally wore the headmaster down—it helped that I was able to find a replacement for my classes—and I've been recommended for artillery on the basis of being skilled at math and trigonometry.

I was as keen as possible to become a soldier and now I am one I feel really happy.

Chapter Thirteen

The night was unremarkable, which, given the circumstances, might have been in itself remarkable.

The wind picked up sometime after midnight, and that was it for me for sleep until sometime in the early morning I remembered my melatonin and groped around and found the bottle and some water with which to swallow the tablets.

How did anyone sleep through this? It wasn't just the howling, though that was bad enough—the first time in my life the word *banshee* came to mind—but even worse was the tent flapping vigorously. No, not vigorously: wildly. It sounded as if it were ripping apart (it wasn't) or that it might at any moment take off altogether (it didn't).

Not the kind of thoughts you want to have deep in a mountain range in the middle of the night.

And I was in a high-tech tent; I couldn't even imagine what George Mallory had felt, on this same mountain, on a night as dark and windy as this. More so, actually. His descriptions in his letters home to Ruth painted a grim picture. "My dearest girl... I arrived first at Camp Three... my boots were frozen hard on my feet. I was a great deal depressed about the situation." Wind, he wrote, was a "determined and bitter enemy."

And in my worry, it seemed, we were as one: "Fierce squalls ... visited our tents and shook and worried them with the disagreeable threat of tearing them away from their moorings."

Of course, Mallory wasn't at Base Camp when he wrote that; he was up on the mountain, on the edge of the Death Zone. I was a lot safer than he'd been. His language was remarkable for the distance at which it held emotions, but sometimes even George couldn't help himself, and I could feel it somehow, the fear behind the insouciance, the terror of that wind that screamed violence and destruction. The canvas that ripped so easily; the lulls when he could almost think it was over, there was a reprieve, and then suddenly starting up again…

I think I felt closer to George Mallory on that night than I ever had before.

I'd eaten supper with the team, Emma sitting next to me and shifting around every few seconds on her seat. Squirming. "Are you okay?" I asked at one point.

And she snapped at me, "I'm fine, I'm fine." The words were innocuous; the tone told me to mind my own business and maybe take a flying leap while I was at it.

There was tension building from all sorts of directions, and it felt almost like another presence in the meal tent, hovering over us, insinuating itself around the people. I couldn't even imagine how many layers of tension I was feeling, never mind those I wasn't privy to, and I didn't think I even began to know the reasons for them all.

Supreme Summits had eight expedition members, seven men and Sylvia.

They were going up in two groups of four, with Jack leading Team A and Richard Team B. Besides Jack and Richard, every climber had an individual climbing sherpa guide as well. They, along with other Sherpa—the kitchen guys, the icefall doctors, the porters—were all loading up on carbs and protein, readying themselves for the climb. More dal bhat, of course, though they had more than twenty-four hours ahead of them. I wondered what they would eat at the higher camps, when they all had only a canister stove on which to cook and melt snow.

That had been one of Mallory's issues, I remembered, on the day he and Irvine went up, never to return: his stove had broken, he hadn't been able to melt snow for drinking water. Some people thought that meant he was being irresponsible.

But I was starting to understand that delay could prove as irresponsible as forging ahead.

Jack was presiding, looking moody and distant. After dinner, Emma told me it was the coordination that was making him crazy—making sure they summited at the same time as the

Chinese team. "And then what?" I demanded. "Just whisk him down the mountain?" I'd had time enough to think about it, and the whole enterprise looked fragile as hell.

"I don't know," said Emma. We were sitting inside her tent; she hadn't sought me out for conversation, but I'd announced myself anyway. I'd watched her at dinner, and something was off. And so I pretty much trapped her in her tent: short of a shoving match, she wasn't getting rid of me.

It was cold, colder than Acorn Street in February, colder than I could remember feeling. Once the sun went down, you didn't want to be outside. I had my gloves on, even in the tent.

And I felt like the only way I wasn't going to go mad was to have a better handle on what was going on. A lot of scary thoughts seemed to be visiting me in the night. "You know, the Chinese aren't going to just pat him on the back and wish him *bon voyage*," I said.

She looked at me sharply. "You think we haven't thought of all this already?" she demanded. "Of course they're not." She took a deep breath, looked away. "It's been confirmed, there's a Party official in the expedition."

"Why on earth? And how do you know?"

"Jack's been on the radio. The Tibet group's all Chinese, so they have to have the minder. If it was westerners, they're only too happy to take their money and make sure they have a good climb. Once they've paid their fees and they're with a recognized outfit, they don't care. And doing the traverse—that's what they call going up on one side and coming down on the other—is illegal; anyone who does it is banned from climbing, at least in Nepal. But this time, it's all Chinese. So they're sending someone along."

I stared at her. "To make sure no one defects," I said. It really was a thing.

She nodded. "To make sure no one defects."

It seemed an outrageous plan, but then I thought that climbing Everest at all—defection or no defection—was an outrageous plan. "Then what is your friend thinking? What are *you* thinking? This is insane! Emma, this official guy, he could be armed!"

"You think we haven't thought of this already?" This time, when she said it, it was a snarl. "Abbie, my guy has the *camera*."

"What are you saying? That someone else has to die on this mountain for that damned camera?"

"I'm saying that this was his idea, not mine. I'm saying that he's willing to take the risk—that he *wants* to take the risk. I'm saying he was going to try with or without our help. I'm saying he'd planned it even without the camera, even before he offered to bring it over. Do you have any idea how many people would *happily* risk their lives for a chance at leaving the People's Republic, no questions asked? Do you have any idea how much defections cost them? His family—if he has one, I don't think his mother's still alive, but anyone he's related to—they'll be interned for sure. It's a risk he wants to take, and he has support at home. In the States, I mean. He's bringing over a lot of forbidden writings with him, stuff he plans to get published in the West. Stuff other Chinese intellectuals have written; he's smuggling it all out. It's a major coup, and—well, there's a price. There's always a price."

"And the camera is incidental." I didn't believe that for a moment.

"The camera makes it worthwhile for Supreme Summits Expeditions to help," she said, and her voice was suddenly calm, measured. Even the fingers had stopped drumming. "The camera makes it feasible for me to help him."

"Jack is that invested in your book getting written?"

"Jack is that invested in being the guy who helped solve the Mallory mystery," she said calmly. "Didn't you get that? You're the one writing *that* book, Abbie. You might be thinking of what the publicity around it will do for you, but do you have any idea what the publicity will do for Supreme Summits? For him to find the definitive word? He'll annihilate those other arguments on the Internet. You know what that's worth to him?"

"I thought Supreme Summits was already one of the major players," I objected, and even to my own ears my voice sounded defensive. "What more does he want? An empire?"

"Oh, he has plans," she said. "Creative plans. Imagine simultaneously sending expeditions on all the best peaks. Everest, K2, Kangchenjunga, Lhotse, I can't even remember them all. He'd have his pick of teams. He'd have his pick of everything. He could be as famous as all the other climbers put together; he could take high-value clients on specialized individual climbs, the way Nims does, faster and more efficiently when there's more money, more attention, more fame. Jack's always wanted to be considered one of the top-ten mountaineers. This is his shortcut."

"And he doesn't care about your friend. Only the camera."

"Jack's a pragmatist," she said. "Two birds, one stone. He won't abandon Yuan Bo, anything like that, it's not like he's *only* about the camera. He's human. But no, he wouldn't be going up there, at least not himself in person, just to help a defector. It's not like he hasn't been approached already."

"Really?" I couldn't hide my astonishment.

"They probably all have, the bigger expeditions. Look east, Abbie," she said, unconsciously echoing Myles. "Defection's a thing. And if you're in a country with borders on another country where people are held against their will, it's always going to be an option. Jack hasn't done it before, but some of the others have. They don't all make the papers."

"One that happens on the top of Mount Everest is sure to," I said.

"If the film from that camera can be developed, the whole world will know," she said.

"And the retribution will be intense," I said. "Have you thought about that?"

"Yes."

"And?"

"And, what? This isn't a decision I made, Abbie. Everyone pays a price when things go wrong in the world. You think Yuan Bo's doing this for the camera? He doesn't care about the camera. The camera's currency for him, that's all. It's his ticket out of China forever. He wants to write dangerous books. He wants to shop where he pleases, vacation where he pleases. He doesn't have children, a wife, no one to keep him connected to the country. He thinks China's lost its soul."

"Like the one it had when it was an empire?" I murmured, just to be difficult.

"No government's perfect," Emma snapped. "But there are degrees of imperfection. He thinks it's his right to choose which one he wants to live under."

"I get it," I said, shrugging. It still seemed like one hell of a risk. "How are they going to do it?"

But Emma was done. "The fewer people know about this, the better," she said. "Especially about the details."

"Wait, what, you're saying maybe someone's outside the tent now, listening? Isn't that a little far-fetched?" We sounded like characters out of a Cold War–era spy thriller. A bad one.

"What I'm saying is we can't be talking about it," she said. "And I'm tired, Abbie."

I can hear an exit cue as well as the next person. "See you tomorrow," I said, turning to unzip the flap. I struggled with it for a moment, as the wind was just picking up, then I managed the Velcro and the zipper. "Night, Emma."

She was already pretending to be asleep.

So I was awake, alone, when the wind really started to pummel Base Camp, and before the melatonin and drifting off again, I remembered Emma's voice. "Everyone pays a price." I wondered what hers was.

I wondered what mine would be.

***

The sun was back out the next morning, bright and piercing without "sunnies," and there was a buzz in the camp. Sometime in the night, apparently, a new group had arrived and pitched tents, and everyone was talking about them.

"So what?" I asked Richard, who was standing in front of me in the Supreme Summits breakfast line. "Who're these people, anyway?"

"Didn't you see? It's Nims," he said, and something almost reverential had crept into his voice.

"What's a nims?" Though somewhere in the back of my mind I'd heard the name before, and recently. Oh, Emma, right. Last night. Something about being famous.

"Not what, who," Richard corrected me. "You should Google him. You'll be amazed. He's one of the fastest climbers in the world. His real name's Nirmal Purja, but everyone calls him Nims. Here," and he handed me my utensils and a bowl for the inevitable dal bhat. "He did this thing years ago, climbed all the fourteen highest mountains in the world in six months."

"That's impressive," I admitted.

"Impressive? It's bloody impossible, is what it is. Watch the documentary. They filmed him. The bloke's a machine. He's out there setting brand-new world records all the time. He takes people up one-on-one, and he only takes the most committed, the most motivated climbers. And that's not all. He does rescues no one else would even consider. Brought people down everyone else would've left for dead. Climbs fast, climbs without oxygen. Up and down the hardest mountains in the world, nothing stands in his way." He waited as the kitchen sherpa—Sonan Norbu, I thought his name was, but didn't want to say in case I was wrong—filled our bowls.

I followed Richard over to a space at one of the tables and we sat down. He was continuing the conversation, his voice low, pitched so only I could hear it. "Listen. I'll tell you something about this bloke. We're leaving Base Camp today. We'll go through the icefall, make it up to Camp Three tonight, members are in good shape, we'll make good time, and then we'll sleep there. Like we've been doing for a week now, up and down, getting acclimatized. Climb high, sleep low, you know the drill from trekking. Tomorrow we're taking on the Lhotse Face and then we'll sleep at Camp Four, which is pretty much at the Death Zone, the last place that's really safe—after that, our bodies start to self-destruct. But we'll be prepared, we'll be rested. We'll get up around eleven or midnight and make the summit push. That's normal, that's what I'm trying to tell you: that's the way normal people do it."

I had been eating steadily while he talked. Now I touched my napkin to my lips. "But this guy isn't normal?"

"I'm telling you, he's not even human. He got here last night. Him and his team, they're getting ready to set out. *This* is their summit push. They don't stop, they don't make camp, they don't do nothing but climb. Their summit push is straight up from Base Camp. One long, hard climb. Without oxygen."

"How do they deal with altitude sickness?" Then I remembered my conversation with Myles. "Do they take drugs? Dex, isn't it, and something else that starts with a d...?"

Richard gave a derisive hoot. "You're kidding, right? These people are *pure*, dude. No oxygen. No drugs. They're *machines*."

"You sound envious."

"There isn't anyone here who isn't, at least a little," he said. "It's not for everybody. He only takes the fittest clients up with him, ever, even when it's not one-on-one. It's a race to the top for him."

"Whereas you prefer to stop and smell the roses?"

He grinned, suddenly. "Maybe, just once, I'd've wanted to try something like that," he admitted. "When I was ten years younger and a hell of a lot fitter. And don't get me wrong, I'm in great shape right now, but I'd never try to summit without O's. But he's an inspiration for sure. It's not for everybody." He finished eating, pushed his chair back slightly, took a long gulp of tea. "Honestly? Here's what I think. At Supreme Summits, we do what we do better than anybody else. Nims does what *he* does better than anybody else. It's like comparing apples to oranges."

"But they're all in danger of falling out of the bushel at any moment, no matter what kind of fruit we're talking about," I pointed out. It seemed that produce was in a lot less danger than climbers.

"There's that," he conceded. "But we minimize risks."

"Does Nims?"

"What do you think?" He finished his tea. "Look, he's friends with all his blokes—no, scratch that, he's *family* with them. He's not Sherpa, but a lot of them are, and they've been working together for years. They call each other brother, and they *mean* it. It's not just words. Any of them would give his life for any of the others, and they'd do it in a heartbeat, it wouldn't even be a question. They put their lives in each other's hands, there's a trust there, there's something a lot of people go through their entire lives without ever experiencing, and he *lives* that trust. He *thrives* on that trust. He'd never knowingly endanger anyone."

He shrugged and stood up. "What can I say? It's changing, sure. Not all the Sherpa like Nims, and truth is, Kristin Harila, this woman climber, she beat his record a few years back, though people don't talk about that. Like I said, the comparison isn't apt, but most people make it anyway. I won't say I wouldn't like to see Supreme Summits be as famous as he is, even though for different reasons."

Then hold on to your hat, I thought. *That might be about to change.* "Good luck with the climb," I said instead.

"Thanks." He grinned suddenly, vividly. "Sometimes I think this is the best part. Just before you leave, when there's nothing more in your way and you know that in a few hours you'll be up there. And whatever is hard about it is still an unknown."

"How many times is it, now, for you? Here on Everest?"

"Fourteen times on the mountain. Ten summits."

That seemed like a lot. "Good luck," I said, and then added, "It'll be different this time, though, won't it?"

He paused. "What do you mean?"

"Everyone's saying Jack's going up with you instead of Mark." Perhaps I could help the cause with a red herring. "Is there something wrong? He doesn't trust Mark?"

Richard shook his head. "No," he said. "No way. Mark's solid. We don't hire beginners. I work with him all the time, I've known him for—how long?" He paused. "Crikey. Almost ten years." He shook his head. "No. There's nothing wrong there."

But there had been, back in Kathmandu. They'd almost come to blows. And Mark had gotten drunk and walked away. "So why's he the one staying at Base Camp?"

"Not my call." He looked at me and softened his gaze. "Don't worry, Abbie," he said. "There's nothing wrong. Jack doesn't get to climb as much as he used to, and it's time for him to get up there. I don't have to tell you climate change is affecting the mountain. It's getting more dangerous up there, not less. And the time's coming faster than we think when we'll have to find new routes. You saw what happened last year when that cornice collapsed. Every year brings more fatalities than the one before. Of course he wants to be aware of it."

It was pretty good thinking on the spur of the moment if he knew what was going to happen up there—and a reasonable explanation even if he didn't. "Good luck," I said again, and later when I'd finished and wandered out of the dining tent I saw him again, helping members get ready, checking carabiners and harnesses and ice axes.

Base Camp, in fact, was buzzing. Everyone, it seemed, wanted to hang out with the famous Nims, including the members of the Russian expedition, who didn't seem to be doing much mourning for the late and apparently unlamented Yevgeny.

Yevgeny was on my mind, mostly because I'd managed to do the unthinkable, cut myself when my gloves were off trying to slice open a packet of peanuts, and with toilet paper wrapped around my hand I set off to the ER tent. A dark-haired Western woman was sitting alone on a camp chair beside a table with an open laptop on it, drinking tea, when I arrived. "Can I help?" Definitely a French accent; I'd found Dr. Yvette.

I held up my hand apologetically. "Seriously clumsy," I confessed. "And I don't have anything in my pack other than Band-Aids."

She put down the cup and put on a pair of glasses. "Let me see."

I sat in another camp chair across from her and proffered my hand. She lifted it by the wrist and blood spattered as she took off my makeshift bandage. "It is not deep," she said. She got up and left me holding it, as though it wasn't part of my body, as she busied herself fetching a bucket and a jug of water and then expertly irrigated the cut, patted it dry with a sterile cloth, and looked again. "You do not need stitches," she said.

"That's a relief."

"I will give you antibiotic dressing," she said, pouring some sickly yellowish goo onto the cut before winding a bandage around my hand.

"Thank you." I was feeling more than a little foolish.

"It is nothing. What I am here for." She was no-nonsense, was Yvette, now busily putting things away. I looked at her curiously. Everything from cuts to frostbite to... "Tell me," I said impulsively. "That Russian climber who died? Someone said he was poisoned."

Her clear gray eyes met mine. If I'd meant to shock her, I'd have been disappointed. "That is so," she said calmly. "Yevgeny Illich Ivanov."

I nodded, as though she'd confirmed something. Well, she had—the rumor, anyway. "How did you know?" I asked.

"Sorry?"

"No, I'm the one who's sorry, I should have been clearer—but it's just, it seemed awfully quick, you know? Because, I don't know, it must be difficult to tell that someone's been poisoned, isn't it? Don't you have to do blood tests?"

If she thought I was mad, she didn't give it away. "There are toxins that manifest themselves immediately," she said. She was methodically putting away her first-aid supplies into a steamer trunk, one of three in the tent. "The symptoms are clear. There is nothing that can be confused with strychnine."

Strychnine? I wasn't sure what I'd been expecting, but now that she'd said it... well, strychnine just seemed terribly old-fashioned. Like something out of Agatha Christie. "What are they?" I asked. "The symptoms, I mean. What are they?"

She closed the first-aid trunk, dusted her hands, straightened up to face me. She could have made her exasperation a little clearer, but only marginally. "Ten to twenty minutes after exposure, the body's muscles begin to spasm, starting with trismus and risus sardonicus in the head and neck."

I knew better than to ask.

"The spasms then spread to every muscle in the body, with nearly continuous convulsions increasing in intensity and frequency until the backbone arches continually. Convulsions lead to lactic acidosis, hyperthermia, and rhabdomyolysis. These are followed by postictal depression. Death comes from asphyxiation caused by paralysis of the neural pathways that control breathing." She paused, her head cocked to the side, looking at me. She resembled a small, intelligent bird. "Does that answer your question?"

"More than enough," I said, wishing I hadn't asked.

She shrugged. "Pathology will confirm my initial diagnosis."

"But how do you *know*?" I persisted. I'd obviously asked the wrong question. "About the symptoms, I mean. Were you there?"

"Of course I was not. He had eaten a meal in his tent. Breakfast. Oatmeal and tea and some black bread. With a friend, who came looking for me. By the time I saw him, his respiration and heartbeat had ended. It had progressed quickly. I tried chest compressions, but there was no possible recourse."

"Who did? Who was with him when he died?"

Yvette wasn't interested. She waved a hand as though to shoo the question away. "The other climber," she said.

"Another Russian?"

"No," she said. "It was an English guide. I do not know his name. He is with—" she frowned, thinking. "Yes, he is with Supreme Summits."

I would have been surprised, I think, if she'd said anything else.

Excerpt from the journal of George Mallory

France, 1916: I've said good-bye to my dearest Ruth and less than twenty-four hours later I found myself having breakfast in a café near Le Havre. I heard the language all around me and it warmed my heart, reminding me as it did of my many happy adventures in the French Alps.

In fact, it was somewhat surreal, if I'm to be honest. We are locked in battles that will decide the future of European humanity, if not that of the entire world, yet life here continues in a plausible facsimile of normality.

They've taught me how to shoot and I expect that if I saw a German twenty yards off and he were to stand very still, allowing me time to aim, I might conceivably hit him. I am fortunate in being assigned to the artillery rather than the infantry, as the chances of survival are appreciably higher, but still I've been assigned to the Fortieth Siege Battery, positioned in the northern part of the Western Front. I am in command of an observation post in order to tell the artillery in what direction to aim the guns.

Ruth is keeping me well stocked, I must say. She sends me packages of tea, food, Grand Marnier, cigarettes, books, and more. She worries a great deal about me, but as I've told her, the sound of shells has become part of the fabric of everyday life here, and one simply goes about one's business.

I've been out there laying telephone wires and am so distressed at all the fine English lads, cut down before their time, their bodies lying unburied and—for the moment, in any case—unmourned.

As for the war… the days all bleed into each other. But the men? The men are exceptional. I can honestly say that no matter what the order, there is no resentment from the men. They listen and they obey, and that is very much that. We all know we are there to do a job of work for our country and our king, and that means everything, even the supreme sacrifice, was acceptable. You wouldn't think so many different chaps could get on so well in such difficult circumstances, and of course the men had it far worse than we officers. But there was a camaraderie there I'd never before experienced, a true brotherhood.

Or perhaps that I only have experienced high on a mountain, putting my life into the hands of my fellow climbers.

Chapter Fourteen

Supreme Summits wasn't the only group on the move: Élite Summiting and GlobeClimbers were gearing up, as were several others that didn't have names emblazoned on everything in sight.

It was difficult not to feel some excitement, the tension of the night before having resolved into a kind of exuberant and almost frenetic activity. They'd all worked and trained and prepared for something they were now on the verge of achieving. Or not. It was hard to remember that some of the faces I was seeing might not come down the mountain again. Hundreds of bodies up there.

I shivered, even in the bright glaring sun.

I pushed those thoughts away—they had to be omens of something, and I didn't want to explore what that might be. I was considering looking for Myles when a familiar voice unexpectedly chirped from behind me. "Miss Abigail! I see you are in good health, good spirits!"

"Anish," I said in surprise, turning around. The small portly figure was now enveloped in a big red snowsuit; if he'd had a beard, he might have passed for a diminutive Nepali Father Christmas.

He was, of course, beaming. "And here you are, enjoying the mountain! As I said you would! You must take many photographs, Miss Abigail, to bring with you back to America! All peoples are interested in Base Camp!"

I smiled; I couldn't help it. "It's good to see you, Anish. But what are you doing up here?"

He nodded as though confirming something. "It is most fortuitous, Miss Abigail! Boss-Man called to ask me to bring him some items from Kathmandu. And now I am able also to see esteemed ladies as well!"

"You didn't trek up," I said. There hadn't been time; and anyway Anish didn't exactly look as though exercise was his thing.

If anything, his smile got wider. "But no! At Supreme Summits Expeditions, we employ only best pilots!"

"You took a *helicopter* up?" That was an expense they probably hadn't counted on. Not that they were pinching pennies or anything—but still I wondered what it was that Jack had needed so badly to bring Our Man in Kathmandu up onto the mountain.

"It is very exciting, the helicopter," Anish said, and I thought I detected a certain wobbliness behind the smile and the words. It probably had been very exciting indeed. Maybe, I found myself thinking, landing in Lukla hadn't been so bad after all.

"I'll bet it is," I said. "You're probably glad to have your feet on the ground."

"I will be happier, Miss Abigail, to have my feet back in my office," said Anish frankly. "But here we are! There is no need to fret! You are enjoying Everest Base Camp!"

"Yes," I said, giving in. He wasn't so much a person as a force of nature. "Of course I'm enjoying it, Anish."

"And Miss Emma? The other esteemed lady? She is well?"

"She's very well, thanks, Anish. Around here somewhere." I gestured a little helplessly; there were more people than ever milling about, the colors of their anoraks and snowsuits clashing in the bright sun, reds and yellows and bright blues. The colors of the prayer flags.

He nodded, as though I'd just confirmed something. "All peoples like Everest Base Camp," he said. "But especially peoples like Supreme Summits Expeditions!"

I laughed; I couldn't help it. "You don't have to convince me anymore, Anish. You're the world's best organizer and Supreme Summits Expeditions is the best-organized company ever."

That got me a look; there had to be something behind the façade, after all. But Anish just nodded and the smile reappeared. "Then we will meet again, Miss Abigail. I must go now to help the Boss-Man. Namaste!"

"Namaste," I echoed, and watched him trundle off. What did Jack need that couldn't have been brought up when he and the others set up camp? As far as I could tell, there wasn't anything he was going to need on the summit when he encountered Yuan Bo but speed. And a lot of luck.

I was still standing there when Emma found me. "There you are, dear."

She was back to that infuriating elderly-aunt-speak. Which either meant that everything was going well or that she was scared out of her wits. I opted to believe the latter. "Anish is up here," I told her.

"I'd heard that. I gather he doesn't, usually."

"He said Jack sent for him. To bring something up." It could only be something heavy, I thought, or bulky; something that others would remark upon during the fast trek into the mountains. "What do you think it was?"

"I don't know," she said and shook her head. "Maybe he just needed Anish for help—later, and saying he was supposed to bring something up was just a cover story."

"Nothing is as it appears, here," I said, agreeing.

She followed my gaze. "Don't pay attention to Nims," she added. "He's not part of our story. Maybe not even part of his own."

"What does that mean?"

"If you listen to the guys," she said, "Nims is a hero. But there are other sides to his story. And, besides, a woman's beaten his record. Broken all the records. But the men won't tell you about *that*." She sniffed.

"Of course they won't," I said automatically. I had started looking for Myles. Nowhere to be seen.

Emma wasn't interested in talking about famous mountaineers. "Jack's doing his motivational speech," she said. "He does that before they all do puja. Let's go listen."

I knew about puja. No Nepali was about to go up the mountain without first securing the permission of the goddess herself in a ceremony that set intentions for a safe journey and a request for a blessing on the enterprise. It made a lot of westerners uncomfortable, listening to words they didn't understand, but there was no expedition without it.

I trailed behind Emma, still looking for Myles. It was silly. We'd had, what? Two conversations? Three? *Enough of that.* Once he came down—and I refused to even consider that he might not come down—he'd be heading back to Auckland, or Perth, or Wellington, or wherever it was he lived, and take his surfer-dude persona and bright blue jay eyes with him, and that would be that.

I was *not* a character in an Emma Caulfield novel. Not at all. But I looked, all the same.

***

Jack had gathered everyone in the main Supreme Summits observation tent.

He and Mark were standing in front of the clear plastic windows, so that the mountain seemed to be within touching distance as they spoke. It was a dramatic gesture, and it worked.

Richard was sitting off to the side, consulting a notebook.

"So this is what we're looking at," Jack was saying as I slipped in, moving quietly behind the other people in the room, finding a chair where I could sit and snap open my laptop to take notes. "It all comes down to this. All your months and years of training, and just hours from now you'll find out if you have what it takes to stand on the top of the world."

Mark picked up the thread. "Practical reminders first," he said. "Understand the oxygen you're gonna need. You've been doing it already, but don't cheat yourself. Start at two and a half, go to three, and turn it up if you need more on tough sections. Yeah?" He looked around; everyone was nodding. "Good. Your final sherpa climbing partners have been assigned. This is your new best friend. Do what your sherpa tells you, and you'll make it down in one piece." He cleared his throat. "Think about how to clear your mask of ice. Your sherpa climbing partner knows how to, and he'll help if you need it, but remember not to panic. It freaks you out when all of sudden you can't breathe due to a clogged mask. Okay?"

Nods all around again. Jack rubbed his hands together and stepped back into the center. "You are all competent and resourceful. You've all done high-altitude work before, so I don't have to remind you that once we're in the Death Zone you won't be nearly as competent and resourceful as you are down here at Base Camp. Trust your training, trust your guide—that's me or Richard—and trust your partner, your sherpa. Don't trust your mind—it's the first thing to betray you once you have that summit in sight."

It sounded like a lot of blah-blah to me. I wondered if the women's expeditions Dawa had told us about included this little exercise in public speaking.

Jack was still talking. "Ask for help when you need it," he was saying. "Use your radio, stay in touch. The weather can close in at any minute and visibility can drop to zero. If this were a walk in the park, we'd have charged you a whole lot less."

That earned him a little nervous laughter. "Be together with the other climbers, and help each other. You're individuals, yeah, but you're also a team. You're in this together. Encourage each other. Slow down if necessary... just keep moving and you'll get there. This year, you're getting a bonus: I'll be up there to kick your ass if you aren't playing nice with the other blokes on the team."

Another wave of restrained laughter and a smattering of applause. Jack waited until it was over, and then made a point—or so it seemed to me—of making eye contact with everyone in the tent. There was a split second when his eyes met mine and flickered off again, and I shivered. Something there I couldn't decipher. "This may sound funky, but now's the time to think about what you're going to do on the summit when you get there. If you have banners or photos, take them along somewhere accessible—remember, you've got twenty minutes, absolutely tops, and probably less." I remembered Mallory and his photograph of Ruth. Now buried in layers of ice.

It hadn't been on his body.

"Decide now who's gonna take your photo, and whose photo you're gonna take. Who's carrying the camera? Will the batteries be warm enough? Do you know what you're gonna say on the video?" He looked around. "Gentlemen—and lady—you are going to be bonked when you reach the summit. You will be exhausted. You'll have used every bit of gumption you had in you and then some. You've been in the Death Zone for too many hours already and your body is feeding on itself. No one makes good decisions there. Make those decisions *now*."

There were nods around the tent. They all knew this already. It was a reminder, not a lesson. I looked around for faces I knew, and for some reason I met Jurgen's eyes. He flicked over me; I was unimportant in his world. For all I knew, he didn't even remember meeting me in Kathmandu.

Jack was still talking. "You don't want to come down saying, 'I should have done this or that...' Write it down if you want. Keep it on a card in your pocket. Your brain is gonna feel like it's full of cotton. Think *now*. Ask your sherpa guide to carry your camera until you get there, because I don't want you messing with it on the way up. You're gonna need your hands for other things."

That seemed to be Mark's cue. "Tomorrow's one of the hardest parts of the climb," he said. "Back up through the Khumbu Icefall." There was a wave of nods all over the tent, but not from the sherpas, who already knew. "You've all been through it twice already this season, but don't get complacent. The ice has already shifted from your last climb. Don't think for one minute that you belong there. Before you leave, just one more time, practice your glove combinations, make sure you know how to grip the ascender with your mitts. It's not easy. It's not natural. Think about everything you're doing before you do it. If your fingers start getting cold, deal with it right away. Don't put it off. Speak to your climbing partner, radio your guide if he's not nearby. Take the warmers out of your boots before you put them on and place them in your mitts, which you may need later. Most of those hand warmers are good for ten hours. Make sure you can pull your fingers out of your regular glove fingers and grab the hand warmer while your hand is still in the glove and you're using it with the ascender."

People were starting to get restless; I could feel it like a current washing through the tent. I glanced at Emma, but she seemed fixated on Jack, who wasn't looking at her.

He took over the lecture. "One more thing," he said. "This is the absolutely optimal time to summit. The weather, the date, everything. This is the week. Winds under thirty miles per hour. We don't have another window, and nobody else does, either. Everyone knows it, too. We're not going to be alone up there. There are expeditions already on the South Col and waiting for the window. There are expeditions from the north side, too, coming from Tibet."

This time, there was a flickering glance at Emma, so fleeting I might have imagined it. But I hadn't. "In other words, it's gonna be crowded. You're not getting a shot of yourself alone up there, so don't even try. Stay with your ropes, stay with your guide, stay with your partners. Especially if we run into any Tibetan expeditions. There's some etiquette up there, but it's not always respected."

There was some movement among the Sherpas, and I wondered about their cousins on the other side—Sherpa communities provided climbers with the same support in Tibet. Did any of them know? Jack had to have taken someone into his confidence, you didn't just grab a climber from another expedition and take off with him. I wondered how deep into the Sherpa community this plan had gone.

"Getting to the top and down to the Col is your goal. If you can get down to Camp Two, that's super, but don't push it; don't try to be a hero and push to Camp Two if you're not up for it. Going down the Lhotse Face is a bitch when you're tired or bonked." There was another round of nervous laughter. "And don't push when the going gets tough. You have to be able to flick the switch: stop, drink, eat something, stay in emotional control, and regroup. You have to keep your mental toughness every moment. If you do bonk, then tell your sherpa, tell your guide, ask for help, and make the right decision. The mountain's always gonna be there. You can climb it anytime. But only if you come down alive."

He took a breath. "I know all of you members, and I know you're all tough and prepared. Every one of you is able to reach the summit. You have the best guides and best climbing sherpas on the mountain. You can do it." He checked his watch. "We're heading up in an hour," he said. "Staying at Camp Two tonight, climbing to Camp Four tomorrow, and leaving Camp Four at midnight tomorrow night. I want everyone to check their equipment with their climbing sherpas before we leave Base Camp. No exceptions."

There were nods and murmurs, and Jack held up his hand. "One more thing," he said. "You know I'm summiting with you." A few low whistles, a smattering of applause and some stamping on the ground. "I'll be there with Richard; it's Mark's turn to man the radio. He'll take good care of us." He paused and there were nods all around; they trusted Mark. "In the meantime, I've got some routes I'm scoping out. I want you to stick with your sherpa and your guide, no matter what happens up there. I might not be on the line with you, but don't worry about that. Keep putting one foot in front of the other. That's how you climb the mountain, and that's how you come down alive."

The meeting broke up then, unevenly, some people getting up slowly, talking together, a couple of them heading right out the door. It had been an odd speech, I thought, and—new routes? That was how he was going to cover up his grabbing Yuan Bo?

Emma had been standing in the back of the tent, and I caught up with her at the door. "He's coming down a different route?"

"Shh!" She looked really shocked and grabbed my elbow. "Get out of here!"

She propelled me, half-running, half-stumbling, out of the tent and along what I'd come to think of as one of Base Camp's boulevards, a wider irregular route among erratic paths connecting different neighborhoods. I started to say something and she tightened her hold on my elbow. It wasn't until we'd reached the edge of the icefall itself that she stopped.

We were both panting. I bent over at the waist, trying to get air into my lungs. I could have done with one of the O2 canisters right then. "What is your *problem*?" I managed to gasp.

"Any of those people," she said, "could have been spying. Jack knows what he's doing. He knows how to talk to these people, to get them to do whatever he says. They don't question him. We'd better not, either, at least in public."

I straightened up. "Fine," I said, though it came out as something of a snarl. I was starting to have enough of this whole secrecy thing. Maybe it was just my nerves, now that we were approaching H-Hour, or maybe I still just couldn't make sense of the whole enterprise. "I don't even pretend to understand any of this," I said to Emma. "And that's fine. Fine. I'm your research assistant. It's none of my business. From now on, I'll just stick to doing research."

"Fine," she said.

"Fine," I said again, and we glared at each other.

"Am I interrupting something?" asked Myles.

***

Emma recovered first. "Not at all," she said pleasantly, turning to him.

"Were you looking for me?" I asked, both because it excluded Emma—with whom I was seriously teed off—and because I did in fact hope he'd been looking for me.

He had the lazy smile on again. "Told you I'd be sure to catch up before we left," he said. "And Mrs. Caulfield still owes me an autograph. Thought I'd come and claim it."

"Two birds, one stone?" I suggested. Emma looked pained.

"Something like that."

She reached out a gloved hand. "Give me something to write on," she said. I hoped she wasn't talking to me. Clearly I wasn't the kind of research assistant who follows the famous author around, pen and clipboard at the ready.

Myles had extracted a small spiral notebook from one of the pockets of his way-too-bright-blue parka, and pulled a pen from another. He presented them to Emma with a flourish. "Her name is Brittany," he said, but he was looking at me, not Emma.

She nodded, bent over her scribbling. "I remember," she said. "Your sister."

He seemed pleased. I, on the other hand, was cranky enough to be thinking, *Well, it's her job, isn't it, to remember fans' names?*

Myles asked, "You ladies out for a stroll?"

I cleared my throat. "Got tired of listening to motivational speeches," I said.

He was looking at me oddly. "Yeah, I see," he said, then took the pad of paper from Emma. "Thanks. She'll be thrilled."

Emma handed him his pen back. "Pleasure," she said briefly. "You kids enjoy yourselves; I'm heading back."

"Emma—" I started, but she raised a hand. "Need to clear my head," she said, and looked at Myles. "Good luck on the mountain tomorrow," she said.

He managed to look surprised. "Tomorrow? What's happening tomorrow?"

She smiled. "Um, climbing Everest?"

He shook his head. "I hadn't heard we were leaving then."

"Everyone's leaving then," said Emma. I couldn't figure out her expression, and we didn't say anything for a time as we stood there watching her pick her way back toward the tent city. "She's not always like that," I said finally. Heaven knew why I was defending Emma.

"Everyone's on edge, ay," said Myles. "You can feel it in the air. There's a kind of tension running through the camp."

I looked at him. "You feel it too? I thought it was just the excitement of the famous Nims being here."

"Oh, Nims," he said dismissively. "I've been in camp before when he's around. Star-power and all. Not the same as what I'm feeling now."

I shivered. "I asked Yvette about the Russian, the guy who was poisoned," I said. "Who was it you said was friendly with the Russians? Was it Mark or Richard?"

Myles was staring at me. "You went to ask Yvette about it?"

I held up my hand, pulled off the mitten to show off my bandage. "Injured on the front lines," I said. I was wondering if I wasn't getting carried away with trusting this guy. I had a secret, and it wasn't mine to share; but he seemed a neutral third party, someone who might bring some perspective to the question. Maybe he knew something.

And he *was* incredibly attractive.

"So that tension," I said, pulling the mitten back on; frostbite wasn't, I hoped, in my future. "What you're feeling in the camp? What do you think's going on?"

He touched my shoulder, briefly, guiding me over to some hefty boulders nearby. That wasn't difficult; there were hefty boulders everywhere. "Have a seat, ay," he said, and while I was perching, he put his sunglasses on, his gaze sweeping up the icefall.

"You know better than I do," I said. "Is it normal?"

He still wasn't looking at me. "There's always something," he said. "But it's—well, okay, laugh at me if you want, Abbie, but the feeling is usually *joyous*, you know? Tension, yeah, but usually there's heaps excitement, too, that comes from being on the edge of something you really, really want and are dead scared of doing. Every climber here's been working for at least a year, usually longer, to be able to do this. It's the accomplishment of a dream, the end of the rainbow. And we've all been working together, learning to count on each other, getting closer." He sounded puzzled. "People should be *happy*," he said.

"So you think it's because of Yevgeny dying?" And who had been with him? To Yvette's French ear, even Jack's broad Australian accent might sound English. Or it could have been one of the expedition members...

"Started before that," Myles said.

I nodded. "At Lukla. Ang Pemba Sherpa."

He shrugged. "Don't know. I just know this year is different." He hesitated and turned to look at me. "There's too much change," he said. "A real sense of something ending. Maybe it's global warming. Maybe it's overcrowding. I don't know. But it feels like this is the end of something. Like the sadness you feel at the end of holidays. Can you feel it?"

"Not like you do," I conceded. "It's all new to me, remember. But I know what you mean. Like everybody's kind of holding their breath." I was pretty sure it had to do with the deaths; they'd certainly done it for me. But he had experience on the mountain; he was probably sensing some undercurrent to the undercurrent.

He nodded, but didn't say anything for a while, his gaze again on the icefall. I cleared my throat. "I should see if Emma's still speaking to me—"

"How long're you staying at Base Camp?" It came out abruptly.

"I don't know," I said. "It's up to Emma. I guess at least until—whenever Supreme Summits finishes summiting." I hesitated. "Well, when they're back," I amended.

He nodded noncommittally. "They'll summit," he predicted. "It's a good outfit."

"They'd better summit," I said. "Jack's reputation's on the line. He's going up with them." Was I supposed to share that? I wasn't giving anything away, surely; it had to be common knowledge.

"I heard," said Myles. "Mark's staying at Base Camp? Working the comms?"

I nodded; in for a penny, in for a pound. "I'm sure Jack just wants to keep his hand in," I said.

I couldn't see his eyes clearly behind his dark glasses, but I could swear they seemed amused. "Jack climbs at least one eight-thousand-meter every year, ay," he said. "But you're probably right. No other reason why he'd want to summit now. Potential clients want to know he knows the terrain, and it's changing." There was a definite edge there, a lingering question. *This is where I should shut up.*

No; this is where I should make sure he doesn't get too close to the truth. "Maybe it's because of what happened," I said. "You know—Ang Pemba Sherpa. Maybe it's in—his honor, you know? As a sort of memorial to him? Something like that?"

"How well do you *know* Jack?" asked Myles. He sounded amazed. "You really think he'd change the plans he's had in place all year for that?"

"People do strange things when they're feeling grief," I said. "You never know."

He looked at me just a little bit longer than that remark deserved, then shook his head. "Jack will take care of Ang Pemba's family," he said. "He'll donate money to the village. He'll do practical things, things that help people. But what he *won't* do is climb the mountain at a moment's notice." He paused. "It's so out of character," he said at length. "And I've never known Jack to do anything that's out of character. He's weird, okay; we're all a little weird, a little mad. But that's part of this feeling, this edginess."

"Edginess about him?"

"Edginess coming from him," he said.

I didn't know what to say to that. It didn't matter, not really. There was no way in hell that Myles would ever guess what Jack was doing on Everest. As long as I kept my mouth shut.

The problem was, my nerves were getting to me. The only person I could talk to about all this was Emma, and we weren't exactly getting along like a house on fire at the moment. And there's something to that whole business of feeling better once you've talked about something—otherwise therapy wouldn't be so prevalent.

And I had no idea how to change the subject. Myles was watching me, and it had to be clear to him that I knew something I wasn't sharing. And since sharing is a major part of flirting...

And there I was again, jumping into an Emma Caulfield novel. I cleared my throat. "You know," I said, "maybe it all fits together. The tension you're feeling, that last-day-of-summer feeling, Jack deciding to climb... everything's changing. You said so yourself, no one trusts the terrain anymore. Maybe soon no one will be able to climb, the glacier won't be safe. Maybe it's just that the party's over. It's frustrating because it's nebulous, but it's probably not— well, you know, evil." Or so I hoped.

Myles snorted with a half-laugh at that. "No, Abbie," he said. "I don't expect it's evil." He stood up and offered me a hand. "Come on, then. It's almost six o'clock; dark in another hour and a half. And you don't want to—"

"—sprain an ankle," I finished for him. It was a perfect echo of our first conversation back in Lukla.

"Or any other body part," said Myles smoothly, smiling.

Excerpt from the journal of George Mallory

Godalming, Surrey, and Chamonix, 1919: And so the Armistice has come, and the war is over. As I wrote to my father, life presents itself very much to me as a gift. It is surprising to find oneself a survivor, and it's not a lot I've always wanted. There has not been much to be said for being alive in the company of the dead.

I'm back teaching at the Charterhouse now, and it seems life has taken a turn for the normal. It will be a long time before we can pick up all the pieces, of course. I find my children a mystery and my home life disordered; but that is a reflection of the country and indeed Europe as a whole. The Great War has ravaged us all.

My climbing has suffered a setback due to surgery I had on my ankle last year, but things could be worse. Geoffrey Young is climbing with an artificial leg; twenty-three of my acquaintances were killed in France, and nineteen of us injured.

I will say that throughout the war I thought often of my beloved mountains, but as my train approached Chamonix, nothing had prepared me for my first sight of the Alps after seven long years away. The thread of my experience with the mountains had been broken, and so it was a vision startlingly fresh and new, as though I were seeing them for the first time all over again. I had held them in my memory; now, again, I held them in my soul.

And Ruth is pregnant again.

Chapter Fifteen

Anish ambushed me at the entrance to the dining tent. "Miss Abigail!"

I was busy looking around for Emma, so I turned to him with more than my usual amount of distraction. "Hello, Anish. You're still here?" Somehow, I'd assumed he'd be flying straight back to Kathmandu. He didn't strike me as a man at home in the elements. Any elements.

"Oh, yes, Miss Abigail. The mountains are beautiful! And I have an excellent assistant. He keeps the office running with no help from me! I could disappear and nothing would change! I would never be missed!"

I allowed him what passed, in my anxious condition, for a smile. "I very much doubt that, Anish."

His own smile became broader. "I do whatever is best for Supreme Summits," he assured me. "And now, as I am here, I will see with my own eyes the triumph of our members when they have summited!"

He made it sound like a military offensive. "Well, good," I said vaguely, edging away. I was starting to get real jitters and needed some reassurance. I had to find Emma.

As though reading my mind, Anish pounced. "Yes! I have been looking for Miss Emma, me! But she is nowhere to be found!" He leaned in and lowered his voice. "But Mr. Jack Boss-Man not around, too. What do you think of that?" He put a finger to his lips, his eyes dancing with mischief. "Perhaps there is time on the mountain for romance, Miss Abigail! What do you think?"

What I thought was that they were in contact somehow with Yuan Bo and that they were making plans for a different kind of *rendez-vous* altogether. "I have no idea," I said.

He smiled and shrugged, palms facing upward. "Love will find a way," he assured me. "And Mr. Jack and Miss Emma, they are very close, they have been for years. So it might happen again!"

Again? Despite my anxiety, I was curious. "Were they a couple, Anish?"

He beamed and put a finger to his mouth. "Shh! It is a secret, Miss Abigail. But I can tell you the truth! Many years ago, when Miss Emma lived in Australia—"

"Wait," I interrupted. "Emma lived in Australia?"

He looked pained. "Miss Emma, she lived many places, Miss Abigail. She is a *writer*." He said it with reverence.

"Not sure that follows," I said. "What happened?"

The smile had vanished. "Some bad things, Miss Abigail. Some sorrows. It was not meant to be." He brightened. "But we do not talk of such things! And many peoples, they meet a specialist person on vacations like this one!"

"I think you mean special, not specialist," I said. Though maybe he didn't. Dinner was being dished out inside the tent, and that seemed as good a social excuse as anything. "Well, it's nice having you here, Anish," I said. "I'm going to go in and—"

"Of course! Supreme Summits always has best food on the mountain! All peoples love Supreme Summits food!"

He was probably right about that, anyway. I smiled again, possibly a little inanely, and slipped inside, leaving Anish standing in the last slanting rays of sunshine in his Santa suit, beaming and nodding.

There were mostly expedition members on the food line, loading their plates, taking advantage of their last kitchen-cooked meal. Later they would crawl into their sleeping bags and then, in the early hours of the morning, make their way in the dark across the icefall, using the day to climb to Camp Four, where they'd heat their rations over camping stoves and try to sleep, ready for the last midnight push to the summit.

No wonder they were hungry.

I snagged some dal bhat and rice and sat down at one of the long tables. I didn't need to carb- and protein-load, but it was probable that at some point Emma would show up here, and anyway, I'm always hungry.

"Hey, Abbie." It wasn't Emma who eventually showed up, but Mark. "Mind if I join you?"

I gestured toward the empty seats around me. "If you can find space, sure."

He settled in beside me, napkin on lap—somebody'd raised him right—took a long swallow of tea, and nodded toward the door flap. "Seems Anish is the only one at Base Camp who hasn't got the jitters," he said.

"He does seem his usual cheery self," I agreed. "And you're right about the jitters. I was talking with—one of the members of another expedition. He says there's tension here he hasn't seen at Base Camp before."

"Myles Walker?" He caught my look. "Don't look so surprised, no-one's been spying on you. Base Camp's a regular soap opera. Everybody knows everybody else's business. It's the only way for it to work."

"What does that mean?"

He shrugged, drank some more tea. He was, I noticed, ignoring the plate of food in front of him. Nerves? But he wasn't even climbing. "It's about trust. The mountain's unforgiving," he said. "You've probably heard the criticisms. About climbers not taking care of each other up there." He waited for my nod. "But the truth is, we all really believe, in our heart of hearts, that in a pinch, someone will look out for us. Within the expedition, that's a given: Supreme Summits don't take anybody up we're not prepared to bring back down again. But not every outfit's like ours."

"So where does the gossip come into it?"

"Not gossip," said Mark. "Not really. Just a hyper-awareness of each other. Knowing where we all stand, so to speak." He still wasn't eating. "I could probably tell you right now who in this tent I'd trust up there."

"And who you wouldn't?"

He smiled, a little grimly. "That, too."

I started recognizing some of the people drifting in. There was a sudden clattering of dishes and someone swearing in German: Jurgen, staying in character, berating one of the Sherpa kitchen crew. Richard came in, waved in our direction, but sat at one of the other tables. I saw some others I hadn't been introduced to, but recognized; I'd probably seen everyone at Base Camp at least once, by now. And certainly everyone from Jack's outfit was familiar.

No Sherpa: they ate separately, in their own dining tent. I didn't know if it was out of colonialism or choice.

Mark was looking around, too, and didn't look happy. "Are you nervous about orchestrating the teams from Base Camp?" I asked.

He looked at me, startled. "No. Why ask?"

I gestured toward his plate. "You're probably the only person in camp not loading up," I said.

He sighed and went back to surveilling the tent. "I'm worried," he said.

Join the club. "Why?"

He shook his head. "Nothing to do with you, Abbie. I know you're just here to—"

"—soak up the atmosphere," I finished for him. "Yeah, yeah. And the atmosphere is so tense it's about to break. Give me a little credit here, okay?"

He didn't even glance at me. "I don't want anybody to get hurt." He took a deep breath. "I don't want anybody to die," he said.

"Of course you don't." I was going to have to feel my way, here. "But why is this—time—different?" I remembered belatedly it had been Mark, back in Kathmandu, who'd first identified Ang Pemba Sherpa's death as murder. "Because of what happened at Lukla," I said, and it wasn't a question. "Because you still don't know how he died."

"Because I still don't know who killed him." He pushed his plate away. "I talked to him before he left for the icefall," he said, abruptly. "We was mates, Ang Pemba and me. I sometimes stayed with him and Ehani at their gaff, when the season was over, if I didn't have another expedition right away. We was that close. And last year—Christ, what a berk, I should've paid attention."

I was probably not the right person to be hearing this, but I was the only one here. I suspected that if Mark had felt he could tell Jack, he'd have told Jack already. "Paid attention to what? What happened?" I hesitated, gauging his reaction. "What did he tell you?" I asked.

He half-turned toward me on the bench, but he was still watching the room. "Not enough," he said. "I should've made him—I don't know." He took in a deep, long breath as though sucking oxygen into depleted lungs. "He said somebody at Supreme Summits was doing something illegal," he said. "I tried to get more out of him, but he wouldn't say. Just that he needed to find out before he said anything to anyone. But he was worried, and that should've worried me more than it did. You didn't know him, but I'm here to tell you, Ang Pemba didn't worry about shit. This was the world's calmest bloke, which is what you want on the mountain. He had to've been pretty damned sure of what he knew to even say that much."

"You've thought a lot about it since," I said. "What do you think he was talking about?"

"Don't know." He drank some more tea. "I just—it doesn't square with what I know about these blokes, you know? Jack—I've known Jack for over a decade. He's moral as hell. He'd never do anything wrong."

Well, maybe nothing *technically* wrong, I thought, but certainly stuff that wasn't part of your basic guide to mountaineering. "Okay, then. Who does that leave?" I asked.

"Who does that *leave?*" he looked at me in astonishment. "You know how many people work for Supreme Summits?"

"You, Richard, Jack, Anish," I said, using my fingers to count them. "Oh, and Laxsmi. And Dawa."

He waved a hand. "All Laxsmi wants is Jack," he said. "She thinks he's gonna marry her and she can live a life of leisure. Not gonna happen. But you don't understand—at any given time, we have maybe eighteen, twenty guides on staff. Year-round, that is. We're not just in the Himalayas, we're on seven continents. We have climbing and trekking programs, last time I looked, close to thirty of them. That's a lot of guides, medics, and a whole lot more of support personnel."

"Okay," I said. I hadn't imagined anything that widespread. "But if Ang Pemba Sherpa was the one who knew something was going on—well, that limits it *geographically* at least, right? It has to be something happening in Nepal?"

"Maybe." He was staring into his now-empty mug. "I just feel that if something's going to happen, if a wheel's coming off—it's gonna be now. Tonight. Tomorrow." He shrugged. "Even at the summit. Why I wish I could be there."

"To look out for people," I suggested.

That earned me a quick, sharp glance. "Mebbe. Mebbe I think I could stop it. Won't know, though, will I?"

"Hard to stop something when you don't know what it is."

"Yeh."

"Are you," I asked, carefully, very carefully, "are you the one who chose to stay by the comms? I mean, did you guys draw straws, or something?"

He shook his head. "Only one way to run an expedition," he said. "Only one opinion matters."

"The Boss-Man," I said, and went on without thinking, "Why do you think he chose you, and not Richard?" Because I was suddenly remembering that Yevgeny hadn't been alone when he died. Richard had been with him. Did Jack want Richard on the mountain so he could keep an eye on him? Or so that Richard wouldn't be using the comms for his own activities? But why would Richard want to kill Ang Pemba, who he'd known for years?

Someone in Supreme Summits was moving drugs over the Silk Road. That was what really mattered here.

"He knows what he's doing," said Mark suddenly, interrupting my thoughts. I'd almost forgotten I'd asked him a question. "Jack does what's right."

It was said with finality, but there was something else there, too. Like a crack in a bell. Like a cream pudding with just the tiniest sliver of glass in it.

I was looking around the tent with interest. Everyone here was Supreme Summits. I saw the Italian couple, sitting stiffly across from each other, obviously tense; as I watched, Sylvia exploded in a flurry of many syllables and gestures. Nerves there, too. Anish had apparently given up looking for Emma and was sitting with Richard, talking, pointing to something on his plate.

Emma! This might be something worth reporting. Or was it too much information to put on Jack, just when he was doing something so inherently dangerous? For the first time, I wondered how exactly the Chinese team was going to react. How was Jack going to grab Yuan Bo, especially if there was a traffic jam at the summit? Useful for losing oneself in a crowd, but potentially deadly on the slow way down. Would the Chinese follow them down the Nepal side?

What if Jack were in fact the person doing something illegal, a man without scruples? I liked him, but I didn't really know him, and I've had notoriously bad judgment about people in the past. What was to keep him from grabbing the camera and leaving Yuan Bo high and dry?

And did Ang Pemba Sherpa's suspected illegal activity have anything to do with the defection, the camera, and—ultimately— George Mallory?

I looked at Mark in dismay. I was so tempted to tell him. I remembered thinking, back in Kathmandu, that Richard was the more thoughtful of the two guides, less impulsive, certainly friendlier; but now I was thinking that Mark's impulses might be good ones, after all. *Not your secret to tell*, I reminded myself. *Not yours.*

"I wish I could help," I said uncomfortably. I had to go find Emma, but I couldn't leave this conversation here. "You know, it might not even have anything to do with—with all this, now. There's tension, I told you, even Myles could feel it, and so maybe that doesn't have anything to do with—well, anything internal to Supreme Summits. Maybe it's just cooking the books, cheating on taxes, or something like that. Something that's more—innocuous." And that put me squarely on the record as Girl With The Stupidest Comments. I didn't look at Mark; didn't want to read his expression.

"Right," he said, standing up. "I'm sure you're right."

I stood up, awkwardly, my empty plate and silverware in my hands, ready to dump in the canvas buckets of soapy water. "I'll come see you later," I said, though how my presence could be interpreted as anything remotely comforting was beyond me. "You'll be in the comms tent?" That was headquarters, where the radio equipment was all kept, where the summit push was plotted and replotted and replotted again.

"Right," said Mark again, and walked out.

I grabbed his plate and cup and dumped them along with mine, his meal untouched. I wanted time to fly; I wanted it all to be over, the climbers to be safely back, nothing untoward having happened to anyone. I briefly considered closing myself in my tent and streaming a movie, blocking out reality, but knew it wouldn't help me focus. And it was getting too cold to spend any time outside, now that the sun was setting; soon it would be very cold indeed.

I headed over to the observation tent—I had no idea how others thought of it, perhaps the recreation tent?—where I could look through the windows and contemplate the heavens or, failing that, drink some hot cider and find somebody to talk to. Maybe even Emma.

I was seriously needing to talk with Emma.

The tent was lively; someone was playing some pop tune on a decent speaker, and there were people there from other expeditions; an atmosphere rather determinedly lighter than what had settled over Base Camp earlier in the evening. Glasses clinking, muted laughter, someone had a climbing video up on the big screen. I looked around; no Myles, no Emma, no Jack. But still preferable to my own tent, and I wasn't going to go stumbling around Base Camp in the dark looking for people who apparently didn't wish to be found.

I settled into one of the beanbag chairs tossed around the floor, tilted my head up, and squinted at the stars, wondering what it was I was looking at. You'd think I might have brought a star guide, or app, or something; but no.

What would George Mallory have made of all this? I had a feeling he'd have dismissed the comforts, though that could be too much of an assumption—I had to remember that even when he and Ruth were at their poorest, wondering how they could make ends meet, she was still happily chatting about hiring cooks and nannies, and they made a point of choosing wallpaper together.

One man's poverty... so there was that basic bedrock of what he considered necessary comfort; but he'd made do with very little in the mountains. Tea, of course—there was no Englishman who could do without tea, and they'd traveled north through India, it was impossible to think that they hadn't gotten provisions along the way. And books; George always traveled with his books, one of which was invariably poetry. If he were here today, I thought, he'd probably have a snifter of brandy and have figured out how to fit a billiards table into the tent.

What I was pretty sure of, however, was what would have been his appetite for the adventure about to take place. Not just summiting, but bringing back an ultimate trophy, something to secure his reputation for all time; yes, I thought, this adventure, with all its dangers and unknowns, would have been very much George Mallory's cup of tea.

I must have nodded off after that; I awoke stiff, the stars brighter than ever above my head, the lights inside dimmer, only a few people engaging in conversation in low voices. I staggered to my feet, stretched, and pulled on my Gore-Tex coat and mittens. I had no idea what time it was.

I fished in my pocket for my flashlight and slipped out into the darkness.

The cold hit me instantly, immediately burning my lungs, and I doubled over, coughing. Hard. Hard enough that it felt I was trying to hack my lungs up, and I remembered, uncomfortably, that Howard Somervell had coughed so hard that he did actually bring up some of the lining of his lungs. The image was there and wasn't going away anytime soon.

He'd survived, but only barely.

I was still thinking these cheery thoughts when I rounded the dining tent and the air ahead of me suddenly swarmed with tiny firefly lights dancing in the darkness. They were at some distance from the outer edge of the camp; I blinked automatically, trying to focus my eyes. Fireflies? At altitude? What the hell...?

Then I had it; not fireflies—the headlamps of climbers, making their way carefully across the Khumbu Icefall, the snow and ice reflecting them, tiny already and moving up and away.

"Impressive, isn't it?" The voice came from behind me, and I turned with something like a gasp. "No, wait," the man said again, and he turned on a flashlight to show himself.

It didn't help: faces lit from below always look demonic. You don't even have to be Jack Nicholson.

But by now I was oriented enough to put both the voice and the features together. "It's—um, Ned, isn't it?" I asked. "Myles's friend?"

"Right." He came up next to me and gestured toward the lights on the icefall. "Just gorgeous, isn't it?"

"It is." I watched for a moment, and then a thought struck me. "Aren't you going up? Isn't your team going up?"

"They're gone," he said. "I was looking for you, actually. Myles asked me to give you something." He pulled a heavy mitten off and I felt rather than saw him fishing in the pocket of his parka. "He went to see you, but you were asleep."

It was a piece of paper, folded around something hard. I thrust it immediately into my own pocket, my fingers closing over it. "Thanks. I didn't realize how tired I was. But—seriously, why're you still here?"

"Acute mountain sickness." He sounded rueful. "AMS. Been dealing with symptoms all day. Dizzy, nauseous. Can't climb like that."

"I thought you spent time getting used to it," I said.

"We did. We do." In the backwash of light from his flashlight, his dark face was impassive. "But it's one of those things—it can happen to anybody any time, no matter what, how matter how you prepare. I was just unlucky." He snorted. "My father will say I made the wrong preparations," he said.

"Why? What would he have advised?"

"A *haka*." Now he sounded amused. "He thinks we're doing battle with the mountain. He climbs, my father, too. A lot of mountaineers of his generation feel that way."

I wanted to get at what Myles had left for me, but my curiosity—and courtesy—got the better of me. "What's a haka?" It sounded vaguely familiar.

"Māori war dance," said Ned. "What, you never seen an All Blacks match?"

"That's rugby, right?"

I could sense rather than see him smile. "It's meant to prepare warriors for the fight," he said. "And, if I'm being truthful, to scare the hell out of the other side. Lots of yelling and stamping and scary facial expressions."

"You're supposed to do a haka to intimidate the *mountain*?"

"My father's got a different mindset from the Sherpa," he said apologetically.

"I should think so." But it was more aligned with what Mallory and the members of his expedition would have felt, I thought. Seeing the mountain as the enemy to be overcome, rather than the goddess to be cared for.

"I won't keep you," said Ned. "I'm for bed, myself. Just seeing them off."

"I'm sorry you couldn't go," I said. He'd sounded wistful.

He shrugged. "Wasn't meant to be," he said. "Next year, maybe. You going back to your tent? I'll walk you, if you'd like."

"That's okay." My fingers found Myles's note in my pocket. "I'll stay here a few more minutes."

"Good night, then," said Ned.

I waited until I couldn't see his headlamp anymore, then started back toward my tent. There was a light on in the comms tent—Mark, tracking the climbers, watching the weather, probably drinking a lot of coffee. I couldn't imagine him getting much sleep over the next day and a half.

And then it struck me. If there were ever an ideal time to snoop, this was it. Everybody in Supreme Summits was either asleep or well into the Khumbu Icefall. The opportunity was just too good to pass up. The fact that I had no idea what I was looking for didn't daunt me in the least. Let's face it, the ideas we come up with at—what time was it?—three o'clock in the morning are very rarely the brightest and best, but that's not ever the way they seem at the time.

And Jack Bailey's tent was directly in my path.

The fireflies had vanished. Emma was probably asleep. Mark was hunched over his computer, Ned was off to bed, and there was nothing but common sense standing between me and that tent flap.

I took a deep breath, and went in.

Excerpt from the journal of George Mallory

Godalming, Surrey, 1921: Which was more momentous in my life, the birth last year of my son John, or the letter I received in January from the Alpine Club's Percy Farrar? "It looks as though Everest would really be tried this summer," he wrote. "Party would leave early April and get back in October. Any aspirations?"

Any aspirations? Delighted to finally have a son after two daughters, of course, but Everest? *The ultimate new frontier, the ultimate exploration.*

There's a bit of redemption in the whole venture, isn't there? A way, perhaps, to atone for the staggering losses, for all the boys who will never climb, never walk, never breathe again?

And of course it must be England, and not just England, but our own Alpine Club, that is to finally conquer the world's highest peak! It is to be a chance for us to show what we're made of, to show the world that we are not undone by the war, that we can still aspire to new heights.

Our leader is Charles Howard-Bury, who first secured the Dalai Lama's permission for us to travel through the Himalayas. Not much of a mountaineer, I'd have thought, but with his heart very much in tune to the necessity of exploration.

The troubling spot is he wants us to have no contact with the press. Ruth in particular is concerned about this problem—well, we're putting all our future into this expedition, are we not? From her point of view, it's rather the whole thing, that. It will allow me to support us through writings and lectures, which I cannot do if there is an embargo on my words! The Society chaps are having their way paid; I do not enjoy those resources, and must be down-to-earth about my prospects.

I've heard rumours that we wouldn't have secured the Dalai Lama's permission to enter the Everest region through Sikkim and Tibet had it not been for some behind-the-scenes arms deal, and that was a little off-putting, to say the least. An exchange that gets both parties what they want is the goal, but with the battlefield of the Somme still in my mind and my dreams, well, it doesn't do to be running about securing arms for others to annihilate each other.

It all got settled, not on the whole to my satisfaction, but I wasn't going to allow this opportunity to elude me.

217

Chapter Sixteen

The first thought that struck me was how tidy Jack was.

The inside of my tent looked as if a tornado—or, alternately, a kindergarten field trip—had been through it recently. Not so here; even in the limited light of my headlamp, the order was clear and possibly—I say this in the kindest possible way—a little OCD.

His camp bed—missing its sleeping bag, which presumably he'd taken with him—was orderly, pillows and blankets neatly folded. A couple of supersized colorful backpacks didn't have a lot of stuff trailing out of them, as mine did, and four or five oxygen tanks were neatly stowed.

He had a metal folding table with a camp chair in front of it, and a laptop computer, several books, a video camera, and a couple of stacks of paper on top.

I didn't have any illusions that the papers would hold anything interesting—that would be a little too retro for someone living of necessity in the digital age—but I was drawn to them anyway. I tried the laptop first, of course, but it was password-protected. So it was either the papers or rummage through dirty clothes from the backpacks, and I didn't allow that particular thought to linger. Still, there probably wouldn't be anything here.

I was wrong.

The top page on the pile was a Wikipedia printout. I've never really understood the point of printouts, not in these days of round-the-clock connectivity, and it's not as if Wikipedia were some obscure site one was likely to forget; but he'd printed it out for a reason and the headline jumped out at me in the yellow light.

Strychnine poisoning.

And the echo of Yvette's voice, close, low under the sound of the wind outside. "The symptoms are clear. There is nothing that can be confused with strychnine." And then: "It was an English guide ... with Supreme Summits."

Maybe it hadn't been Richard who'd been with Yevgeny when he died.

But why would Jack Bailey ever poison another climber? There was plenty of competition among groups on the mountain, but killing another team off one at a time seemed a bit extreme. And then there was the whole get-the-defector-down-Everest thing. He didn't have *time* to kill Yevgeny.

I breathed in, held the breath, let it out again. It was all about dates and times. Like the timing it took to figure out when and how to summit; like the time Mallory and Irvine left Camp Four; but this was a little more exact.

Had Jack made the printout before or after the Russian was killed? Was he researching strychnine as a means of murder, or looking into it after the fact?

It had to be after the fact. Aside from everything else, Jack was a consummate planner, and anyway no one would just happen to have some rat poison on them at Everest Base Camp on the off-chance they might want to commit a little murder along with summiting.

I moved my headlamp closer to the page, peering at the date. There it was, in the top left corner, smaller print than the rest of the page: he'd printed it today. Or, technically, yesterday. But at this point it was academic. Yvette had told Jack it was strychnine and that the last person to see the Russian alive was from Supreme Summits Expeditions. Either Mark or Richard.

So either Mark or Richard had killed Yevgeny, or else Yevgeny'd accidentally ingested poison meant for one of them.

And Myles's voice. *A lot of Russians on the mountain this year.*

I shivered and looked around the tent again, my light picking out the neatness, the order. It felt ... military. Had he served? Did it matter?

There wasn't anything else there to find. I wasn't even sure why I'd tried.

By the time I got to my tent the wind had picked up even more and I could feel the cold all the way through to my bones. I kicked off my boots and climbed into my sleeping bag with everything still on me, even the coat; I even pulled its hood up over my head for a little additional warmth.

Enough with the *if George Mallory can deal with the cold, so can I* mantra. I was never, ever going to complain about Boston winters again.

There was something besides the cold that was keeping me awake. It was as though some creature were out there, moving through Base Camp, searching, hunting… something more primal than even the wind and the snow, some living breathing blood-lusting creature. Nepal's yeti might be a friendly being, but this was something different, something wild and brutish and intent on harm. I could almost sense it right beside the opening to my tent, scrabbling at the corners, testing the fabric, sniffing for my scent, coming closer, its breath fetid in the thin air.

I turned over restlessly, still shivering, both from the cold and the apprehension. Something was wrong, something was *danger-ous*, and I still for the life of me couldn't sort out what it could be.

***

I awoke to the light and to a tropical stickiness: during the night my body temperature had risen, and I found I'd partially unzipped the sleeping bag and my coat along with it, and was still drenched in sweat. I crawled out of the bag and stumbled to my feet. I felt like I had one hell of a hangover, achieved without any consumption of alcohol, which felt ridiculously unfair; if it stayed around I was going to have to pay attention that it wasn't a start of altitude sickness.

Just to add a little fun to the party.

I stripped quickly and grabbed some hygienic body-wipes to do a quick number; I wasn't taking the time or the energy to see if the solar shower in the Supreme Summits facilities tent was up to par. A couple of base layers of clean clothes, a sweatshirt, and

I was lacing up my boots to head to the toilet when I heard Emma's voice. "Ahoy! Aren't you awake yet?"

I didn't bother answering, and she unzipped the tent entrance and came in. "Good," she said, seeing me. "You were dead to the world this morning."

"This morning?" I scowled at her. "What time is it?"

"Almost noon." She looked around. "You weren't here when I went to bed," she said.

I ignored the implied question. "You sound remarkably cheerful," I said. How on earth had I slept so long?

"They're fine." She was nodding. We seemed to have two separate conversations going on in tandem. "I've been on the radio; Mark's taking a break."

I nodded, too, automatically. Focus. "Where are they?"

"Camp Three," she said. "Resting, then they'll push on for Camp Four this afternoon. Sleep there and start the summit bid at midnight."

She hadn't lowered her voice; apparently we weren't keeping anything secret anymore. "Things good with Jack?" I asked tentatively.

She nodded. "Do you want some breakfast?"

"Yeah." I finished lacing the boots and rose less than gracefully to my feet, sliding into my parka and doing all the getting-ready, remember-when-you-were-little-and-in-snowsuits routine. Zip and button the parka; scarf wound round the neck; sun protection clip-ons, hand warmers, and gloves. "Good to go," I said.

Emma hadn't waited, was already on the move. I was suddenly famished and hoped she hadn't been talking euphemistically about food as an excuse to have a private conversation outdoors.

I caught up with her outside the dining tent, and wasted no time going inside—I had a feeling I'd need all the sustenance I could get. Besides, I'd been looking for Emma for nearly twenty-four hours; it could wait another one.

There were only a few people in the tent, a couple of westerners who did some sort of logistics for Supreme Summits; we hadn't been introduced. I snagged a tin cup of tea and a plate of dal bhat the Nepali servers seemed to always have on the hob and went to sit where Emma had already staked out a place.

I gulped some tea. "Anyway," I said, as though continuing a conversation, "don't tell me you couldn't find me last night; I spent the evening looking for *you*."

She nodded, unconcerned. She had somehow relaxed since I'd seen her last. Either something had happened to give her hope, or she'd scored some really nice mood elevators. "I was talking with Jack," she said.

I looked at her, taking in the posture, the almost dreamy look. "Wait," I said. "When you say talking with Jack... are you talking *romance*?"

"Possibly," she said.

"In the middle of everything?" The words were out before I could stop them.

It brought her back from the edge, though. She seemed to focus on my face. "One of the members might be coming down," she said. "He developed a cough during the climb. Weather's good so far, and looking good for tonight. Mark's pleased."

I'd been eating steadily and was starting to feel a little more human. And ready, perhaps, for some conversation about her once and possibly future dreamboat. "Jack," I said, as casually as I could, "has been researching strychnine poisoning."

That got me a fast, sharp look. Whatever she saw in my expression must have been reassuring, because she dropped her shoulders and took a deep breath. "I know," she said. "He's worried."

"Does it have to do with—the other thing?" Even with so few other people in the tent, I didn't feel like I should be saying Yuan Bo's name out loud.

"Everything has to do with everything," she said, which was either very Zen or way too much wishful thinking. "Are you done?"

"I am now." My brain had caught up with my body; I would happily skip the rest of my belated breakfast if it meant Emma finally opening up to me.

She was ready; she grabbed my bowl and cup before I could and took them over to the used-crockery table. I looked around for the tight silk gloves I put on under the bulky mittens, and fished in my pocket for them. My fingers closed around something small and hard, and I remembered: something Myles had given Ned to give to me.

I pulled it out slowly and looked at it: just paper folded around something hard. Maybe a piece of jewelry? Now I was back to the romance side of things.

Emma was standing next to me. "What's that?"

"I don't know." I left it in the palm of my left hand and unwrapped the paper with my right, oddly reluctant to do this in front of anyone. Just in case.

I needn't have bothered. There, sitting incongruously on my bright pink silk glove, was Emma's missing flash drive.

Excerpt from the journal of George Mallory

Himalayan Mountains, 1921: And so, nearly just like that, we were off.

The ship was called the Sardinia, bound for Calcutta, India, on the beginning of what I was sure would be the greatest adventure of my life. We docked in Calcutta on May tenth, and then onto a train bound for Darjeeling, with plenty to organize.

Still, I had high hopes as we set off. In Darjeeling there were Sherpa who'd come over to us from the Everest region of Nepal—closed to all westerners, of course—serving as cooks and porters for the expedition. On June nineteenth, at Rongbuk, we finally had our first glimpse of the mountain itself. In the back of my mind were a host of questions clamouring for answers, but the sight of it now banished every thought. We asked no questions and made no comments, but simply looked.

This was not a peak like the ones I'd experienced in the Alps. It had the most stupendous ridges and appalling precipices that I had ever seen, and I knew right away that all the talk of easy snow slopes was a myth.

We established our Base Camp and over the next days and weeks attempted to locate the best route up the mountain. That first day, I rose before dawn to watch the mountain unfold itself before us, and I was surprised to see it suffused with a faint blue light; but then I looked beyond, and there was the summit, white-hot and blazing in the morning sun.

By September our prospects were looking bleak, and I found myself missing Ruth more than I could bear. Then, on the twenty-second the weather improved, and we set out at last, making camp beneath a cliff below the North Col. But that night the wind picked up, screaming eerily and shaking the tents with such violence I feared they would tear away and be carried up into the air, with us perchance still inside.

And so it was the wind, finally, that kept us from attaining our goal. But I rested in the knowledge that no one had stayed as high as we had for as long as we had, and we learned invaluable lessons.

I'd been separated from my family for seven long months, and it was going to take a colossal effort to be able to part from them again.

Chapter Seventeen

"Where did you get that?" It came out as a hiss.

"It might not be yours." But I knew it was.

She hadn't taken her eyes off the drive. Neither of us wanted to touch it, as though it were a scorpion that could sting at any moment. "Did you take it, after all?" Emma asked.

"No." I couldn't even work up any indignation anymore. I was back to feeling scared; the creature from the night before was palpable now, snuffling around us. I looked at Emma. "What is going on here? Why would anyone borrow it?"

She was still staring at it. "I don't know," she said slowly. "Notes. Emails. Nothing."

"It's not nothing." I roused myself and closed my fingers around the drive. "Come on, let's get out of here. We have to find out."

She nodded. She was looking dazed, as though she'd just been in a crash, survived an earthquake. Not, I thought, the cheeriest of analogies.

Emma's laptop was in the observation tent, which—fortunately—was empty. "Don't sign on to the Wi-Fi," I warned her. I didn't know exactly how these things all worked, but being connected to the world while looking for a secret—a potentially lethal secret—didn't seem a good idea.

She nodded and opened it, and it belatedly dawned on me that the paper wrapped around the drive might have some clue. I handed her the drive and smoothed out the wrapping and saw an unfamiliar cursive.

Abbie, sorry I didn't get to see you. We're leaving earlier than I'd thought. I've tried to see Jack but he's been unavailable, and I don't know what else to do with it. I only gave it a quick look.... It fell out of the pocket of one of the Supreme Summits guys, don't know which one, he was sitting in on a talk

Yvette was giving yesterday. She didn't know who he was but he was wearing the gear. So maybe you can get it to Jack. See you on the flip side, Myles.

Emma had opened the drive on her screen and I edged closer to I could look at it with her. A few folders; a lot of Word documents and PDFs. "Here's stuff on Mallory—before I engaged you to do it, dear—and this is a bunch of notes on other characters. Chapter One. Oh, that one's my condo association. And—"

"What's that?" I asked, pointing at one of the folders labeled JB.

"Oh, Jack," said Emma, as though remembering. "Yeah… when we were first talking about Yuan Bo, he sent me this folder. Just to keep it safe. I haven't looked at it."

"Look at it now."

She shook her head. "I didn't exactly promise I wouldn't," she said uncertainly. "But there was that—assumption."

"Emma," I said urgently. "Listen. That ship has sailed. There had to be a reason he needed to keep this safe and not in his possession, and somebody *from Supreme Summits* knew enough about it to steal it. Two people are dead—no, two people have been murdered. Don't you think Jack might be in danger?" The truth was, if he were, there was absolutely nothing that we could do about it from Base Camp, though perhaps Mark might radio a warning to him.

If Mark wasn't the guy who'd stolen the drive in the first place. Or had it stolen. Or…

"Open the folder," I said to Emma.

She bit her lower lip and nodded, then clicked on the folder icon.

At the top of the list view was a document labeled TIMELINE. Emma opened it; and that's exactly what was there: timing from Kathmandu to Lukla and from Lukla to Base Camp. Timing for various forays up the mountain for acclimatization. Timing to be coordinated with the Tibetan party… "Who's Gyalzen Sherpa?" I asked.

"Yuan Bo's guide," she said. "He's related to—oh, no." She looked at me in horror.

"Ang Pemba Sherpa," I said. It seemed inevitable.

"His cousin," she said, and closed the file. "We'd better look at the texts."

And that was when the ground shifted.

***

Mark was talking urgently into his satellite phone when we got to the comms tent. "Where's it centered? Over."

He had it on speaker; another English voice answered, speech clipped and calm. "One hundred eighty-four kilometers east-northeast of Saga. Magnitude reading four point three. Over."

"Where's Saga?" I whispered to Emma, but she shook her head.

"Thanks," Mark said. "Supreme Summits, out."

I was feeling as shaky as the ground. "So that *was* an earthquake?" Possibly the silliest question I'd ever asked.

He glanced at me, and I was taken aback by the fatigue in his eyes, the puffiness around them, and remembered that even before all this he hadn't been eating, was worried about something.

"Yeah." He was scrolling through some weather site on his laptop, and we were probably bothering the hell out of him just by being there.

Emma had no such qualms. "Is it going to affect the climbers?" she asked. "Has it?"

He didn't look up. "Not yet. But could've been a foreshock. Megathrust events usually come in pairs."

"Wait," I said. "There's going to be another?" I'd read about the earthquake in 2015. It hadn't just shaken Kathmandu—literally—to its foundations; a resulting avalanche had wiped out a whole lot of Base Camp and killed a substantial number of people there.

Not "there"; *here.*

Mark was still focused on his weather maps. "What do you think? We're sitting on top of a collision zone between two tectonic plates," he said. "Stress builds up and produces earth-quakes." He glanced up, as though he could feel the panic emanating off me. "It probably won't, Abbie," he said, his voice gentle. "Now go away and let me work."

I turned to Emma. "Maybe we should tell him—"

She stopped me by grabbing my wrist and yanking it toward the door. "We're going," she said.

Outside, I confronted her. Honestly, that seemed to be the only thing we were really good at together, Emma and I: having arguments. "Something's going to happen up there," I said. "Something with Yuan Bo and Jack and Ang Pemba's cousin and—"

"Stop it," she said. She was hurrying away; I had to scramble to keep up with her. "We're to tell no one. Don't you understand that?"

"Don't you think maybe a natural disaster overrides all these other things?"

"It's not yet. We don't know," said Emma. She stopped so abruptly I ran into her. "Listen. We need to find out everything we can from those files Jack gave me. And maybe warn him, if that's what's necessary. And we don't even know whose side Mark is on."

It was the first time anyone had said it: that there were two sides at work here, maybe working against each other. I shivered.

"Let's read the texts," I said.

She nodded. "Let's read the texts."

And they were as damning as we'd feared.

From Jack to Ang Pemba Sherpa: *We're getting close to the wire now. What have you heard from Gyalzen?*

Ang Pemba replied a few minutes later: *Everything is ready. Officer from People's Police for climb is now Liu Gang. He say not difficult for distraction.*

Emma hadn't reacted to that; she knew already about whatever plan they had to take care of Yuan Bo's minder at the summit.

Jack followed up. *Then what's the problem?*

That got the reaction; Emma caught her breath. "What problem?" I whispered.

She shook her head. "I don't know. He didn't tell me. He wouldn't tell me."

Ang Pemba: *You must know it is someone in the company doing it. You know why I watch so closely. Person in Supreme Summits Expeditions, in your company. Two shipments always in same time as expeditions.*

Seconds later, Jack came back. *In Nepal? You're sure?*

Ang Pemba: *I do not know for sure. But getting to Kathmandu eventually. You cancel Nuptse trip and we see.*

You could feel Jack's frustration coming off the screen. *If it's one of our people I need to know now. We're going up Everest in another two weeks. I trust these blokes with my life. If one of them's been doing something illegal that betrays everything we're supposed to stand for I need to know for sure.*

Ang Pemba: *It is one of them.* No room for doubt there.

"What are they talking about?" I asked. "What's illegal?"

She was staring at me. "Oh. My. God."

"What? What, Emma?"

She took a breath as though starved for oxygen. "It's about drugs."

"What?" I felt like everyone else was a couple of moves ahead of me on the chessboard. Or maybe playing a different game altogether. "What're you talking about?"

She nodded. "Listen. It's clear Jack doesn't know whom to trust, right? He's going up the mountain for the first time in forever."

"Because of Yuan Bo."

"Because he doesn't know if he can trust either Richard or Mark, and this way he can keep one off the mountain and the other under his eyes."

I stared at her. Mark had been acting strangely; Richard had been in the tent when another climber was poisoned. It could easily be either of them. *I trust these blokes with my life.* But—

"Why drugs? What makes you think it's about drugs?"

"Because it's the Silk Road," Emma said. "Don't look like that. Remember? We all talked about it, back—oh, I don't remember where. On the trek up. Fentanyl processed in China and brought over the mountains. And Supreme Summits sending people up every climbable mountain in the Himalayas." She took another deep breath. "Someone who works for Jack," she said, and there was real sorrow in her voice.

"And Ang Pemba Sherpa found out," I said slowly. "And he was the worst guy to figure it out, because of his son. He must *hate* drug runners. And they knew he knew. So he gets lured to Lukla and killed."

"And Yevgeny got killed, too—he must have been part of it," she said, "and maybe he was going to give them up, or go off on his own, or something… there've been more Russians climbing these past two seasons than ever before. So that fits in—"

I cut her off. "Unless the strychnine was meant for Richard. He's one of the guys under suspicion, after all. Maybe he was taking too much of the pie and the Russians wanted to get rid of him."

"It's not just Yuan Bo and the camera they're grabbing up there," Emma said, following her own train of thought. "And if it's Richard, and Jack tries to stop him, or confronts him…"

"Wait," I said. "Let's not go too far down the rabbit hole. Think about it: Jack knows all this already. It's only new to us. He's had these texts for weeks. He *participated* in them. So what's he planning?"

"And why did he choose Richard?" she added. "Because he knew he'd be safe up there with him?"

We stared at each other, horrified. "What do we do about it now?" I asked. "They're leaving the high camp for the summit, tonight. I mean—really soon."

"If it's Mark, he could be in touch with the Chinese at the same time that he's guiding Jack," she said.

We needed to haul ourselves back from the edge, I thought. "Jack knows the mountain," I said. "Listen, Emma, we're getting too wild here. Deep breath. You know Jack; you have to trust him.

He knows the mountain, he knows the players, he knows the situation. There's nothing we can do here but wait." *And worry*, I thought.

She stood up. "I'm going back to the comms tent," she said. "I want to talk to Jack."

"It won't help—" I started. But then I saw her face and remembered. Whatever had happened between her and Jack, this had become even more personal for Emma now. Yuan Bo, the camera, her book... and now a revived emotional attachment of some kind.

"Okay," I said.

It wasn't until after she'd left and I was replaying our conversation in my head that I realized Emma hadn't been present when I'd had the conversation with Myles about drugs.

How had she known?

Jeannette de Beauvoir

Excerpt from the journal of George Mallory

Himalaya Mountains, 1922: As it happened, I didn't have much choice. As soon as I debarked at Marseille, plans were underway for a new attempt on Everest. There wasn't much time to talk it over or even think about it; since I'd left my teaching job, the welfare of our family depended on my mountaineering.

I very clearly saw the mountain as unfinished business. I was the one who'd found the route to the top; I was dashed if I would stand idly by and watch some other climbers get my prize!

So with a February departure date set, I had barely three months to complete thirty lectures, write my chapters—and spend time with my dear Ruth and our children. And, meanwhile, of course, the new expedition was taking shape.

We were all filled with such hope!

This time we were taking woolen waistcoats, Jaeger pants, tight-woven windproof cotton smocks, and a range of footwear that included ski boots and knee-length felt boots. And, this time, we brought along those odd heavy metal canisters with compressed oxygen. We'd already found out what happens to the body and mind at high altitudes, and Bruce was emphatic that we would climb faster and more safely with these strapped to our backs.

We arrived in Bombay and travelled by train to Darjeeling where everyone met up, including the Nepalese Sherpa. I initially viewed Tibet as an old acquaintance, but we were soon overtaken by a blizzard and when I wrote to Ruth, despite wearing every piece of clothing I'd brought along, my fingers were so cold I could scarcely hold the pen.

But the storm moved off and we moved on, and finally came that magical moment, our first glimpse of the mountain itself. Base Camp to Camp Three was more technical than we'd expected, and mid-May saw me and Somervell alone up there waiting for the porters to arrive, reading to each other from Shakespeare, discussing political and social issues, and generally passing the time.

Norton and Morshead joined us, and with the porters we ferried supplies up to the North Col. We set out for the summit later than I'd wanted, and were met by another horrifying wind from Tibet. We soldiered on, but we'd abandoned our crampons and we started to freeze up. We made camp at

25,000 feet and had the most excruciating night, during which we all nursed our frostbite, and six more inches of snow engulfed our tents. We set out but were rebuffed and it was clear to me that we'd still be climbing by nightfall. Descending, we had a near catastrophe when the three others lost their footing and began to fall; I was able to put in my ice axe and belay them, but it was a near miss.

We stumbled into Base Camp and were dispirited indeed. We had early on lost our provisions and I was convinced the lack of hydration had proved just as deadly as the lack of oxygen at altitude.

I thought it was safe to assume, as I wrote to Ruth, that the expedition was over. We'd gone higher than anyone before us. Five of the party had frostbite and we all suffered with exhaustion, and it would have made sense for us all to live to fight another day. But there was pressure from home, and so Bruce and Finch decided on another attempt, this time using the oxygen canisters. And perhaps we were all a little mad. Some clearly could not go on, and I had frostbite, but surely the game was worth a finger!

Thus it was that on June seventh, with the weather finally fine, we prepared to depart for the North Col—myself in charge, and Somervell and Crawford, with fourteen Sherpa porters, the whole of us on four separate ropes.

I had of course considered the risk of avalanche, but we'd run some tests and believed we were quite safe.

We were, of course, quite wrong.

I cannot write about the avalanche. Not now, perhaps not ever. It is powerful and tremendously fast, and the worst of it was that seven of the Sherpa were killed. I may never forgive myself for those lives. I experienced grief and guilt over their loss, and yet when I went back over the events in my mind, I do not see what else I could have done. We did not know there could be variations in the snowpack.

We did not know... so much.

Chapter Eighteen

It started snowing shortly after sunset.

No one seemed particularly perturbed; there were enough other things to be perturbed about, and I just zipped up my interior hoodie so it was covering my nose and made my way to the dining tent.

It was oddly busy, as though others hadn't wanted to be alone on this night. Mark came in and drank some tea and left; he was clearly getting cranky and fed up with Emma, who was fluttering around him like a demented butterfly.

She spotted me across the tent and hurried over. "News from the camp," she said. Her eyes were bright, her cheeks flushed; if I didn't know better, I'd have said she was high. "Your friend stole a march on us."

"What does that even mean?"

"Top Ascent summited," she said. "They're nearly down to Camp Four by now."

"Everyone?" I asked, and she smiled. "The New Zealander was with them," she said. "He'll be at Base Camp sometime tomorrow. You can celebrate then."

"We can all celebrate then, maybe," I said cautiously.

"Maybe," she said, patted my shoulder, and left.

So Myles had done it. I wondered what happened now; what do you do for an encore, when you've summited the highest mountain in the world? And a small voice at the back of my mind reminded me, *You don't call it a summit if you don't return.*

But of course he was going to return. Tomorrow.

I didn't know most of the people in the tent, though I recognized them by sight: technicians, a guy whose job seemed to be documenting everything on video, a woman I thought I'd heard was a scientist. As usual, the Sherpa were on their own; I hadn't once seen them mix with the members or indeed any of the westerners outside of meetings and required interactions.

I was a little surprised when someone sat down with a grunt beside me. "Anish! You're still here!"

The bloom was a little off the rose of his good humor, but he made a valiant effort. "Of course, Miss Abigail! I could not return to the city without seeing the brave peoples returning and celebrating their achievements!"

As far as I'd been able to tell, there wasn't a lot of partying done when they came down after their summit bids—exhaustion and injury and sometimes grief took that off the table—but I was willing to be pulled into his cheery worldview. "So you think Supreme Summits will make it to the top?"

He looked shocked. "But of course, Miss Abigail! It is what we do!"

"So it is," I said and raised my tin teacup to hide my smile.

"I have forgotten sometimes," he said, his eyes roving the scene inside the tent, "how—what do you say, Miss Abigail? Primitive?—the mountain can feel."

"You look like you're well outfitted for it, anyway," I said. He was still in his red Santa suit. And this tent was every bit as well-appointed as some of the teahouses we'd stayed at during the trek, but whatever. Perhaps Anish liked his luxuries.

He pulled his attention back to me. "But Miss Emma is not with you! Is she well? I will never forgive myself if esteemed ladies regret their experiences!"

I laughed. "She's fine, Anish. It's late, hadn't you noticed?" I made a show of stretching. "In fact, I'm heading back to my tent myself now. Time to try and sleep."

He was on his feet at once. "Then I shall escort you, Miss Abigail! And the staff will come and remove the snow from your tent! It is all part of the service we offer at Supreme Summits Expeditions!"

In spite of my anxiety spiking about the sheer number of things that could be going wrong up on the mountain, I had to smile. Anish was an excellent antidote to worry. And I actually wouldn't mind the escort. Now that there was some sense that others—notably Mark—might be involved in all sorts of devious actions, I wasn't sure that I really wanted to be wandering around Base Camp alone after dark. "Thanks, Anish," I said. "It's kind of you."

The wind and snow together hit us as we exited the tent, spicules of snow as sharp as razors in my face, the wind making me stagger back. If it was anything like this up at Camp Four, they were going to have their work cut out for them to make any progress at all.

It wasn't really clear who was escorting whom. Anish had taken my elbow as though I were a grandmother, but he was the one who slipped a couple of times and grabbed me for balance. I dropped my flashlight once and spent a moment of panic finding it and making sure it still worked. We more or less stumbled along together, snow swirling around us—not gentle snowflakes, but heavy, painful needles—until we got to my tent. I'd left a light on, low, inside; Emma's was still dark. She was either still over in the comms tent with Mark or had decided to try and sleep.

I turned to Anish. "Will you be all right getting back?" Belatedly, I didn't know where in our "neighborhood" he was staying, and he hadn't seemed any too steady to me. The blind leading the blind, it felt more like.

Or, as Shakespeare would have it, the madman leading the blind. I didn't know which of us was which.

He was unconcerned. "But of course, Miss Abigail! Do not worry for me! I will always brave all the elements for the esteemed ladies!"

"Be careful, then," I said. I was fumbling with my heavy-duty mittens, my heavy-duty flashlight, and the heavy-duty zipper on my doorway. I was never, ever going to complain about anything being awkward during Boston winters again.

And I wasn't going to stand here freezing to death while exchanging niceties with Our Man in Kathmandu.

I didn't even watch him go. I was literally shaking by the time I got inside and was zipping up the door flap against the snow and wind. This was quite the worst I'd experienced here yet, and I fervently hoped it would prove to be the last.

And hoped like hell it was better up above Camp Four.

**

I can't say what it was that woke me; I was pretty sure I hadn't been sleeping at all, between the cold and the worry. I could vaguely remember a dream starting up and dissipating, something else reforming and disappearing, the shadowy liminal space where I seemed to spend a lot of my time trying to sleep at altitude.

But I know I was already awake and out of my sleeping bag when it happened.

I'd just checked my watch: four-thirty. Supreme Summits could be reaching the top right now. Emma would know; for all I knew, she was watching their progress with a stopwatch in hand. But something had disturbed me.

It was too late to try and get any more sleep; I went through the tiresome rituals I'd learned as I made my transformation into my version of the Michelin Man: zip into everything warm, knit hat down around my ears, parka and gloves and bigger insulated mittens. I picked up my flashlight and fought the wind to open my tent flap.

There were people moving around, and the sky was turning a steely gray; sunrise wasn't far off. I tossed the flashlight back inside and secured the tent, without really having anywhere to go or any reason to go there. Other than my nerves. And a strange sense of foreboding.

Emma had been in with the radio all night, I was sure. She couldn't know anything, yet. She hadn't come to wake me, to say they'd made it up, to say Yuan Bo was safe, to say the camera was recovered.

And there was a joker in the pack now, too: whoever was moving fentanyl down the mountain was up there. And I couldn't imagine what might happen if anything—or anyone—got in the way. That joker could rip through the pack at any moment.

Worrying wasn't going to do anything for anyone; and Myles might even be on his way down to Base Camp, now that it was nearly light enough. Maybe things had worked out. Maybe there was going to be a happy ending here.

I shivered and headed toward the dining tent. What I needed was hot strong tea and news; the comms tent was next door, I could bring some tea to Emma and Mark and find out what was going on.

I passed by the stone stupa, stones piled high and prayer flags fluttering around. It hadn't been that long ago when climbers had been clustered around it, listening for hours to the prayers, tossing rice and flour, doing puja, asking the goddess for both permission and forgiveness. The westerners all tolerated the interruption to their preparations; the Sherpa all reiterated how sorry they were to be once again treading on the holy mountain. It was easy to think that all the things that were going wrong, that could go wrong, were the result of her displeasure. She'd only allow a certain number to pass, and she'd grab whomever she could. The stupa was the center of life at Base Camp and I felt its magnetism and—

It sounded like someone was moving boulders around somewhere nearby; absurdly, that was all I could think of. Some of the neighborhoods did that, to make room for space they needed.

And then the earth moved under my feet, again. The goddess herself, flexing, discontent, ready to make herself known...

Yesterday it had happened, and it was an earthquake, perfectly prosaic, no goddess involvement. But despite my immediate panic at the word, that was okay, somehow, too: we were, after all, in a tent city; what's going to happen? There were no tall buildings here. Nothing to come crashing down. Tents don't fall down during an earthquake.

It never occurred to me that the *mountains* were going to fall down.

241

Emma and Anish were standing in the doorway of the dining tent and were looking outside; I could see Anish pointing to something behind me. I turned to look and the rising sun was so beautiful that it was all I could absorb in the moment, it was the most perfect dawn ever, and then I looked across toward Mount Pumori and it looked like the top of the mountain was exploding.

I heard Emma's voice. "It's okay. It's far away. We're not that close. It's okay," but suddenly it wasn't, it wasn't even close to being okay. I think I said something, but I don't remember what it was, and something big was coming at us, and I turned and screamed, "Run!"

But they were already running, Emma and Anish clinging to each other in some insane way, and then I tripped and fell and kept going, crawling, wanting to head toward the tents and not toward the stupa because anything that big was going to dislodge those boulders like they were some kid's playthings.

It didn't matter. I heard Emma cry out and then it hit us.

It was a cloud of snow and rocks and wind, and it was overpowering. *So this is how I die. I've always wondered, and now I know.* It lasted, I'm told, only a few seconds, but it felt like forever, I was fighting to stand up, fighting to breathe. It was hard and wet and cold and I was panicking, not getting enough sir into my lungs, stumbling and falling and…

I'd seen videos on YouTube about mountain rescues and there was some strange part of my brain that went there. *It'll be all right. They'll send a dog to find us. Those mountain rescue dogs. I just need to find a pocket of air, and the dogs will find me.*

The last part, about the air pockets, was the only rational bit I could grab out of those racing thoughts, and I put both my hands over my face to try to create an air pocket, on my knees but trying to stay upright. *It's no use. It's going to bury you. There's no time for any dogs. I wish I didn't have to die so I could tell Phillip what a harebrained idea this trip was. Maybe it'll just knock me out. That would be good. Maybe I won't realize when I die.*

It was an enormously strange mix of thoughts going through my head, and I didn't actually know how long the snow pounded the camp around us. I just remember it was probably less than a minute, but at a certain point I found myself thinking, *Okay, I'm still conscious. I'm awake, I'm not dead.* Some snow started to clear in front of me and then, belatedly, I realized I wasn't buried.

To test that theory, I put my hand in front of my face, and I felt a surge of excitement: I could see the hand! Things cleared; there's an expression about dust settling; what I saw was snow settling.

At first I couldn't see anybody else, and for a single insane frightening moment I thought I was alone, that everyone in Base Camp had been killed, that I was on some strange *Twilight Zone* episode. The cloud of snow coming off Mount Pumori had felt— apocalyptic, somehow. I couldn't imagine how we'd survived it, how anyone had survived it. Maybe the whole world was covered in snow.

I was pretty shocked that I wasn't buried. I was pretty shocked that I was okay.

The avalanche had hit a gully below the camp, so Base Camp wasn't buried, but hurricane-force winds ricocheted up the slope, hurling snow and rocks with deadly intensity.

In the next few hours, I learned, some people had indeed gotten very hurt from rocks and boulders the wind blast had picked up and hurled around. I'd been shielded from the worst of it.

I was still on my knees beside the stupa, which actually hadn't moved and in fact had protected me from much of the blast. I realized I was alive and the fear I hadn't had time to feel came screaming back inside me and I started shouting for Emma.

Excerpt from the journal of George Mallory

America, 1923: I think that, left to my own devices, I might never have returned to Everest.

The avalanche disaster had shaken me to my core, and the lost lives weighed heavily on my conscience. In September, safely home again, I settled back into family life, and it gave me great relief from the pain and guilt I'd been feeling. Ruth really is the most marvellous girl always, but especially in that time of doubt and sorrow.

By winter I was back on the lecture circuit. Even though catastrophe had visited us, the public, it seemed, couldn't get enough of tales from the snows, and the lecture halls were packed.

But Everest was still unconquered, and I was still keen to be the man to do it.

So it was that in January I sailed for New York. I was in many places the man of the hour, despite my own crushing feelings about how the last expedition had ended; I kept those well to myself whilst regaling audiences with tales of adventure and pictures of hidden Himalayan wonders.

My name was finally in The New York Times, but only because an answer I gave caught a reporter's fancy. Why climb Everest, he'd asked, scarcely interested in the answer, and so I was equally short with him. "Because it's there," I said, dismissively, before turning to another question.

But as I pondered the question on my journey back home, I realised that my hasty answer in fact rang with truth. Everest was the highest mountain in the world, and no man had reached its summit. Its very existence was a challenge. I suppose we go to Everest because we can't help it. We go because we are mountaineers.

And yet all the while there was something deeper, a heartbeat beneath the heartbeat, a longing in the soul to be part of the wild places, and the inner journey that every man must navigate if he wishes to attain the as-yet-unattained. For me to have said, "because it is there" was to assert all of those things, and even to turn the question back toward the questioner. Why do we do anything? Because something has presented itself to us, something worthwhile, perhaps even something marvellous, and we cannot but respond.

Chapter Nineteen

After that, the day turned absurdly, unabashedly beautiful.

The sun had risen in a sky so blue and brilliant it could have been a Maxfield Parrish evening scene, dotted with impossibly white and fluffy clouds. A perfect day on the mountain, in fact. It was as though the Earth had said, "Look, that wasn't so bad, we're all okay now, nothing to get worried about." Even the wind had died down, and as I pawed through my pockets for my sunglare clip-ons I realized that I was actually, impossibly, overheating.

Everything around me seemed to be moving in slow motion. There were a lot of voices, but they felt muffled, as though I'd somehow damaged my eardrums; and people were moving around but they looked odd to me, as though I were seeing them from a distance, or on a piece of old film. It took me a few moments—minutes, hours, I couldn't tell—for my brain to sort it out and see what was happening.

We'd gotten off lightly, that much was immediately clear; this was nothing like the destruction I'd seen on YouTube in the aftermath of the 2015 avalanche.

Around me people had staggered to their feet, looking around them, most of them as dazed as I felt. A couple of flattened tents already had small groups digging furiously to liberate anyone who'd been inside.

I was just trying to orient myself—for a few seconds I wasn't sure what direction was up, never mind any of the cardinal points. It had all happened so fast; that was what made it feel so impossible. It had been a minute. It had felt like a lifetime.

Finally I grasped the stupa and hauled myself to my feet. A couple of prayer flags had come loose and one flapped into my face; I pulled it off and cast it aside. Another insult to the goddess, no doubt. Everything even looked reasonably normal; there was more snow cover than there'd been before, and a lot of tents looked like they'd collapsed, but then it seemed as if the entire camp took a gigantic breath and flicked back to life.

I didn't have to look for anything to do; almost immediately a guy in a snowsuit and goggles grabbed my elbow. "Help me here," he said in heavily accented English, and I saw he was pulling at a boot protruding from the snow—a person. I started digging.

It was almost with a jolt of surprise that I remembered what the focus of my fear had been since arriving at Base Camp: the teams up on the mountain. It hadn't occurred to me there could be danger in this modern made-to-order city.

We were unutterably fortunate that the avalanche wasn't as bad as the earlier one; most of the camp was still standing, and later I'd learn that there had been only two fatalities, though a lot of people got hurt. At the time, though, I just found myself staggering from one task to another. I did whatever I could: digging tents out, bringing tea to shivering survivors, grabbing a shovel or whatever was to hand to help. It puts you into a zone, that kind of work: you don't think about anything other than what you're doing. There are no philosophers at avalanche sites.

When I finally realized that I was completely exhausted—no amount of personal training in a Boston gym will prepare you for digging out after an avalanche—I went looking for the Supreme Summits comms tent. It was where I'd last seen Emma, standing there with Anish. I hadn't gone back to find her, because too many people had been shouting at me, needing help, and I didn't know how to say no. Now I wondered if I'd made the right decision; maybe I should have gone to her first. I'd caught sight of her once or twice in the mêlée; I knew she was alive. But Mark? I didn't realize how scared I'd been, how I was unconsciously holding my breath, until I saw the tent, bright yellow and reassuring in the slanting morning sunlight, all in one piece.

It seemed the goddess was looking out for at least some of us.

Footing was treacherous: Base Camp was already strewn with rocks, from pebbles to boulders, and now they were all coated with snow so their shapes and sizes were camouflaged. I went down two more times before I made it to the tent. The door flap was pinned open and I tried to stamp some of the snow off my boots in the doorway. I started talking before I could even take off my dark clip-ons and see who was there. "I'm so glad you're all right," I said, shoving them in a pocket and brushing my hood back off my head.

Mark was hunched over the table with the big computer screen and the clutter of electronic gadgets I'd seen before. The computer screen was black—probably EverestLink had gone off—and he was holding his walkie-talkie in one hand while plotting something on a map. Emma wasn't there.

"Hold on," he said to me, pressed a button on his receiver, and said, "I still can't reach him. Still rotating through the frequencies. Over."

There was a burst of static, and then Jack's voice filled the tent, all broad vowels and swagger. "Mad bastard. All right." There was another bit of buzzing on the line and his voice came back in. "...approaching Camp One, but there's been damage. We're cracking on. Over."

Mark depressed his button. "Yeah, we heard," he said. "I'll let you know if anything changes. Base Camp out."

He pushed his chair back and turned to me. He was a mess: hair standing on end, eyes bloodshot. I probably looked a good deal worse. "What's going on?" I asked.

"Richard," he said. "MIA."

"Damn." I sank onto the camp chair across from him. "Just him, or...?"

He nodded, passed a hand over his face. "Thing is, it didn't affect the high camps," he said. "Avalanche was low: icefall, Base Camp, yeah, some damage at Camp One. But our blokes were above it."

I didn't waste my time—or his—asking how he knew all that. "Did the snow wipe out the GPS?" I asked instead. "You've been tracking them since they left."

He nodded. "Iridium works fine, there's a satellite every hour even when there's blockage. But it only sees you if you let it.

Device has to be turned on," he said. "They're off. And the avalanche transponders ain't so hot either."

"What do you mean, they're off?" I asked. "You mean—they turned them off?"

"They didn't self-destruct," he said. "*Someone* turned 'em off."

We stared at each other for a long moment. It took every bit of self-restraint I had to ask if Jack had added anybody to his team. Mark cleared his throat. "Erm, Emma says you know Myles? Member from Top Ascent?"

I nodded. "Why?"

A shadow seemed to pass over his face, and I knew it then. "They was in the icefall," he said. "Coming down through it."

"Did—how do you know?"

He shrugged. "Avalanche. All the outfits; we're all checking on each other."

There was something twisting in my stomach. "Is Myles—are they all right?" But I already knew the answer.

"Don't know, Abbie. I won't lie to you: bad place to be. You don't need an avalanche."

I nodded, feeling numb. Of course you didn't need an external avalanche, the Khumbu Icefall was very good at creating them itself, an avalanche killed sixteen sherpa guides there one year. It was a looming unavoidable presence. I'd looked up at it every day I'd been in Base Camp and heard people talking about it—more than even about summiting. Three miles of constantly moving ice, moving crevasses, holes, cliffs. Three miles of lashed-together ladders that could suddenly not fit as designed, and woe to the person on them. Icefall doctor *extraordinaire* Ang Pemba's murder, terrible as it seemed, probably had just precipitated the inevitable—one way or the other, that mountain was going to get him.

And now, maybe, it had gotten Myles.

"Helicopters can reach the icefall," I said now, a little desperately, to Mark. "The new regs say they can use helicopters for rescue above Base Camp, right? They can tell if they're okay?" I stopped speaking then, his eyes both tired and sympathetic, too intense in their kindness; Mark had lost people to this mountain.

People he had cared about, people he had known for years, who'd held his life in their hands, perhaps, as he'd sometimes held theirs; and here I was, the rich white westerner, feeling sorry for herself because a man she'd known and flirted with a few weeks could have joined the mysterious company of the dead on the mountain. I drew in a shaky breath. "I'm sorry," I said. "Of course not."

"There'll be search parties," he said. "The Sherpa are already organizing it; they sent people into the icefall a couple hours ago." Of course, for every Western climber in Myles's expedition, there would be at least one and possibly two climbing sherpa guides as well. Far more Sherpa are lost to avalanches on the mountain than are their wealthy clients.

Their loss would be more profound than anything I could even imagine.

"Okay," I said, as much to my own thoughts as I was saying it to Mark. There would be time to grieve, once I knew for sure. That time was not now. "Okay." My voice sounded shaky, even to myself. "And Jack—Jack's okay?"

He nodded, his eyes drifting back to the table. "He's coming down pretty fast. They're running low on O's, and with everything else, faster is better." He hesitated. "Still have to make it through the icefall, though."

Sounded like a lot of people in the Khumbu Icefall, and with it even more unstable than usual. "It's the crevasses, isn't it?" I asked, a little uncertainly. "They can—close up again."

"Can do." He'd already dismissed me: he'd given me the news he thought I needed about Top Ascent and had better things to do. I sat for a moment, staring a little sightlessly at the blank empty screen of his computer. Crevasses hold bodies, I'd read, trapped them in the moving glacier, closing up as though they'd never opened. It was a bad place for a body.

It was an even worse place for a soon-to-be-body.

I stood up, then, suddenly not wanting to be in the tent. I didn't want to think about Myles. Jack was far from out of danger, whether or not he had Yuan Bo with him. The man had looked up strychnine; chances were, whoever had administered it knew that, too. And how many natural disasters had provided convenient backdrops for scores to be settled, tracks to be covered, murders to be done? "I'll leave you with it, then," I said to Mark, a little helplessly, and he didn't even bother to respond.

I'll never forget that day, the absolute aching beauty of it, all brilliant blues and blinding whites, the air sharp and cold, the sun getting higher and hotter. and the snow, snow everywhere, on the peaks and in the camp. The camp itself filled with people, rescue workers coming in, helicopters buzzing overhead, all the dining tents thrown open to serve anyone.

I'd glimpsed Emma a couple of times in the immediate aftermath of the avalanche, but now I went looking for her in earnest, checking out any smallish figures in yellow. Not in any of the Supreme Summits tents.

I finally tracked her down at the Base Camp ER—*why*? "I couldn't find you," I said, a little breathlessly, probably sounding like I was accusing her of something.

She didn't spare me a glance. "I volunteered with an NGO in Africa," she said, calmly, not looking up from the bandage she was winding around a climber's wrist.

"I didn't know."

"Of course you didn't." She fastened the Velcro and nodded to the climber. "You're all set."

I sat down in his place once he'd left. Emma was putting tape and plaster methodically back into a satchel beside her. "Is that where you met Jack?" It was a bit of a wild guess, but not entirely.

She looked up briefly, nodded, and went back to what she was doing. "Funny how the skills come back when you need them," she said.

"I wondered about your past," I confessed. We might be in the middle of a disaster, but I wasn't passing up an opportunity to solve this one riddle, at least for myself. "I mean, you and Jack. How a novelist would even ever meet someone who ran a mountaineering outfit."

"Oh, we novelists get around," she said.

"Anish told me you used to live in Australia, and you'd met Jack there."

She gave me a tired smile. "Anish needs to know everything," she said. "He's like artificial intelligence: if he doesn't know it, he'll make it up." But she hadn't denied it.

"Was it somewhere you'd learned to administer first aid?"

She was staring at me, but I didn't think she was focused; it was as though in her head she was somewhere else altogether. Finally she took a deep breath, clasping her hands in her lap, and nodded; apparently she'd decided to take pity on me. Or had nothing better to do at the moment.

"When I first started doing well, really well, financially I mean," she said, "I felt—like I'd done what I'd always wanted to do, and what was next? And not long after that, my husband died, and that just solidified my sense of wanting something more—transcendent, I guess you'd say—out of life. So I volunteered with an NGO. They trained me and sent me to the Democratic Republic of the Congo."

I didn't have anything to say to that. I doubted very much I could even locate the Democratic Republic of the Congo on a map.

A map with countries' names labeled.

"It was terrible," Emma said. "I mean—everything. The country's been in crisis for decades. It's one of the most violent places in the world, with security deteriorating all the time, and so—so many people displaced, living in camps, living by the side of the road."

Now she was watching the activity in the tent. I kept watching her.

"That spring, there were terrible rains—more than usual during the season—and all these mudslides started. Everywhere, really, but the worst were on Mount Karisimbi, up on the border with Rwanda. Three of us were sent up there to help, not that we could do much at all. Fifty people died." She took a deep breath. "Jack was there, doing rescue work. And when you're thrown together like that, working eighteen hours a day under terrible

circumstances, literally life and death situations all around you…"
Her voice trailed off.

I could see it. Working together in a nightmare situation, with a common goal, and knowing you could die at any moment. The intensity of the connections you'd make in that situation would be profound; the immediacy of death could provide an erotic charge to things. I was soberly impressed; my volunteer work consisted mostly of writing checks for organizations like the one Emma was talking about. "Did you see each other after?" I asked.

"We tried," she said. "He came to Boston for a summer; I was in Sydney for a month. But… it's hard to keep Jack off a mountain." Her voice was rueful.

"Have you heard from him today?" I figured she'd told me as much as she was going to, and anyway there were more pressing things to talk about.

She nodded, and the faraway look left her eyes. "Oh, yes. They're getting evacuated."

"Really?" Mark hadn't told me that. "From where?"

"Just above the Icefall. There are rescuers there, it's not a good time to move through it."

I took a deep breath. "And Yuan Bo?"

She nodded. "I think so. Jack couldn't say over the radio. But he said they'd picked up a couple of climbers on their way down. I think that must've been him, and maybe his climbing sherpa too."

Now that things seemed to be settling down in terms of the immediate emergency, it was a relief to talk about why we were really there. "I hope so! Oh, Emma, do you think—"

I was cut off by a medic—I assumed that was what he was, he had a red cross on his helmet, he was a westerner I didn't recognize. "Can you come help?" he asked Emma. "Chap's got his leg under a rock. We've got him out but need some help relocating it. All hands on deck, that sort of thing."

"Of course." She stood up, then glanced at me. "Can you help, Abbie?"

"I can try." I felt decidedly queasy about manipulating some-one's broken limb, but all hands on deck...

"Not with him." She already had her mind elsewhere. "Can you go to my tent and grab my vanity bag? I have some Percocet in there."

"Oh. Yeah, sure." No wonder she hadn't been in as much pain as I'd been on the trek.

"Just bring it back here," she said. "Thanks."

"Of course." I set off across camp. Things seemed to be set-tling down some, fewer people moving fast, more people just set-tling in. Helicopters still coming in, though, and I wondered which one Jack would be on. And whether Yuan Bo would be with him.

It wasn't until I was in Emma's tent and rooting around in her backpack searching for the vanity bag that I realized someone had come in between me and the entrance. And then it was too late.

I turned around, bag in hand, and found myself looking into the lethal end of a gun.

Jeannette de Beauvoir

Excerpt from the journal of George Mallory

Mount Everest, 1923: So much planning was engaged in, this time around.

Everyone on the team was fit and prepared, and we allowed time for our bodies and those of our support porters to adjust to the thinner air.

Including the terrible weather. In Camp Three the storm intensified; by morning there were two inches of snow inside my tent, while outside the spindrift was gusting into miniature whirlwinds. The porters had already suffered injuries from falls and frostbite and several chaps were snow-blind, and more than fifty of them deserted us after the first day.

Young Irvine had the winning spirit—he'd been wonderfully hard-working and brilliantly skillful about the oxygen. I'd been concerned about his lack of experience in the mountains but concluded he would make an ideal companion and with as stout a heart as anyone could wish to find.

I wasn't forgetting meanwhile that there was the old monsoon to be reckoned with, and a hundred possible slips between the Base Camp and the summit, but I felt strong for the battle even though I knew every ounce of strength would be wanted.

The expedition made its new start as planned. Norton, Somervell, and I arrived at Camp Three and the next day headed up the frozen 1000-foot slope to the North Col. I led the way up a series of easy-angled convex snowfields to a wall of nearly vertical ice crowned with a chimney, which took a careful, neat climbing technique. Above the chimney we traversed the upper section of the snow basin which had avalanched in 1922 and arrived at the familiar shelf below the crest of the col.

Somervell was forced to turn back through altitude sickness, but Odell and the Sherpa Lhakpa followed us up, helping to make the route safe for the porters by driving in stakes and installing fixed ropes on the most difficult sections. We pitched a tent and dumped some supplies and then, after a brief reconnaissance of the route above, set off back to Camp Three. I had an alarming moment when I fell ten feet into a crevasse, leaving me wedged in place by my ice axe above a very unpleasant black hole, and no one heard me shouting for help, but I did manage to hack my way out.

And then the blizzards returned, and the temperature plunged to a new low; there was a further setback when four porters were marooned overnight on the North Col, and together with Norton and Somervell I had to head up to rescue them. New storms came up and we all had to descend to Camp Two.

I looked back on tremendous efforts and exhaustion and dismay looking out of a tent door on to a world of snow and vanishing hopes—and yet, and yet, and yet there have been a good many thanks to set on the other side. The party has played up wonderfully, and the ascent to the North Col was a triumph for the old gang. In the high camp my cough was the devil. Even after the day's exercise I couldn't sleep, but was distressed with bursts of coughing fit to tear one's guts—and so I had headache and general misery together; besides which of course it had a very bad effect on going on the mountain.

Despite all that, Norton was determined, and of course Noel and Somervell, both dedicated photographers, were anxious to record the mountain for posterity. The weather turned again, and we could see clearing. But they had to turn back—again, the wretched porters who couldn't go on—and it seemed we were destined to give it up.

That was when I had a brainwave. What about going up fast and light—two men, oxygen, starting out early and just going hell for leather?

That meant, of course, me and Sandy Irvine.

Throughout my mountaineering career I'd always pushed as hard and as far as I could, refusing to give up until I was convinced beyond all possible doubt that there was no other choice. Now that the weather remained fair, and I was still on my feet, and I had a willing partner, and there was oxygen equipment at Camp Three, I couldn't renounce my hope of going to the summit. As I'd declared in New York, a climber was what I was, and this was what climbers did.

There was more. If I went back to Ruth with Everest unclimbed, I'd face the anguish of wondering whether I should leave her and the children for yet another try. I simply couldn't see my way to inflicting that on her again. It was only by making another attempt now that I could be true to Ruth and all we'd gone through together, and to the ideals of honesty and integrity we'd embodied in our love.

The weather had turned again, warm and sunny, and Irvine and I congratulated ourselves on an auspicious beginning to our trek. I outfitted myself well. Since I'd be wearing the oxygen equipment on my back, I stuffed my personal items into the pockets of my windproof cotton Shackleton jacket and a pair of pouches slung around my neck.

Jeannette de Beauvoir

I also carried three recently arrived letters wrapped in one of the handkerchiefs, as well as a photograph of my beloved Ruth; in my latest letter to her, I'd promised to leave it at the summit of the mountain, so that she could forever be there in spirit, the place I loved most in the world other than the comfort of our home.

At the last minute, Somervell pressed a small camera into my hand as well. He'd nearly died on his most recent descent from the North Col, and I knew it galled him that he wouldn't be able to make another attempt. I gladly took the apparatus from him and promised I would take photographs when we reached the summit.

We scarcely could eat our breakfast of fried sardines, biscuits, chocolate, and tea, for the excitement of the moment. I had a sudden sense that this was it: this was the right time, the moment I'd been longing for—the moment the whole world had been longing for—and now that it was upon us, it was with the wonder of a small child at Christmas that I beheld the next twenty-four hours.

I was going to be the first man on top of the world.

We made it up to Camp Six in good time, and sent some of the porters back down, along with a note for Noel, who I knew would be watching with his camera trained on the slopes. I left a note that told him "to start looking for us either crossing the rock band under the pyramid or going up skyline at 8.0o. Yours ever, G. Mallory." And then, out of courtesy, I included a hasty scribble for Odell as well: "We're awfully sorry to have left things in such a mess—our Unna Cooker rolled down the slope at the last moment. Be sure of getting back to IV to-morrow in time to evacuate by dark, as I hope to. In the tent I must have left a compass—for the Lord's sake rescue it: we are without. To here on 90 atmospheres for the two days—we'll probably go on two cylinders—but it's a bloody load for climbing. Perfect weather for the job! Yours ever, G. Mallory."

We checked each other's oxygen tanks, and I made sure I had both Ruth's picture and Somervell's camera quite accessible.

I will need them both when I reach the top.

Chapter Twenty

He was still in the bright red Santa Claus snowsuit, though he was looking anything but jolly. "Miss Abigail," said Anish. "Please not to move."

"What the hell, Anish?" I was more surprised than scared. At that moment, anyway. "What are you doing?" Possibly the silliest thing I could have said, but then again, this was my first encounter with a handgun.

I was hoping strenuously it would be my last.

"Please do not scream," he said.

Screaming hadn't actually occurred to me. "Okay," I said. This was feeling more and more surreal. At any moment he was going to ask how the esteemed ladies were enjoying their trip. "What do you want me to do instead?"

He gestured with the gun toward Emma's messy camp bed. "Please to sit," he said.

"Okay." He was silhouetted between me and the tent doorway, with the bright sunshine outside; I couldn't really tell anything about his expression. But the gun added a level of seriousness to the endeavor. I sat.

"It is easy," Anish said, as though outlining the trek he had planned for his guests. "I need you to return to me the computer drive you have. That Miss Emma has."

I stared at him. "The computer drive?" I wasn't connecting.

"The drive," he repeated, impatiently. He was waving the gun up and down for emphasis, and I hoped to hell it had some sort of safety device on it. "I know you have it."

I'd finally understood what he was talking about: Emma's flash drive, stolen at Phakding. Someone who worked for Supreme Summits Expeditions had dropped it, was what Myles's note had said.

Anish had dropped it. "Why?" I asked.

"Miss Abigail," Anish said, and for the first time he sounded less jolly and more exasperated. "This is not for your research. You do not ask me questions. If you give it to me, I will not shoot you."

That sounded like a pretty good deal to me, the unfortunate obstacle being that I had no idea where the drive was. "It isn't still in her laptop?" I asked hopefully, looking around the tent. I saw neither laptop nor flash drive.

"You believe I have not looked already? That would not be efficient," said Anish. Our Man in Kathmandu: efficiency first. All peoples trusted Supreme Summits Expeditions. "I have waited too long," he added. "Waited for Miss Emma to return. I wish to leave now. I do not know where she is."

"She's in the medical tent," I said. I didn't see how not telling him was going to help me, and maybe he'd take cooperation as a positive sign. "Why do you need it?" I hesitated. "Anish, what's going on?" You seemed so nice, I almost said.

"You know," he said. "It is no secret. I have heard you and Miss Emma talking to peoples." So much for our attempts at discretion. "But it does not matter. We are closing it down, now."

It came to me then; he wasn't talking about Yuan Bo. "You're the one," I said slowly. "You've been smuggling drugs out of China." With the bright sunshine behind him, I couldn't see his face, couldn't watch for a reaction. But I already knew. Anish had been the first person to tell me about it. You are sitting on it right now! Kathmandu is part of the Silk Road. It is the route that connects the mysterious exotic East to the West.

He nodded, as though following my thought, my memory; the gun moved up and down again. "You see? I always say you are smart cookie. Not all peoples as smart, but I know Miss Emma and Miss Abigail maybe real problems."

"Not so much," I confessed. My interest in the drug-smuggling was secondary to the people-smuggling plan. Best not to mention that; there was a chance Anish didn't know about Yuan Bo. Stick to the fentanyl. "You work with the Russians," I guessed. And again heard Myles's voice: There are a lot of Russians on the mountain this year.

"You see? You do know."

"Why did you have to poison Yevgeny?" Maybe if I kept him talking, Emma would return. Oh good, and get two of us shot instead of just me. Maybe it was just instinct: if he was talking, he wasn't shooting. "Was he getting cold feet?"

"Sorry?"

"Cold feet," I repeated. "Did he want to stop?"

Anish shook his head; the gun didn't move. He was already seeming less awkward wielding it than he had at first. That couldn't be good news for me. "No. Quite the contrary. He wanted more of—the loot."

"Maybe he thought he was taking more of the risk."

"I do not care what he was thinking!" Temper, a side to Anish I hadn't seen. "I have to stop it right away. He did not wish us to end the run here. He was unpredictable. I cannot have... loose something?"

"A loose cannon?" I suggested.

"No. Loose... ends. That is the expression, I think? I have to tie up loose ends."

For just a second the absurdity of wrangling words together with one of us pointing a gun at the other nearly had me laughing. Nearly. "So you brought the strychnine with you when you came up," I said. "Where d'you get something like that?"

He stared at me. "In Kathmandu," he said, as though the answer were obvious. "All peoples, all drugs."

That made sense. Now for the sixty-five-thousand-dollar question. "Who's working with you, Anish? Who's been bringing it down?" Myles, again: There are labs in Beijing... connecting to Lhasa through Highway 108. The old Silk Road, still at it, still selling dreams to the West... Another thought hit me. "And why are you closing it down?" Seemed a lot of people might not like that happening.

"It is time," he said. "Too many peoples are climbing now. Ten years ago, it was easy. Now? Not anymore. And the mountain changing, too. Climate changing." He seemed pleased with his little wordplay.

Sure, whatever, as long as it keeps your finger from pressing that trigger. "So who else do you have to kill, Anish? To close it down?" Belatedly, I realized his list was probably going to include me. No need to rush things, Abbie. Red herring time. "Is it Jack? Has he been running it with you?"

Anish chuckled. "Boss-Man? He too straight. And has plenty of money already."

"Whereas you don't? Doesn't he pay you enough, Anish?" Eventually he was going to come round to the flash drive again, and I had no idea where Emma had stashed it. And she wasn't coming back to find it, either. Surely we weren't going to walk back across Base Camp with him pointing his pistol at my back.

"No one pays me enough," he said simply. "I am not Sherpa."

I think I might have finally grasped it then. The Sherpa were a small minority in Nepal, but they were absolute kings—and queens—of the mountains, possessing physical traits and skills that were unrivaled. I imagined Anish back in the office, sending wealthy clients up to pour money into the pockets of the climbing sherpas, tipping everyone with their largesse... but not Our Man in Kathmandu, who did all the planning, securing all the permits, sweating all the details. He got a paycheck; they saw multiple paydays, with bonuses and more. Not much by Western standards; a fortune for subsistence farmers.

"Is that why you killed Ang Pemba, too? Because he was Sherpa?" It had to be Anish who'd written the letter luring Ang Pemba to Lukla. Anish, who knew the details of everyone connected with Supreme Summits Expeditions.

"I do not know," said Anish. "I never liked him. He is Boss-Man's favorite." Again, that simmering jealousy, that seething years-long hatred he'd kept in check so elegantly for so long. "He only work in the season; I work all year long. But still, Boss-Man liked him best." He shrugged and the gun's muzzle jumped—and I jumped with it. "But also I think he learn of the drugs route. And he hates drugs. I could not let him find out for sure."

"Because of his son," I said, nodding, willing my pounding heart to calm down a little.

There was a moment of silence. I couldn't come up with any more questions. Anish was clearly uncomfortable holding the gun—a fact that could go either way, as far as I was concerned.

"Now," he said finally, "you can give me the drive."

"But there's nothing on it!" I said, my voice rising ridiculously high. "Emma and I read it. It's her notes, it's some stuff Jack put there."

"It is proof of what we are doing," said Anish calmly. "The Boss-Man has not read it all. He just put it on the drive, just gave it to Miss Emma." His title of respect seemed grotesque now. "He will not be able to, now. It is important he does not know."

"What do you mean—Anish, you're not going to carry on, are you?"

"I am closing Everest route," he said. "There are many others." And many other people to work with him, I thought.

"It's Richard, isn't it?" I asked suddenly. It had to be. Richard who'd gone up the mountain this one last time. Richard whose group had gotten separated from Jack's. Richard who'd always seemed the nicest man in the room. "You and Richard are going to keep doing this?" Supreme Summits, I remembered belatedly, climbed all over the world. There were other opportunities for a compromised expedition company. "You're crazy. Jack must know."

"Anish, for God's sake, put the gun down." The voice came from just outside the tent. Anish didn't turn to look; he'd been expecting this. He lowered his hand. "You took your time," he complained. "It's heavy."

"You don't have to hold it on her. She's not going anywhere." An English voice, just not the one I'd been half-expecting.

It was Mark.

***

He came inside the tent, and it only took one glance to see he was looking a lot better than he had back in comms; something had happened to lighten whatever load he'd been carrying. He reached over and took the gun out of Anish's hand. "You shouldn't be waving this around," he said. "You could hurt somebody."

"I do not know how to use it," Anish acknowledged. Now you tell me, I thought.

"I know." Mark wasn't moving, still standing behind Anish, blocking the tent doorway; I thought that was odd. Strange what you notice; I would have thought that by now my life would be unspooling in front of me. That's what I'd heard happens, at times like these. An avalanche and a gun, all in one day.

I decided I might be seriously overdoing the I-need-an-adventure thing.

"Anish," said Mark, "sorry and all that, but this isn't happening."

Anish took a step toward me and I put my hands up, instinctively, still grasping Emma's bag. But he turned to look at Mark. "Pardon?"

"Richard's been arrested," Mark said. "You will be, too. It's unfortunate, to be candid. I really liked you." He spared me a glance. "You all right?"

I nodded; wasn't sure I could speak at all.

"Good news for you, anyway," Mark said. "Your New Zealander's been evacuated. Broken leg, but he'll survive."

I felt as if I couldn't breathe, and this time it wasn't because of the thin air. Too much going on inside my head. I wasn't going to die. Myles wasn't dead. Seemed like we had a lot in common.

Anish had turned to face Mark. He shook his head, as though to clear it; I could appreciate his feeling of disorientation. I was feeling a little disoriented myself. "But you have been part of it! Why are you saying this?"

"Correction," said Mark. "I've been working with you over the past two months, and that's only so I could help stop it." He hefted the gun slightly, as though to remind us of its presence; I certainly hadn't forgotten. "Richard, man, we were best mates. You took him away. You took Ang Pemba away, too. You really think I wouldn't care about them?"

Anish may have tried to answer, but then there was suddenly a tremendous clattering noise, as loud as the avalanche, as loud as thunder, beating at the air and I thought, this is it again, but no one told me that when you die angel wings are so damned loud. And someone had me by the wrist and was pulling me up and out of the tent and I realized that, extraordinarily, I wasn't dead. That the sound was the rotors of the helicopter hovering just a few feet over the tents, they were all flapping in the backwash, and Mark was asking me if I was all right.

I looked up and they had all climbed out of the helicopter, Jack and one of the Italians, and a diminutive Asian man. Standing beside him was Emma, with the broadest smile I'd ever seen on anyone's face.

And she held up what was in her hand.

A camera.

Author's Note

About Everest

The world is changing, and it's changing fast. The descriptions I've given here of Everest and its Base Camp are accurate as of this writing—late 2024—but will not stay that way. There are enormous problems brewing, the most immediate and obvious of which is global warming. I don't think people will ever stop climbing the mountain, but the experience will change from year to year as the glacier disappears.

More issues include the increased overload of humans on the mountain, and the garbage—organic and otherwise—that many still leave there. The yak supply chain is already problematic, and with the possibility of new regulations to keep non-emergency helicopters off the mountain, yak transportation will be needed more than ever.

The Khumbu Icefall will see the most change in the near future. It's essentially five kilometers of ice that's constantly on the move—up to one meter every day. That means all the cliffs, the "holes," the crevasses are also constantly moving. Mini-avalanches can occur, and new crevasses can appear. Even now, the safest way to cross the Icefall is to leave Base Camp during the night and cross it in the dark, so there isn't any snowmelt from the sun adding to the dangers.

All of that is to say that if you're reading this five or ten or even just two years after I've written it, the landscape and climbing may have changed quite radically. As of the 2024 climbing season, this is a pretty accurate portrayal of trekking and climbing.

Experienced climbers will note that I did a little time-telescoping with the Supreme Summits summiting bid and subsequent descent down the mountain. Purely a bit of literary license; the actual climb involves a great deal of back-and-forth, much more than could sustain my fictional tension at Base Camp. If you'd like to

see how it would really happen, check out the animation here:
https://www.alanarnette.com/everest/everestsouthroutes.php

So… if the mountain has changed when you read this, then welcome to the world of once-upon-a-time. I hope you still enjoyed the story.

About George Mallory

George Mallory was every bit as romantic a figure as I've described here. He wrote constantly about himself and his exploits in many different media, though to the best of my knowledge did not keep "journals" per se. Magdalene College has digitized his letters to Ruth, and they were my main source for his timeline in this book; when possible, I've tried to use some of his own words in creating his journal entries.

One of mountaineering's greatest mysteries remains the question of whether Mallory and Irvine summited Everest thirty years before Norgay and Hillary. Mallory's body was discovered by Conrad Anker in 1999, at 26,700 feet on a rubble-covered snow ledge on the North Face of Everest. He was face-down, his fingers dug into the gravel, with a severed rope tied to his waist. Irvine was nowhere to be seen, and nor was the infamous VPK (Vest Pocket Kodak) camera they were said to be carrying. Technicians at Eastman Kodak have long held that the film, deep frozen for decades, might still be salvageable, though other experts are more skeptical.

There's much more to the Mallory and Irvine story, including Mallory's own book, and it all makes for great reading. It seems to me that it's at the very least reasonable that they might have made it. You can make up your own mind.

An excellent biography, which includes a lot of Mallory's letters, is Peter and Leni Gillman's *The Wildest Dream*. It was made into a film. The review is at *https://clive-w.blogspot.com/2012/04/*, where you can also see photos, including the famous headshot of George and Ruth Mallory.

About Sandy Irvine

Timing is everything! While this book was still in the editing stage, news came that a National Geographic documentary team, led by Jimmy Chin, found part of Irvine's remains on the Central Rongbuk Glacier. The remains included a detached foot inside a boot and sock with "A. C. Irvine" on a name tag. So it's very possible that events will overwrite my story, and the mystery of the camera will be solved.

Life always moves on, and novels—at best—produce a snapshot of a given time. I hope this mystery was still fun to read, no matter whether the camera is or isn't eventually found.

Acknowledgments

I am indebted to so many people!

First of all, many, many thanks to mountaineer Jeannette McGill (*mcgills-mountains.com*) for her invaluable perspective on climbing in general and Everest in particular.

Thanks to Reddit's mountaineering community, including the following individuals by their screen names: infamous_advantage37, apathy-sofa, LosWranglos, nek1981az, Sanfords_Son, mountainerdy, mtntris19, ecstatic-solid8936, sherpa_8000, and lovesmtns.

My editor, Bill Bowers, has a sharp eye and (occasionally) a sharp tongue, both of which are beyond useful. My Beta Readers—Kimberlee Sams, Carem Bennett, Margo Nash, Corinne Diana, and A.C. Burch—have the difficult task of reading the book when it's not quite ready for primetime... and helping it become so. I turn to Pat Medina for help whenever I encounter a tricky plot problem, and talking it through with her is invaluable. Susan Squires introduced me to Nepal and I will be forever grateful.

Others help in ways too numerous to mention: Doni Angell, Indira Ganesan (for "Pizza and Poirot"), Colin Kegler, Marge Piercy, Dianne Kopser, Julie Blackburn, Bob Allen, Edward Franchuk, Chip Capelli.

Thanks to my own local booksellers, East End Books, the Provincetown Bookshop, and Tim's Used Books, and especially to my wonderful local heroes at the Provincetown Public Library, Amy Raff, Nan Cinnater, Deborah Karacozian, and Courtney Francis.

To Kyre Song, who is so much more than just my web guy.

And you, my readers—I am so very grateful you continue to give me so much of your time and your attention. You trust me to take you somewhere you've never gone, and every day I hope I live up to that trust.

About the Author

Jeannette de Beauvoir is a bestselling author of mysteries and historical fiction as well as a poet who lives and works at Land's End in Provincetown, Massachusetts. Her work has appeared in myriad literary reviews and anthologies, and she's a member of the Authors Guild, the Mystery Writers of America, Sisters in Crime, and the Historical Novel Society.

Find out more, and sign up for her newsletter, at jeannettedebeauvoir.com.

Did You Enjoy This Book?

If you did, please…

1) **share your opinion** on Goodreads and/or Amazon;

2) **visit my Amazon page** and check out some of my other books;

3) give the book a boost by **telling people about** it on social media;

4) **subscribe to my newsletter** for book reviews, short stories, quizzes, free stuff, previews of upcoming work, and more;

5) ask your local bookseller **to stock** my mysteries;

6) make them your **choice for your next book club** meeting (I'll even join you by Zoom if you'd like!);

7) **email me** at jeannettedebeauvoir@gmail.com;

8) and **watch for** the next Abbie Bradford mystery!